SHA
UNIC

SHAMPOO UNICORN

SAWYER LOVETT

HYPERION

Los Angeles   New York

First Edition, May 2025
10 9 8 7 6 5 4 3 2 1
FAC-004510-25079
Printed in the United States of America

This book is set in Cochin/Monotype
Designed by Marci Senders

Library of Congress Cataloging-in-Publication Data
Names: Lovett, Sawyer, author.
Title: Shampoo unicorn / by Sawyer Lovett.
Description: First edition. • Los Angeles ; New York : Hyperion, 2025. •
Audience term: Teenagers • Audience: Ages 14–18. • Audience: Grades
10–12. • Summary: After a hit-and-run leaves Greg, a closeted jock,
unconscious, Brian, the secret host of a popular podcast, uses his
platform to investigate the crime and reveal harsh truths about their
small town, which inspires others to show support and organize a pride
festival that gains national attention.
Identifiers: LCCN 2024012185 • ISBN 9781368108959 (hardcover) •
ISBN 9781368113830 (ebook)
Subjects: CYAC: Podcasts—Fiction. • LGBTQ+ people—Fiction. •
Identity—Fiction. • Hit-and-run drivers—Fiction. • LCGFT: Novels.
Classification: LCC PZ7.1.L73818 Sh 2025 • DDC [Fic]—dc23
LC record available at https://lccn.loc.gov/2024012185

Reinforced binding

Visit www.HyperionTeens.com

FOR EVERYONE QUEER
FOR YOU, IF YOU NEED IT
FOR MY GHOSTS
& FOR RYAN

SHAMPOO UNICORN
Episode 307: "Everybody's All-American"

SASS:

Hello, and welcome to another thrilling episode of *Shampoo Unicorn*, the podcast where I, your humble host, parse out the hell that is being a high school queer in small-town rural America. This week, we'll talk about prom, graduation, and all the other rites of passage I'm supposed to look back on in my golden years.

[SHAMPOO UNICORN THEME SONG PLAYS.]

SASS:

Lights up on the football field of Anytown, USA. It's Friday night, and our team is up against some pretty big dudes for their first game at home of the season. For the graduating seniors it will be the last season of their high school careers, and everyone's just feeling sentimental as hell about it. The band kids are decked out in their uniforms, and the weather is starting to get crisp enough for coats and scarves. Almost everyone in the stands is wearing some article of clothing with the high school mascot on it. Most of the kids at my school wait all week for the home games. There's a mandatory pep rally every Friday in which the entire school files out of their shortened last period class and into the gym, where cheerleaders cheer, the principal says something inspiring, and either the coach or a football player tries to get everyone excited about the big game by using sports as a metaphor for life. It's . . . a lot.

Imagine a soundtrack of brassy country music over a high school football game. It's the weekend and the mating rituals of the heterosexual American teen are on full display. A couple walks by with their hands in each other's back pockets, a move obviously lifted from some '80s Brat Pack movie. Homecoming Queen and Mr. Congeniality are fused together in a knot of writhing limbs in an impressive display of dexterity and obliviousness to the world around them. Are they mere moments away from creating future little rootin'-tootin' soldiers for the Lord? Who knows? Our health classes favor an abstinence-only curriculum, so it's possible that neither of these passionate souls knows how to operate a prophylactic. I'd put decent odds on neither of them being able to spell it.

[MUFFLED INTERCOM NOISES FOLLOWED
BY THE NATIONAL ANTHEM.]

SASS:

And here we are, high in the stands looking down upon the people. Because it's Friday night, and as much as I'd rather be at home playing video games or reading, my best friend claims to have a hankering for shitty football booster hot dogs. That's right, internet, it's the Bert to my Ernie, the peanut butter to my jelly, the SpongeBob to my Patrick.

MIMI:

Hi, internet! It's your girl Mimi, here to balance out Sass's cynicism with a dose of small-town realness. This is the last football season of our high school careers and we've only ever been to, like, two games before? And those were only because Sass had a crush on Tromboner.

SASS:

Long-time listeners will remember my unfortunate crush on the trombone player from the marching band and how my tender heart was broken into a million pieces when he cut his beautiful flowing locks and started listening exclusively to jam bands.

MIMI:

RIP, Tromboner, you will live on in our spank banks for years to come.

SASS:

Anyhoo, word around the school is that Quarterback

has some sort of epic HoCo proposal for Cheerleader, so I allowed myself to be dragged along with this chick's wiener quest.

MIMI:

WIENER QUEST! Would that be the best or worst video game ever?

SASS:

Should we be paying attention to the sportsball match?

MIMI:

Do you know what's happening?

SASS:

Fair point. How's that hot dog treating you?

MIMI:

Like it's just passing through, to be honest. If there's a culinary institution in this town less reputable than the cafeteria, it has to be the concession stand run by the booster club. It's a crime against nature that they're so tasty. Why are forbidden fruits always the sweetest?

SASS:

Girl, if that hot dog is sweet, there's more wrong with it than the wine-drunk football moms in lululemon cooking them.

MIMI:

Bless 'em.

[*BACKGROUND CHEERING OVER
MUFFLED INTERCOM NOISES.*]

MIMI:

It appears that the home team scored! And that
Homecoming Queen and Mr. Congeniality didn't even
come up for air. This is an unprecedented moment in
the history of PDA. I wonder if there's a world record
for this sort of thing? They must be uncomfortable. It's
pretty chilly out, and while it was chivalrous of him to
give her his jacket, it was an obvious excuse to cover up
his roving hands. Would we say he's landed on first or is
rounding second? What exactly are the bases? Are the
bases different for gay people?

SASS:

A sports question! A gay sports question, even.

[*BACKGROUND NOISES: VOICES, WIND,
AND CRUMPLING OF PAPER.*]

SASS:

I don't know. I mean, most of the experience I have is
from, *ahem*, online research. There's only one other suit-
able gay in the village, and while we did mess around
once or twice, he's so deep in the closet he's wearing
mothball deodorant.

MIMI:

I mean, the bases are mostly the same, right? First base is making out, second base is over-the-clothes stuff, third base is, like, oral, and a home run is intercourse.

SASS:

But, wait. What? What if you're just interested in oral? Or hand stuff? And who defines intercourse? I know that P in V is the standard. But, like, what is it for boys? P in B?

MIMI:

What's the B?

SASS:

(whispering)

Uh, butt.

MIMI:

I don't know. I've never thought about the gay bases.

SASS:

Why would you have? The real question is why have I never once thought about the gay bases? Crap. If any of you listeners have any feedback about all this, please do holler.

MIMI:

Oh, look. Halftime is starting.

SASS:

I cannot wait to see what this "epic homecoming proposal" is.

MIMI:

Okay, here comes the football team . . . leading what looks like . . .

SASS:

Is that . . . On a leash? How'd they get it all . . . so evenly?

MIMI:

Oh. My. God.
                *[INDISTINCT BULLHORN NOISES
                        IN THE BACKGROUND.]*

SASS:

(laughs)

Look, we can't say exactly what is happening because there's no WAY this homecoming proposal isn't gonna make it to YouTube, but trust me when I say this is some hella country bullshit.

MIMI:

PETA would have a field day, I'm *so* sure.

SASS:

Better still, Homecoming Queen and Mr. C finally came

up for air to see what the fuss was about. Wait, are they arguing? Trouble in paradise?

MIMI:

Homecoming Queen is pissed that Mr. C didn't do anything that romantic for his proposal! Seems he wrote something inside a pizza box?

SASS:

Oh shit, Cheerleader and Homecoming Queen are both crying!

MIMI:

Tears of joy, tears of sorrow.

SASS:

And the great world spins on. Join us right after we hear from our sponsors, won't you? On *Shampoo Unicorn*, the only podcast with more teen drama than an entire season of *Riverdale*.

MIMI:

Sass, will you go to homecoming with me?
[TRANSITION MUSIC PLAYS.]

1

FROM A CERTAIN PERSPECTIVE
Greg

Your mind was a maze with no map.

You were always lost before a game. It helped you be oblivious to the boys' bodies around you. If you zoned out, you wouldn't be distracted by all the sweaty naked skin, or the wildly different bodies of your teammates, or their junk flopping everywhere.

In particular, this evening, you were thinking about language; how the same dudes who called one another homos or queers for missing a pass changed their whole manner of speaking in front of adults or girls. How girls were always *hot* or *fine* or *stacked*, never *beautiful* or *pretty*. That sort of earnestness was for people who gave a crap, and most of your bros tried hard not to get caught caring. Except Paul, your team's quarterback, who was such a genuinely nice guy that almost no one gave him any real shit—even the good-natured shit talk that you traded with the bros you liked best. He sincerely loved God, country, family, his girl, his truck, and his dog. You had almost no doubt that he'd marry his high school sweetheart and die in his hometown satisfied with a small but honest life.

He wasn't beautiful in the way that Derek was—he lacked the sinew and elegance of a small but compact frame. It would be overly generous to call him hot. He was a big guy, thick, with just a little belly fluff and light, messy hair. His nose had been knocked out of place a couple of times, which added character to his wide face. He was the effortless type of masculine that you deeply, deeply longed to inhabit.

Today, his ruddy cheeks were redder with the excitement of staging what he would not stop calling "an epic homecoming proposal, man. I mean, one for the books." He had phoned in every favor possible to get the rest of the team to agree, but despite being well-compensated, blackmailed, or bribed, some of the guys freaked out when they saw the goat.

"The fuck is this about?" Derek had said. When Paul explained, even you admitted that it was a good plan, romantic even, from a certain perspective. The other guys had traded high fives, back pats, and chest bumps and headed out onto the field.

Spectators in the stands roared when you and your teammates broke through the paper banner the cheerleaders stretched out across the home goalpost. The smell of fresh-cut grass filled your nose, and a cool autumn breeze brushed your face. Stadium lights brightened the field, and it was as if you were on a stage, examined and watched. Could they see through your facade? See the fear hanging over you like a dark cloud? Was your secret safely hidden behind the face mask of your helmet?

"Hey, Burke," Derek shouted, running past you. "Pick it up. You afraid of the other team or what?"

You shook off your thoughts, your fears, and charged after him, beating him to the sideline.

Your team played a good first half. You were so used to one another by now that you could tell when to flex a play, which opposition players offered the most advantage for rushing, who was open for a pass at any given time. The other team was bigger, from a city far away, and they were really good. But this game wasn't about sports. Not for you and maybe not for your teammates, either. It was about recognizing that this season was the last time you'd ever play football with your friends. After this year, you'd never see their faces closed in concentration against the crowds and the floodlights, never see Paul hike an arm back to send the ball spiraling across the sky into the waiting arms of one of the running backs, and never watch Derek zigzag through the opposition so fast it looked like he was floating.

When defense was out on the field and offense on the sidelines, when you had a breather, you searched the stands. Just below the bleachers, Beth moved in sync with the rest of the cheerleaders. Her sharp voice cut through the crowd with the other girls echoing her. That sexy gamer guy from your geometry class ate a hot dog like he knew you were watching. On the fifty-yard line, Derek's dad, in a wool blazer, gesticulated to a bunch of other guys in expensive-looking suits. In the next row, your principal and his wife, both decked out in the school's teal and white, sat with a respectable amount of space between them. And there, perched high in the stands, was Riley, wearing a gold-sequined jacket. From this far away, you could see how few other Black people there were in the stands and wondered what that felt like for her. And beside her, like a small white shadow, was Brian.

You wondered briefly why they were there because they hated violent sports, but then, of course, figured it had something to do with Brian's secret podcast. Secret to everyone but you because you'd figured out it was him behind the curtain from the start. Brian was always talking about *rites of passage* and *glory days* like they were quests in a video game he was losing. And you knew his voice. It was the inescapable sound of your conscience.

A shrill whistle called your attention back to the field. The referee headed off. It was halftime. You ran back to the locker room with your teammates.

"Hey, man," Paul said, stopping you. "Lead the goat out for me, okay?"

You followed Paul. "Why me? Can't someone else do it?"

"I trust you." He clapped you on the shoulder with an enormous meaty ham hand.

One of the shower heads dripped, the plunking of water hit the tiles below. Coach had three plumbers in to fix it, but after a few days, the leak would return. It gave off a mildew smell, and it mixed with something else. An animal scent. While you were on the field, someone had delivered a cage with the goat inside and placed it in the showers. Paul lifted the latch, opened it, and led the goat out by a leash. "Meet Kobe."

You rubbed the back of your neck. "I don't know. Is it legal? The goat is purple."

A wide grin pulled across Paul's lips. "It's fine. We used nontoxic dyes. The kind Charlie's mom uses on the dogs at her grooming shop. It's humane and shit. Here." He handed you the leash and a couple of carrots.

On your way out, Paul snatched up a bullhorn from a bench. The goat resisted at the sight of the crowd and lights, but you negotiated a reasonable pace once it became clear that you were in charge of the snacks. You couldn't make out what they were saying except for the occasional "It's a goat."

Beth and a couple of other cheerleaders grasped Brooke's arms and guided her to the middle of the field. She shook her head several times and pulled back on their lead a few. She ducked behind Beth, shyly blushing.

Paul joined them and raised the bullhorn to his lips. "Brooke Mayfield, you are the greatest of all time, and I would be the luckiest of all time if you would GOAT to homecoming with me. Will you be my date?"

The crowd laughed first and then applauded. Brooke covered her face with her hands. She waited a beat before she looked up and nodded, then leaped into Paul's arms, causing him to drop the bullhorn. It made a loud squelch before it went silent, and the crowd went wild.

You wondered what Riley and Brian thought about the spectacle. God, you probably looked like such an idiot. You could just see Brian, casually examining his nails before arching a devastating eyebrow and delivering some line of shade that would bury you in the dirt, where you belonged. Was he going to homecoming? With a boy? What would it feel like to see him dancing with someone else? The thought made your pulse race dangerously and you pulled yourself back to reality so you wouldn't have to look too hard at why it made you so uncomfortable.

Paul was definitely living his glory days, you thought. Once you had a stadium full of people cheering for you, you'd definitely peaked, right? Where could you even go from there?

2

GIRLS JUST WANNA HAVE FUN
Leslie

Leslie thinks about performance.

She's not part of any theater or performance group, but she could be if she had to choose a clique. After all, her whole life is an act.

Like right now, she's pounding the treadmill, watching girls on the machines in front of her. To the naked eye, you'd think she was a normal teenage boy, looking at normal teenage girls. You'd think *He's an athlete, a track star*. You might think he was kind of a creep for staring. But you'd think *he*, not *she*.

But you'd be wrong. She prays to God that she won't always be stuck in this small town, in this school, in this body.

The girls are gossiping about some friend who got ghosted by a basketball player. Leslie turns up the volume on her phone and the podcast she's listening to gets louder over her earbuds. She wonders what it would be like to have casual girlfriends, what that word might mean platonically and romantically.

Her treadmill beeps to start the cool-down phase, and her heart hammers more from anxiety than from the run. She slows to a fast walk, then to a regular walk. Her boy drag is so generic it could be a uniform. T-shirt, basketball shorts, plain socks, and Nikes.

She slams her hand on the stop button, tugs the towel from her waistband, and wipes down her machine. For a minute she checks her reflection in the mirror, then slips her hoodie over her head to cover up her sweaty hair and flushed cheeks. The locker room is a hell she can't face today, so without another look at the girls, she weaves through the barbell racks and goes outside, into the bright sun.

Leslie doesn't know Sass personally; she found their podcast on the internet searching for reasons to stay alive in a small town when no one knows you're queer.

The sidewalk is uneven, and her sneakers are so worn and bare on the soles the edges bite her feet. She heads for the pharmacy by the gym where she buys a protein bar and a water every day.

She's been listening to *Shampoo Unicorn* for a year now. Back when she wasn't sure what particular genre or strain of queer she was. She spent hours on incognito mode, using clandestine accounts she built with a fake email address. She took clickbait tests and read legitimate resources and was surprised for the first of many times about the volume and quality of pornography. She knew she wasn't straight the way her classmates were, and she knew she wasn't a boy like her cousins.

And now?

She yanks the door open and the bell above it rings.

Now, every day she chooses something to do tomorrow that's worth sticking around for. Yesterday she had ice cream for breakfast, lunch, and dinner. Today, she'll shoplift a tube of lipstick.

She's been thinking about this quiet act of defiance for a while now, aimlessly wandering the aisles so it looks less shady when she lands in the makeup section. She downloaded a couple of makeover apps to see what shades will look most flattering, which brands are long-lasting. She affects an air of boredom and restlessness so that if anyone asks what she, in her boy skin looking as though she doesn't belong here, is doing. If questioned, she could say she's shopping for her girlfriend. That this nonexistent girl asked her to pick up lip gloss. Do girlfriends send their boyfriends to get makeup for them? Never having been on either side of that coin, she doesn't know.

The disinterested cashier looks up from his phone only long enough to give her a nod. He's new. His dark hair is dyed an unnatural black and he has quarter-size ear gauges. Workers come and go so fast in this store, which is good for her, especially on a day when she's up to no good. He has chipped nail polish and is scrolling through videos in between customers, so he's not paying much attention to Leslie.

Her first stop is the candy aisle, always tempted by the chocolate but constantly calculating calories, worrying what any extra body fat could do to her when she finally gets access to hormones. She's studied message boards and timeline photos and tried to figure out where her particular body and genetics factor into this math.

She moves quickly past temptation, killing time in the magazine section. Picking up *GQ, Esquire*. Men's magazines, even though she'd rather grab *Cosmopolitan* or a gossip magazine and find out what Miley and Gaga are up to.

Leslie considers buying a birthday card for her mom, but she's spent the last couple of weeks only buying a protein bar and drink. A break in the routine she's built will raise suspicion.

Closer now, shampoos, hair gel, dye. Could she ever be the sort of girl who rocks blue hair and doesn't blink when strangers stare at her? She imagines pale blue hair, matching ripped gingham leggings, with a frilly white baby-doll dress, holding a wicker basket of apples like some punk trans version of Dorothy Gale. Even now, as unassuming as she can make her face and clothing—which she thinks of as packaging—she feels like pulling her shoulders in, collapsing her spine, and gradually disappearing. When she's called on in class or addressed in casual situations, she feels the same. Like being perceived is physically painful and she'd very much like not to be. Calling attention to herself on purpose seems masochistic. Could she command attention as a woman the way she tried to avoid it as a boy?

And oh, what's this? However could she have ended up in cosmetics, looking at a perfect red tube of lipstick? It's the cheapest brand, but the color reminds her of poppies, of stop signs. She palms it and easily slides the tube into her pocket, leaving her hands there, casually.

Next, she's onto the nail supplies. Leslie stands in front of the practical tools—clippers, files, cuticle cutters—but her eye is drawn to the polishes. To the red that matches the lipstick stowed away in her pocket. This time she doesn't hesitate, just grabs the small bottle and puts it into her other pocket.

On the shelf over, she spots a highlighter palette and lifts it off the display. She rotates it in her hand to let it glimmer in the light, Ariel admiring herself in the reflection of a clamshell, she can almost see herself staring back, longer hair framing her face, teal sparkly highlighter and a fierce purple mermaid eye. Buying it is out of the question. It's too big to take. She places it back on the shelf. But she'd like to experiment with it and other stuff, like mascara, eyeliner, and primer. It's not as if she doesn't know how to apply it all. She watches beauty channels by women so beautiful and elegant that it's hard to imagine her ever looking anything like them.

Ordinarily, now is when she'd look at the family planning section—perusing the condoms and lubes, morning-after pills, and personal massagers, wondering why all of these things make sex seem scarier and more awkward than the actual act of two bodies rubbing against each other. But the cosmetics hidden in her pockets are like glowing vacancy signs about to alert the dude at the counter of her crime, and she might anxiety-barf right here in aisle six.

She breezes past the coolers and grabs a water and a mint chocolate protein bar. The cashier barely looks up as he scans her purchases, oblivious to the life-changing scene he doesn't know he's witnessing.

She scans her card, takes her receipt, and darts out of the shop, then hops on a well-timed bus. There's no one chasing her when the bus pulls away from the stop, no angry mob with pitchforks and torches as she feared.

She got away with it, and she'll wear the polish on her toenails, hidden safely in shoes and socks like a secret impenetrable shield.

3

ABSENCE IS AN ABSCESS
Greg

The stagnant cloud of your dad's cigarette smoke came from the living room. Great, the old man was up early. You swore that the stale odor of Marlboro Reds clung to everything you owned. You groaned into your sweaty pillow and rolled over, squinting against the sun filtering through the faded, threadbare beach towel you used as a curtain.

"Thanks for joining us on another episode of *Shampoo Unicorn*," a voice soft like home said into the earbud wedged in one ear. From the living room, the roar of a NASCAR race competed for your attention before you jammed your other earbud in.

You'd known about Brian's podcast since almost the beginning.

No one else at school did, as far as you could tell. He'd done a good job of keeping things pretty anonymous. It was weirdly nostalgic, sharing a secret with Brian and Riley, even if they didn't know you knew. And the podcast was good. It wasn't perfect, and it would be a stretch to even really call it professional. But it was fun and funny, and it made you smile.

It made you homesick for your childhood friends. It made you secretly proud of them, too. You admired Brian for walking through the world in his own skin, and you admired his podcast persona, Sass, for the barbed wit you could see was a response to the petty bullshit your friends put him through. You missed Riley's deadpan humor and the way she made everything she was part of better.

You missed them so much it felt like an abscess where your heart should be, the simpler times of acting out plays and making up choreography in the boxcar clubhouse behind your subdivision. You tried not to make eye contact when you passed them in the hallways, and when your teammates gave Brian shit in the cafeteria or in the hallways, you tried to distract them by reminding them where you were all supposed to be. Your heart always started pounding in your ears, and you could feel sweat break out between your shoulder blades just thinking about it.

"Ayo, Brennon." Derek hip-checked Brian one day in seventh grade. "Your boyfriend wants to know why you're not carrying his books." He grabbed Brian, easily six inches shorter, around the shoulders and planted a wet kiss on the smaller boy's cheek. "Brianna, why don't you join the cheerleaders. You know Mitchem would work a lot harder on the field if he could watch you shaking that tight can for the team."

Brian's shame and fear as his eyes met yours was an image you would never forget. He could have told them then. He could have spilled your secret and ruined your life. He didn't look away, but he didn't hide his tears, either. And when he brought his fist down into the tenderest part of Derek's nutsack, you knew for sure by the way Derek's eyes crossed that Brian's fist had found its mark with more force than anyone expected. You laughed as you dragged him away, hunched over and walking with wide strides back to the gym. The rest of your bros followed you, grabbing Derek by the elbow and figuratively busting the nuts that Brian literally had. When you looked back, he was standing with his spine straight and his shoulders squared, but when he looked at you, there was hate in his eyes. Brian called you a coward with his whole body, and silently, you agreed.

You wondered if you could ever be friends again. You thought constantly about apologizing. But then you remembered the hot stench of your dad's breath telling you that a football scholarship was the only way you would ever get out of your Podunk town. That all you were good for was taking a tackle, that your value fluctuated based on how many yards you ran. That you were otherwise a shitless freeloader, eating your parents out of house and home, bringing in no money, running up bills, and for what? His voice at that first football game, the one where you'd scored the winning touchdown, was full of regret, like maybe his biggest failure was not making it out of Canon before your mom got pregnant and his dreams withered like salted slugs.

Always figured you for a fruit, but hell's bells, son, maybe there's a chance for you after all.

Your dad never let you forget all the things he'd given you. How he'd taken on janitorial work, even though it was beneath him, so you could afford football camp. Gotten you a beater car so that you could drive back and forth to practice. Had always made sure you got three squares a day, taken you to church so you'd have a strong moral compass and knew what the world expected from a man. He never quite called you a faggot, but you could feel violence lurking at the bottom of his next drink. You itched for it. Sometimes you could feel your hands balling up into fists and wondered what they'd feel like against the old man's jaw. But your mom deserved more. She worked so hard. And she loved you so much that the kindness in her eyes made you want to protect her from his bullshit.

You liked Brian's podcast. He created a whole online persona for himself and gave your classmates generic names to maintain his anonymity while still describing what it felt like to be "the only gay in the village," even though you watched the *Little Britain* sketch that title came from together so he definitely knew he wasn't. There was something comforting in being lonely together, and his secret felt like an ember in your chest, some piece of him you could carry to warm you against the chill of who you had outwardly become.

His rebellious courage was the flame that kept you from freezing with constant fear.

SHAMPOO UNICORN
Episode 308: "Gossip Boy"

SASS:

I wouldn't normally post an episode so soon after the last one, but there's been big haps here in Anytown, USA. A couple of varsity athletes got caught with their pants down doing something gay.

[FOOTBALL NOISES, COUNT, SNAP, WHISTLE.]

SASS:

It's a very special episode of *Shampoo Unicorn* this week, in which we talk about gay gossip, the closet, and consequences.

[SHAMPOO UNICORN THEME SONG PLAYS.]

SASS:

First, we should talk about what it's like to be the only

out gay kid in a small town. As you might imagine, it's sometimes . . . not great. I know that I'm pretty flippant on this podcast, but at school, I'm someone different. I'm not closeted, but I also never had to come out. I'm what my mom generously calls naturally flambunctious; that is: flamboyant and somewhat rambunctious. I tamp that down a lot in my everyday life. It's easier to fly under the radar sometimes. Direct from the unicorn's mouth, here's my mom, a longtime fan of the pod and a first-time guest.

SASS'S MOM:

Did I always know you were gay? Hmm. Well, starting around when you were four or so, I thought it might not surprise me. You very specifically wanted to be Belle for Halloween. I wondered if you might be trans, and I never wanted to limit you, so I told you I thought people might not be kind about it, and you said, and I quote: "Let them eat cakes." I still have *no* idea where you heard that.

SASS:

I was quoting Miss Piggy, not Marie Antoinette.

That was my mom, by the way. Think of her with with same capital M *mother* vibes you would Sasha Colby or Mama Ru. My mom almost entirely exists for me, her dearly beloved cherub, who she treasures above all else in life, whose very breath —

SASS'S MOM:

Excuse me. Let's not forget that I had many, many vibrant years before I was your mother. I got it in, kiddo. Every now and then—

SASS:

I am not sex-positive enough to hear about you fuuu—

SASS'S MOM:

You can see now why I had some inkling you'd be gay, right? You also told me you wanted to marry Mr. Candle when you were older. Clearly, I let you watch *Beauty and the Beast* too many times, though I'm glad you didn't grow up romanticizing Stockholm syndrome.

SASS:

Look, I maintain that Lumiere was the real catch from that movie. Every other guy in it is terrible. I'm getting off track, though. My point is, I'm kind of an easy target for bullying.

There's not a super easy way to say that I was bullied without it sounding like I'm trolling for sympathy. I'm not. I'm just saying that there's some amount of irony about being bodychecked and called a queer by a dude who later would get caught blowing another dude after sports practice. Internalized homophobia much?

Here's the other piece: One of the parties involved

in Lockergate is my former best friend. We grew up together. He, Mimi, and I all lived on the same block and played together all the time.

MIMI:

I mean, we knew he was gay, right? We've always, like, known. But we're staunchly against outing people, regardless of them turning into douchebags. Like my girl Michelle O said: When they go low, we go high.

SASS:

I mean, she said it during the campaign that Hillary Clinton lost, so maybe that's not the best example. But yeah. The sort of unspoken rule was that if he left us alone, we'd leave him alone. And he did, mostly. He laughed when his asshole friends said something homophobic to me, but he never directly instigated anything. And I do genuinely think he tried to redirect their attention.

MIMI:

Not that his complicity wasn't bad enough, for the record.

SASS:

No, I'm not saying that. I'm saying, in some ways, I get it. It's easier to be popular, to go with the flow. And his parents are super religious.

MIMI:

They weren't always, though. I mean, they were normal amounts of religious growing up. Christmas and Easter churchgoers, or whatever. But then the coal mines closed down and his dad lost his job. And his mom got a job, and his dad went entirely out of his goddamned mind with the whitest of Holy Roller nonsense. Which is weird if you're not from the area, but mining is a big part of the culture around here, and for a certain type of good old boy, their identities revolve around this really brutal, hostile industry that just chews people up and spits them back out broken with no real support.

SASS:

And Gr— Uh, let's call him Gaybor. Because he's gay and we were neighbors. Gaybor's mom started working at the nursing home and his dad started going to the Pentecostal church. It really shook that whole family up. They eventually moved when the bank foreclosed on their house. Gaybor and his parents wound up in a trailer park a couple of miles outside city limits.

MIMI:

And it's not like we didn't try to stay in touch. But by the following school year, everything had changed. The other kid from the locker room incident moved to town, joined the same Little League team, and he and Gaybor had gotten super close. Hmm. We need a nickname for the other party. We can't keep saying *other party*. How about Jocko since sports is his whole deal?

SASS:

I tried to check in with Gaybor the summer after his family moved. I invited him over and would call and text, but he stopped answering at all.

MIMI:

And when I reached out, his answers were really shady, like he was trying to hit on me or something. It was super performative, and I didn't put it together until he showed up with Jocko that he was trying to flex for some new kid.

SASS:

I was pretty much done with him then. But later, in freshman year, he told people that he—

MIMI:

Fucked me in the bathroom of the "good" Italian restaurant, as if.

SASS:

Good being a relative term to differentiate Olive Garden from the place with the red-and-white checkered plastic tablecloths. I'm still unsure about which establishment this rendezvous was meant to take place at.

MIMI:

Anyway, the whole school has been talking about the locker-room incident all week. This happened Monday morning and by Monday afternoon, they were both expelled. No one person's story matches anyone else's and wild speculation is the only constant. There's not really anything on the local news, and I haven't seen anyone post about it on social media, but I feel like there are pages of texts and DMs speculating because we definitely have been eavesdropping on some wild rumors.

SASS:

We did some undercover investigation, and by that, I mean we poked around and secretly recorded people's responses. And just so we don't get sued, we ran the voices through an audio-distortion filter, which is why the clips sound kind of like robo-Muppets.

THE MOST POPULAR GIRL IN SCHOOL:

I mean, I just can't imagine! I dated him in junior year and let me tell you what, he was not one bit the homo then. He was very handsy at homecoming and made no secret of grinding his boner against me. Oh god. Did I do this? Did I turn him gay with blue balls or something?

MIMI:

I promise you didn't. That's impossible.

THE MOST POPULAR GIRL IN SCHOOL:

I have made a man gay. Oh god, I have to be very careful with this power I never even knew I had.

[FADING FOOTSTEPS AS SHE WALKS AWAY.]

MIMI:

(shouting after her)

You didn't! That's . . . actually impossible. No one can make anyone anything else.

Jesus Christ.

TRACK STAR:

I mean, I never would have guessed he was queer. He was a crazy-fast athlete. And, like, he set the school record for running the mile. My coach practically begged him to run track with us, but there was some sort of schedule overlap or conflict with football stuff.

SASS:

What about the other party?

TRACK STAR:

No way that dude's gay. He nailed at least half the cheerleading team last year.

SASS:

According to whom?

TRACK STAR:

Well, y'know. Locker-room talk. But . . . I believe it.

SASS:

He could be bi?

TRACK STAR:

Yeah, I don't know, man. I know you're a homo and that's cool or whatever, but I feel like bi is just something gay dudes say on the way to the bone zone. Maybe they were stoned or it was a dare or an experiment.

SASS:

The . . . bone zone?

TRACK STAR:

Gayville. Homotown. You get what I'm saying, right? I don't mean it in a bad way. Just, I don't think those two were permanent residents. Maybe they were just passing through or it was a misunderstanding or whatever.

SASS:

I see. Welp. Thanks for your time. And your . . . somewhat abstract thoughts on sexuality. This has been very illuminating.

(in voiceover)

While it has been amazing not to be the gay center of attention, the gossip feels really pointed, with a fair amount of homophobia attached to it. It's hard to ignore, but also, I'm dying to know what is happening outside of school with Gaybor and Jocko.

MIMI:

Do you think Gaybor's dad locked him in his room or do you think there's some sort of church cellar he's locked in?

SASS:

Shit. I hadn't even thought of that. How bad do you think things are for him? I wonder what Jocko's parents are like?

MIMI:

Pretty uninvolved from what I understand. I don't think there's a maternal figure in the picture. I know his dad owns a couple of houses and cars and a boat. They're, like, rich-rich. We all met at his house once for a group English project. It was huge, with a full staff, housekeeper, gardener, chef, the whole *Downton Abbey* meets *Beverly Hillbillies* vibe. And the garage was wild. Like, a full-on showroom of cars and bikes and trucks he sold privately outside of the dealership.

SASS:

So, lots of questions and lots of gossip. Which means lots to look forward to after this brief commercial break.
[TRANSITION MUSIC PLAYS.]

4

SHADOW SISTERS
Leslie

Leslie thinks about depth.

She's flat in real life, going through the motions, filling the roles prescribed by school and family. She has casual friends, kids she's known since elementary school. But nothing more emotionally intimate than lab partnership or group assignments. There's just too much risk of eventual rejection involved in getting to know someone before she's ready to let herself be known. There are just so many steps to transitioning that it looms large, exhausting and dangerous, just ahead of her, like a boss battle in a video game she never agreed to play. She doesn't do extra-curriculars, doesn't hang out with anyone. It's so uncomfortable to live in a skin where no one can see her, and it's too risky to start peeling her mask away yet.

The parts of Leslie's life that she loves most take place in binary code. In pictures, memes, and messages zapped magically to the laptops and smartphones and various devices of strangers she believes are her real friends. People in similar situations, experimenting with names and pronouns and secret ways to fight dysphoria without outing themselves.

She has always wanted to be beautiful, always played with her mom's makeup and heels. When she was around ten, the last time her mom caught Leslie leaving her mom's closet (this time in a black flapper dress that must have been a Halloween costume or something), there was no big confrontation and Leslie doesn't even remember feeling ashamed, just confused. Her mother told Leslie that ten was too old to be playing dress-up, and then she'd taken away the tube of Ruby Woo lipstick and shut the door to her bedroom. They never talked about it again.

From the internet, where all of Leslie's shadow sisters live, she's learned how to look at herself in the mirror and recognize the girl she could be. She has grown out her hair, wears shirts with a deeper V, shaves all her body hair with an electric shaver, and keeps her skin smooth with razors and lotions that she keeps hidden in a kit in her gym bag. Her parents most likely assume she's jacking off during her long showers, but she only leaves the water running to create steam. Lathers up her legs and runs a cheap disposable pink razor to rid herself of the stubble on her legs. Some days, shaving is the best thing she does all day. After hearing about guy swimmers keeping their skin smooth to glide better through the water, she considered taking up the sport to justify hairlessness. Only to drop the idea because she couldn't stomach the idea of undressing in a men's locker room.

The podcast she listens to helps. The hosts are a gay kid and his straight biracial best friend. While Leslie is neither of those things, she's known what it's like to be what they call "an only." People assume she's a gay guy, even though she's never raised the question of gender or sexuality. Her responses to other people's questions about it have always been right enough to redirect or confuse them.

Deflection is her best chance of survival. So now, that's what she does. Deflect, distract, and blend in. She'd like to be invisible, like a Victorian lady ghost haunting the halls of her high school in something high necked but formfitting with a long train. She stays as close to the walls between classes as she can, avoiding detection, pulling her shoulders in to avoid the inevitable collisions with other students. She can stand still during the breaks and people almost walk right through her.

She feels her parents' curiosity. Sometimes, they ask if she's interested in anyone at school, careful to avoid asking if she has a girlfriend or a boyfriend, which makes her think maybe they'd be okay with her transitioning. But occasionally, something about Caitlyn Jenner or Laverne Cox will come up in the news or on TV, and she can't gauge their reaction. They both describe themselves as "fiscally conservative and socially liberal" when asked, but they have a strict policy of not talking about who they vote for, lest they influence Leslie while she figures out her own values. Still, they spend a lot of time watching old sitcoms that really don't hold up to a lens trained on the racism, sexism, or homophobic tropes some mediocre director decided to augment with a laugh track. She knows, from talking to her shadow sisters, that being cool with gay people isn't the same as being cool with trans people. Honestly, she's not really sure her parents are cool with anyone. They're mostly a quiet family who avoids making waves. She's learned to swim below the surface, like an anglerfish, looking only as far as she can see in front of her, with no real idea of what the future might hold in terms of romance or work. Her transness is the light that makes the lurking darkness hopeful and not terrifying.

The truth is there's not anyone she's interested in. Girls definitely turn her head, but sometimes it's because she envies their style, or thinks they could be friends under different circumstances. Boys, while not unattractive, are dangerous. They grow into men who have the potential to be violent. She's spent enough time reading about other trans women,

35

historical and celebrity, for sure, but also the trans women who had the audacity to live lives of quiet dignity, grocery shopping and throwing dinner parties and paying parking tickets and falling in and out of love. She also knows the statistics and cautionary tales of the brave people living their truths out loud. It's fucked-up that this mundane crap is so complicated and dangerous for women like her.

Leslie has decided to live. Stubbornly, defiantly. No matter what else, she will not go gently into the bad night her ancestors have railed so hard against. High school might be a waiting game, she might be biding time until her real life can start, but she will fucking live. She swears on this to the shadow sisters who made her life easier, the ones who never had shadows to hide in. To her ideals from yesteryears, the drag queens of the Stonewall uprising. *By the power of Marsha P. Johnson*, she says to herself during difficult moments. *In the name of Sylvia Rivera*, when she overhears a classmate being especially homo- or transphobic. *For the honor and heritage of Christine Jorgensen*, when breathing air into a hostile body seems like a chore. She has read so much about the trans women who built this road she is standing on. She wishes they could speak to her, tell her things will be okay, tell her how to live the sort of life she needs. But then, she reasons, maybe they wouldn't know. She wonders at how many other trans women, trans femme girls, and nonbinary and genderless people exist on the internet. Is the void of disconnection more or less isolating than living alone in an Appalachian town feeling like you are wrong, unnatural, because some Bible-thumper told you so and your church community and family affirmed it time and time again?

And so she chooses a reason every day to wake up. Sometimes it is something small and kind, like putting quarters in all the machines outside of the supermarket so, on their way out, little kids won't have to ask their parents' permission for a piece of gum or a palm-size toy in a plastic bubble. Some days it's an app that lets her apply a gender filter.

Some days it's significant, like the first time she posted in an online trans community as herself. Her real self.

She carries the responses to that post around with her like a warm pink bubble in her chest for days. The encouragement and shared coming-out stories, questions inviting her further into the group, and their gentle kidding, all remind her there is a broader world outside her hometown where she might make a place for herself.

On *Shampoo Unicorn*, Sass and Mimi talk about a boy who was outed at their school. A coach caught him and another boy in a locker room after practice and they were both expelled. That's at least one thing about being trans; you don't need anyone's help to get caught. But if her parents or classmates see her toenails, they may not even guess her girl-ishness is related to gender dysphoria. They may wonder first if she is gay. And honestly, she can't say she isn't. But she can't even begin thinking about being physical with someone else until she's more comfortable occupying her own body. Leslie refuses to sweat the question of who she is attracted to until she can walk around the world as a self she loves.

Sometimes, she runs a hand along her flat chest, wondering what it will feel like when there are curves there, wishing hips grew from her sides where bones poke out now. Even her body feels flat. She thinks of it as a fallow field for a future she is building. She reads about estradiol, about hormone blockers, online. The first time she sees someone call them anti-cistamines, she laughs out loud. The laugh is so round and full she can feel it resting in her belly right below her rib cage for the rest of the day—the joke, a little golden bubble of joy she keeps returning to.

Today, the boy from the podcast, Gaybor, is on her mind. What are the differences in being outed as a cis gay man versus being outed as a trans woman? Being outed to a potential partner is more physically dangerous for trans women. There's that whole trope of trans panic, the story that unless everyone knows your particular anatomy and identity, you're somehow lying and deceiving people as though a person's individual truth is up for public debate.

What would happen at school, at home, if people knew? She can hold out. Suffer her prison a little longer. She just needs to get through graduation and summer before college will let her live on her own with more independence. She could join a queer student union. She could go to a hairdresser for a woman's haircut. She could have clothes she's only looked at and dreamed about online delivered to her at school. She could get a post office box. A job. Maybe even an off-campus apartment.

She doesn't have a timeline for coming out. Her scholarships are substantial, but her parents are still paying for her room and board at school, and she's heard enough horror stories about parents yanking financial support or worse after their kid came out. And based on their comments and unaware slurs, those microaggressions that add up, she's still not sure where they'd fall on the trans acceptance scale.

Her heart is heavy for the outed boy. What is his real name? She's sure it's not Gaybor. Names are so weird. The one she responds to every day feels like a pair of underpants left too long in the dryer. Every time someone uses it, she feels constricted. It's not yet a deadname, because she is living quietly for the day she can answer to something else. But responding to it weighs her down, like she's being buried at the bottom of a river. What are Gaybor's parents like? Do they support him? Shun him? What future does he imagine for himself when he dares to dream limitlessly? Is it similar to hers? A loving relationship? A circle of warm friendship? What does he fear in his worst moments?

If Gaybor was caught with a girl instead of a boy, he would've gotten suspended, not expelled. Hell, a couple of freshmen from her school were caught behind the bleachers and only got detention. The world is unfair. It's cruel and lonely. When you're different or other or don't have the right skin color, when they can't fit you in the normal mold, you're discarded.

And it's tiring being discarded, being less than. Leslie wants to change things. Wants people to see her. To know the real her.

The podcast's closing theme pulls Leslie out of her thoughts. The soundtrack of the school around her is only slightly muffled by her earbuds. Through the plastic clouds, she hears her name, yanks them out, and returns to the record scratch of reality.

Someone touches her shoulder and she flinches. "   ," Mr. Infante, her geography teacher, says. "The bell just rang. Better get to your next class, son."

5

ALL QUESTIONS, NO ANSWERS
Greg

It happened in slow motion.

The locker-room door slamming, the footsteps, Coach Winsor's and Principal Matthews's stunned silence, you on your knees, Derek shoving you onto your back, and you, naked except for a threadbare pair of boxer briefs. The smell of deodorant barely masking the musky scent of bodies, sweat, soap, and something less tangible but wildly masculine. You tried to cover yourself, groped for a towel that wasn't there, and waited, your junk in your hands, until they told you both to get dressed and meet in the principal's office.

Derek didn't look at you. He gathered his clothes, got dressed on the other side of the room with his back to you, and left without saying anything. Not that there was anything to be said; still, you felt like you should apologize but you didn't know where to start.

You kept your head down for the entire walk to the principal's office, ignoring all your classmates and avoiding eye contact. You walked this same hallway for four years. You never spent this much time looking at the floor, just focused on making it from one point to another with minimal human interaction before. You wondered if, on your deathbed, this would be one of the things you'd see when your entire life flashed before your eyes. You kept your head down during the entire meeting with your principal and Coach Winsor, Derek silent beside you. Only daring to look up when you heard the word *expelled* ring in your ears like a verdict from on high. When Principal Matthews mentioned your parents, you felt the hammer of your heart smash your chest from the inside. Your dad will kill you. Your mom will want to die.

The office was like a set from a generic teen movie. Diplomas hung on the walls behind the principal, and bookcases flanked the desk on either side. One held a set of encyclopedias and matching leather-bound books. The other had a bunch of matching teal binders labeled by year. There were photos of his family on the desk beside his name plate. Principal Matthews with a wife and a son. The kid must have been about seven or so. You wondered what he'd say to his son in this situation. If he'd be angry or disappointed, compassionate or distant.

"Do you have to tell my parents?" you asked, your voice cracking midway through the question.

"I'm afraid so, Greg," he said. "I won't tell them any graphic details, of course. But they're your legal guardians, so they do have to be informed of any disciplinary actions."

You felt Derek sit upright beside you. "What are our legal rights for appeal?" he asked, in a cold, haughty voice you'd never heard him use.

"You can request a hearing with the Canon School Board. I'll put together the paperwork and mail it to you both if you'd like," Principal Matthews said.

"Excellent," Derek replied. "You should expect to hear from my lawyer by the end of the week."

It never occurred to you to envy Derek's wealth before. Sure, he had nicer things, but he was really generous because he didn't want to make you feel shitty about your secondhand clothes and ratty shoes. This was the first time you could remember ever really resenting him. An attorney, an appeal, an alternative. These were never options for you. And without the athletic scholarship you'd earned, college wasn't an option now, either.

You felt like a stranger wearing someone else's skin for the entire drive home, dread sitting in the pit of your stomach like a heavy deuce. Your dad would be there, but your mom wouldn't. No telling if he'd be drunk or sober, awake or asleep. No telling if the school had called or emailed, or if they'd go old school and send a letter in the mail. These days he worked third shift while she slept. They saw each other for church and in passing. If the air was tense, at least it was quiet. The drive home felt like it took hours. Even though in peak Canon traffic it couldn't take more than twenty minutes.

You wondered how badly it would hurt to die by collision, but then put the thought away. Collision involved someone else, and you'd already put the people in your life through enough without dragging anyone else into your shameful, stupid bullshit.

6

WE MEET AGAIN
Brian

I stalked Greg online all week.

Hunted him at school, even though I knew neither he nor Derek would be there. Eavesdropping on gossip, I tried to parse out what was likely and what was hyperbole. From being the subject of so much slander myself, I knew to believe little, but I paid attention anyway, hoping for a kernel of truth. I haunted the hallways, listening for his name over the slamming of teal lockers, even braving the stench of cigarettes hanging in the boys' restroom to see if any of the smokers knew anything.

"I keep thinking about how shitty things must be for Greg at home right now," I said to Riley between classes. She leaned against the locker next to mine, her head resting back in thought. I gripped my neck and grasped my elbow with my other hand to stretch, slightly self-conscious that the motion caused my tightest-fitting Janelle Monáe shirt to ride up.

A girl I didn't know with black braids and an oversize cardigan, probably a freshman by how young she looked, came up to the locker beside us and spun her combination lock.

"Weird," Riley said, side-eyeing the girl, then leaning closer to me and lowering her voice. "That's been on my mind, too. And also, realizing how little I know about Derek's family, besides his dad being the self-proclaimed 'New and Used Car and Truck King of Canon County.' It was hella corny how much the guy loved it. He wore that outfit in the back of a convertible for the Christmas parade on Main Street for a couple years afterward." She smirked.

"OMG, that's right," I said, and returned her smile. Riley's amber eyes were beautiful with their golden specks and deep warmth. And distracting. "Remember when he had all those billboards along the four-lane highway with him in a crown and a fur cape? And how everyone called Derek Your Highness or Your Majesty that year?"

"Yeah, sure I do. I'd have felt sorry for Derek if he wasn't such a dick." Riley snorted. "Greg's dad, on the other hand . . ."

"Yeah . . ." We both let the thought take us to different places. It felt weird caring after pretending so long not to care about Greg, who'd become a stranger to us, who had also cosigned to my torture. He was this sweet boy I'd loved so much when we were younger and this enigmatic stranger.

After school, I drove to the gas station across from Greg's trailer park, waited until his dad's truck left their carport, and walked down the gravel road to his trailer. The wooden porch rocked and the thin, metal door rattled when I knocked on it. I'd only visited once, right after he moved, and then my friend disappeared from my life, only to emerge months later as this masc-presenting athlete. He opened it, and I tried not to let my face give away my shock. Most of the left side of his face was discolored, all black and blue and sick green around the edges of the bruises. Where his eyeball was supposed to be white, it was clouded with blood, and a cast covered his right hand and forearm.

"What are you doing here?" Greg asked.

"I . . . You weren't in school, so I wanted to check in." Tinny country music played in the trailer next door, just audible over a persistent smoker's cough.

"I'm expelled, so I won't be back." He loomed large against the doorframe with his arms folded across his chest, blocking my view of his living room.

I tried not to stare at him, his mottled bruises and pained expression made my heart ache. Instead, I looked at the porch, its red paint, cracked and fading, the wood splintered in places.

"Jesus Christ, Brian, you have to go." He raked a hand through his dark, messy curls. "My dad will be back in a few; he just went to pick my mom up from work. He can't catch you here."

"Did he do this to you?" I asked, furious and worried. "Come home with me and we'll figure it out." I reached out to touch him, and he jumped back as though suddenly electrocuted. His movement shook my confidence. I barely knew him anymore. How could I figure his life out?

Greg pushed his head past me, shifting his gaze up and down the dirt road. "Look, I can see you tonight, okay? My parents took away my laptop and cut service on my phone. But I'll meet you at the clubhouse. They'll be asleep by eleven, so I can be there about midnight."

"Okay, should I do—"

"Look, you gotta go. I'll see you tonight." He shut the door, and I spun on my heel and scampered back to my mom's rusty old Camry.

• • •

Stepping into the still night, I was a phantom. The houses lining the street were silent and dark inside, like empty shells except for the occasional porch light left hopefully on or the quiet sound of late-night TV shows. My footsteps crunched over the autumn leaves, and my heartbeat thudded dully in my ears. When I got to the clubhouse, I could see him lit by the blue screen of his phone, leaning a hip against the empty doorframe.

"I thought your phone was cut off?"

He flashed Angry Birds at me. "Oh yeah, this is just a stupid game. No service required."

I shoved my hands into my pockets and waited for him to talk. After a few uncomfortable minutes, Greg told me that his parents were making him take the GED and enroll in community college. He'd have to get a job to earn his keep until he graduated, and his parents had been praying over him night and day, inviting the pastor of their church over to witness to him, as well.

When I asked about what happened with Derek, he said he didn't think Derek was gay, but that they'd been screwing around for a while. Just, y'know, guys being guys. The whole thing started at a party where they'd both been super drunk and Greg made a pass at Derek and things just sort of happened. It kept happening, Greg said, and while it was never reciprocal or affectionate, self-loathing semi-sex was better than no sex at all, right?

"I'm so sorry, Brian. I have been such an incredible douche to you. I hated myself every goddamn day, and I felt like a huge chickenshit every time I didn't say anything when those guys fucked with you. I am so, so fucking sorry."

I thought about his apology for so long that it felt like the sun should have risen and set again. Looking at his beautiful, bruised face was hard. There had been abuse, and at times it had been fucking brutal. But I never had to wear any vest of hypocrisy. All the shame. All the humiliation and fear we both felt but he couldn't say, not to anyone else, not even to me across the chasm he'd created between us. This time, he waited me out. "I'm not going to say it's okay. Because it's not. You hurt me in ways I might not realize until I'm old and unpacking the trauma of my formative years in therapy. But you can't ask me to forgive you, standing here, looking like that. It's not real, and it's not fair."

Greg dropped his head and sniffled.

"It must have been pretty hard for you, too, though," I said. "At least I never had to lie about who I am."

And then he was crying in earnest. He wasn't the same kid who, when we were fifteen, let his football buddies pants me in the science hallway. But neither was he the same kid who learned "The Imperial March" on a kazoo and dressed up as a stormtrooper for my eighth birthday. His face had hollowed out and his hair had gotten darker. Stubble dotted his jawline, and a river of tears ran down his face through the tiny hairs. Under a microscope, his face might look like hundreds of trees, fallen and flooded.

I touched his face, wiping away his tears with my fingertips, and then he was kissing me, and not at all gently. The pressure of his lips against mine was sudden—ferocious, warm, and wet against the cold, dry air. We were wrapped up in each other, his face damp and rough against mine, and his body shivering against mine, through all our clothes. He felt like the only solid thing in a spectral world.

"Are you cold?" I asked against his lips.

"Nope." He laughed against mine, and then I was trembling, too.

All the things he and his friends had said and done replayed in my mind, and it felt like kissing him was a betrayal of myself. As much as I hurt, I hurt for him, too. My pain and his wove together, and I wanted to knit ourselves inside of it, safe from harm. It must've been scary for him to be found out. He wrapped his arms around me, and I wanted more than anything to turn my brain off.

If only I could rewind to the kid I knew—the sweet Greg who delivered my homework every day with a new chapter of Pokémon fanfiction when I had chicken pox in third grade. The only boy I knew who could eat a dozen deviled eggs in one sitting without barfing and still have room for dessert. By the time we were in fifth grade, Greg knew the choreography for both "Thriller" and "Bye Bye Bye." I thought he was the coolest person I'd ever met, then.

I pulled my shirt off over my head first, and then his as well, unprepared for the heat of his chest against mine. My fingertips and the cold made goose pimples on his skin. I wanted to touch him for hours, to make up for the tenderness that Derek hadn't shown him, wanted my hands and mouth to heal his wounded places. Red and purple mottled bruises on his ribs caused me to gasp. I swallowed tears and grazed the bruises with my lips as gently as I could, just a whisper of a kiss.

There are limits to what two boys can do to each other in the middle of the crisp autumn woods without condoms, especially when one of them is badly injured. You can do enough, though.

We stayed out as late as we could, talking and making out and holding each other and occasionally crying and laughing. When the sky started to get light, we untangled our limbs, and he walked me back to my car.

"Can I drive you home?"

"Brian." He kissed me so sweetly, pulling my bottom lip between his teeth. My body twitched in response as he pulled away. "You know you can't."

"What happens now? Like, you've had way more dude-on-dude experience here. Are we dating? Is that . . . even a thing we could do?" A million unanswerable questions stampeded through my head like zebras, and I could feel my heart beating like hooves. I knew there was no chance of a traditional dating situation, but maybe we could meet here, in our boyhood clubhouse outside of time, in secret like forbidden lovers. The drama appealed to me, even if the danger did not.

"I'm not sure. I have your number. Can I call you when things are . . . less complicated?" Greg dove into his shirt first, then his coat, and finally buttoned his pants and cinched his belt around his waist.

"You can call me even if they aren't."

He smiled, patted the hood of my car, and waved until I could no longer see him in my rearview mirror.

It's not what I imagined my first time would be like. I had imagined a worst-case scenario in which it would be a seedy hookup in the first bar I could legally get into. On the flip side, my best-case scenario would be that I'd meet my soulmate in some perfectly sweet, wholesome way, we'd fall in love, have picturesque sex in a field of daisies and dress our adopted children in matching pajamas every year for the family Christmas card.

Lying in bed staring at the ceiling, what I came to was this: There's no ideal way to lose your virginity. It's an outdated social construct for straight people and fucking irrelevant to queer folks. However your first consensual encounter happens is right. It wasn't about positions or where, how many times, or if you got off at all. It was the unimaginable beauty of his moan and the way his back arched when you did something that made him feel awesome. I knew what his kiss felt like and how his skin was salty in some places and earthy in others. How the moonlight had danced on his eyelashes. Remembering lit a bittersweet ache in my chest and an electric current in my thighs. I had read about and watched people having sex on the internet, but I hadn't actually done it. I could divide my life into before and after, and there was no doubt that the experience had changed me.

You could be pressed closely enough against someone to feel their heartbeat against your chest, hear their breath in your ears, and the whole thing would open your eyes to the wonder and awe that existed in the world that maybe you'd never even known about.

I wondered what Greg was thinking and how long I'd have to wait to ask him.

What if he thought this was all a mistake?

7

LIFE IN THE AFTERMATH
Greg

Boredom was a curse.

Your parents had you locked down tight, no phone, no laptop, no car. Your parents could barely look at you. You hardly saw your mom. She'd be gone to work before you woke, leaving her usual note on the fridge with how to prepare the Tupperware meal she'd left inside. When your dad did speak to you, it was from the recliner where he was usually watching NASCAR or WWE, which you thought was super homoerotic but never said so for fear of the back of your dad's knuckled hand.

He loved to go in on how much he'd sacrificed for you, how hard he'd worked and how you'd never been expected to earn your keep at the expense of your athletics or academics. He'd wanted to raise a good, God-fearing son who would work hard and uphold the morals and values he'd tried so hard to instill.

"I'm sorry," you said, folding your arms over your chest and cramming your fists into your armpits so no one could see your balled-up rage. You weren't sorry, but you couldn't defend yourself any more emotionally than you could physically at the moment, still bruised and oozing pus from fresh cuts.

"You're right," you added, your voice resigned, face pointed at the ground to hide the shame and fear on it.

You stumbled out of bed, stretched, and picked up the least-dirty shirt and shorts from a pile on your bedroom floor, then layered them over your boxers. You flipped through the Bible magazines your mom brought, old *Guideposts* with wrinkled pages, some devotionals swollen with your mom's ballpoint underlining, a copy of some crap book by a washed-up teen actor whose career had not survived puberty. You pushed back the day for as long as you could. Finally, you wandered into the living room and your father's eyes snapped to you like a magnet.

"Listen, boy. You listening?"

"Yessir." You stifled a yawn and sniffed to see if your dad had made coffee. Judging from the bouquet of cigarette smoke, rye whiskey, and mothballs that hung in the air, he hadn't.

"You ain't just gonna stay home all day eating all my food and burning up all my 'lectricity just because you messed up your future." He was stretched out in his recliner with a *Dukes of Hazzard* rerun on mute. "You got to get a job and get your school shit figured out so you can contribute something to this household."

"All right," you said as Bo and Luke slid across the hood of the General Lee.

"There's a GED class starting at the vocational tech school next week. You got to sign up on the internet. It's not what we wanted for you, but you can start some sort of trade program and earn a good enough living to support your family later in life."

"Yessir."

"Least this way, you won't be a total failure, even if you are a total disappointment." He looked full on at you then, and you could feel his challenge. He was drunk and spoiling for a fight. The atmosphere was incendiary, and you treaded carefully, cautious not to cause a spark. You could see the amber bottle on the TV tray by his recliner. Less than half full. Your old man was lit, and so was his fuse.

"Yessir," you responded. "Maybe I can fill out some applications online?"

Your dad pushed himself painfully out of the recliner, as though suction were holding him back. His bones popped, and he groaned, shuffling to the bedroom he shared with your mom. From the closed door, the stubborn closet whined open and hangers scraped across the clothes bar, revealing where your father had stashed your laptop.

The bedroom door slamming jolted you out of your thoughts.

"Jus' use it in the living room when me or your mom is home," your dad slurred, practically throwing the laptop at you. He lowered himself into his chair, pushing back to raise his feet. Flicking his lighter, he lit another cigarette and glared at you suspiciously through the smoke until you finally opened the device and started typing. Less than one *Dukes of Hazzard* episode later, you had filled out a dozen applications and the wet sucking of your dad taking long pulls from his whiskey bottle set your spine on edge. You closed the laptop, careful not to slam it, lest that motion spark his rage, and placed it on the chair. After nodding to your dad, you went quietly back to your room.

To relieve boredom, you'd start reading whatever was around the house and doing crunches and pushups in your room. Anything to pass the time. Your parents relented when they realized you'd have job interviews and eventually work. They restored service to your phone, but not your computer, so that you could at least get and return calls from potential employers.

The first thing you did after getting it back was read your missed texts and social media messages. You almost responded to a couple of friends who claimed to be checking in, but it felt false to pretend like you were okay, and it was too exhausting to lie. You left them on read, and when scrolling got boring, you popped your headphones in and watched videos for a while. Nothing from Derek, which was what you were looking for.

You couldn't stop thinking about Brian. You couldn't stop thinking about how his face looked in the cold moon glow, his face all eyelashes and hot breath and perfect lips swollen from kissing. How could you have fucked up this badly? How could you hurt a boy so soft? You wanted to apologize to him for a million things but nothing you thought of to say seemed anywhere close to enough, and anyway, you weren't sure he'd want to hear from you. You couldn't stop thinking about the billion ways your bros had tortured him. And how you let them. You just laughed or redirected them when you should have been protecting him. You could have saved him so many times if you weren't such a coward. Derek had always been the ringleader. You never thought to ask why, but now that all you had was time to think, you wondered if it was because of the time you and he spent fucking around. If maybe he wasn't scared he was at least a little bit gay. Did targeting Brian make him feel less so? And if that was true, the whole thing came full circle to wind up right back at the place where everything was your fault. Your fault he needed to prove himself. Your fault that his future was in jeopardy. Your fault for all the bullshit he caused Brian. You were like the middle of a tangled knot where all the strings were razors covered in poison.

In the end, you went back to books, which at least kept you out of your own head for hours at a time.

You thought you'd be waiting to hear back from your applications for a while, since Canon wasn't what you'd have called a bastion of industry. Someone from Jolene's called you back almost right away, surprising you. Your mom smiled when you told her, which made you suspect that she pulled some strings somewhere.

The night before, you ironed and laid out your clothes. Showered, brushed your teeth, and combed your hair the next morning. You were almost out of the house before your dad grabbed you hard by the elbow and reminded you to come home right afterward.

"No fucking around," he said, so close to your face you could feel his hot, pungent breath. When you finally escaped his painful grasp, you sprayed your clothes with cologne to cover up the cigarette smoke that permeated everything you owned.

The manager asked a lot of questions, but overall was pretty cool. He said he'd gone to high school with your parents, had recognized your last name on your application. You felt like you'd nailed the interview. It wasn't a great job, but it paid more than minimum wage, and the guy who interviewed you said that servers tipped out the cooks, bussers, and hosts every night, so you'd have walking-around money, too.

You'd parked in the employee lot, toward the back, so you'd have some privacy in case you finally decided you might call or text Brian. Images of that night kept playing in your head, everything that happened between the two of you. The rest of your life was so hard and complicated that thinking about his pale, thin body shining in the moonlight was a lifeline. You had many questions for him, and no answers to offer in return. You started the conversation several times in your head but couldn't come up with the right things to say.

You stared at your phone, halfway between the building and your car, wondering what you'd even say. The sun was shining half-heartedly, and it was the sort of generic Thursday morning that you had taken for granted before being kicked out of school. A slight breeze brushed your hair off your forehead, the song of traffic and distant nature stilled your heart, and you took a pause. Just for a minute. This could work. You could make a life. All was not lost.

Tires squealed behind you right before something struck your side, knocking you forward.

Your head thumped hard against the pavement, and you fell into darkness.

SHAMPOO UNICORN
Episode 309: "The Truth behind the News"

NEWS ANNOUNCER:

A high school senior was found yesterday in the parking lot of a local restaurant following what appears to be a hit-and-run. The victim, identified as Gregory Burke, is a senior at Canon High School and remains unconscious in the intensive care unit at Canon General Hospital following the incident. Due to a recent episode in which Greg was caught in a sexual act with another boy at the school, it's speculated that this was a hate crime. Local officials are asking anyone with information to please step forward at this time.

*[*SHAMPOO UNICORN *THEME SONG PLAYS.]*

SASS:

(clearing throat nervously)

I've done a lot to keep this podcast fairly anonymous. In the past, it was important that queer people from other small towns be able to relate to what was happening here. And maybe they . . . maybe *you* still will. I don't know. I don't know what will happen. But it would be fairly easy to figure out who I am by what I've said on this channel. All anyone has to do is a quick Google search of the information. I'm usually strongly opposed to outing anyone, but the news released Greg's name, so I've decided, after a lot of consideration, to share it here.

MIMI:

Sass, you don't have to—

SASS:

My name is Brian. I'm a senior at Canon High School. Earlier this year, a couple of kids got caught having gay sex in the locker room. One of them was this guy, Greg. He and I grew up together. He, Mimi, and I used to be best friends. And then we weren't. I don't know what to say about that. People grow apart. They make different choices, have different priorities. That isn't the point. I've never had the luxury of invisibility. My mannerisms, my voice . . . give me away. But having this anonymous space to be unselfconsciously gay gave me a place to be more honest about how much that shit weighs after you carry it around for so long.

Shampoo Unicorn has been a place for me to be coy and catty and try out the personality I curb in public on the daily. It's been for me. But . . . this isn't just a space for me anymore. So lifting the veil on who and where I am will . . . somehow maybe help us figure out what happened to Greg. This feels important, bigger than me, and if being . . . openly myself makes me more credible or creates a wider arc to what happened to Greg, I think it's worth it.

Greg's in a coma right now. He was hit by a car in a parking lot. I don't know if it was a hate crime or not, but the timing is, to me, very suspicious. We weren't close, and hadn't been for years, but he was gay and had recently been through a whole bunch of shit that no one's talking about.

So, that's what I want the subject of this episode to be about.

MIMI:

If you're coming out as a host, I'm coming out, too. We're coming out together. Coming out swinging, in fact. My real name is Riley.

As a contributor to this show and someone who listens to a fair amount of true crime, this checks a lot of boxes for me. Like, I've listened to those shows without having any concept that there are people involved in these "cases" I've been a spectator for. Now that I know someone who could arguably be the subject of a podcast, my being casually entertained by someone else's deep, painful experiences feels . . . pretty fucking ghoulish. So I want to underline the humanity of what's happening. This is a guy we knew. We were friends with him once upon a time. He was an athlete, a student, a son, and a friend. A person. And that's important. Actually, this episode is important for quite a few reasons.

BRIAN:

What do you mean?

RILEY:

Well, it's your coming-out episode.

BRIAN:

Huh?

RILEY:

I mean, I love every single person that you are, but you're someone different on this show than you are IRL. This is, like, *the you* that you are when no one's looking. And I love that. But I also love how thoughtful you are as Brian in your everyday life, too. I hope you're in your new violently flaming era, bestie.

BRIAN:

I wouldn't have thought of it that way.

RILEY:

Which is why I'm your most valuable and constant guest.

BRIAN:

There's a long list of reasons that's true.

RILEY:

Anyway, the point is: This terrible thing happened in our town, and no one is really talking much about why or what will happen so much as they're just gossiping about the most irrelevant and inane things.

BRIAN:

Mostly it's being talked about online. His Facebook page is full of thoughts and prayers from the same kids who throw homophobic language around like beach balls, and who have to clarify "no homo" every time they compliment someone of the same gender. But I hear about it in the halls, too.

I'm not a hundred percent sure that it was a hate crime. There are too many questions right now to figure any of that out. But because there was so much hallway speculation, Riley and I set out to do what we do best.

RILEY:

Fuck shit up? Smash the patriarchy? Cause shenanigans?

BRIAN:

Riley and I set out to do what we do fourth best.

RILEY:

Ask questions. Report. Find answers.

[HOSPITAL BACKGROUND NOISES.]

BRIAN:

(whispering)

The normal hospital smells hang in the air. We're at the hospital. We're approaching a woman in faded blue scrubs with a *Star Wars* lanyard hanging from her neck. The ID says she's an RN.

(talks louder)

Excuse me. I was wondering if you could answer a few questions.

NURSE:

Uh, I'm sorry, about what, exactly?

BRIAN:

About Greg Burke. He's on this floor, right?

NURSE:

Oh, darlin', I'm sorry. HIPAA laws prevent me from talking about people's medical information.

BRIAN:

Oh, no. Not like that. I mean, just, has he gotten any other visitors? Have a lot of people come to see him? Stuff like that.

NURSE:

Well, I mostly work during evening visiting hours, and there have been some people in and out, sure. His mama's been there almost the whole time, and his daddy came in a couple times. Beyond that, I couldn't tell you. Maybe you ought to ask his parents? Why'd you wanna know, sugar?

BRIAN:

Well, mostly I'm just curious. Have the police been here at all?

NURSE:

Not that I know of, but like I said, I'm just here in the evenings. There's no way I can keep track of everybody's comings and goings. Besides, I can't really talk about any of this.

RILEY:

(in voiceover)

When we didn't find much out at the hospital, we tried the police station, but they were initially super dismissive of us after leaving us sitting around for over an hour, so we bailed. Instead, we hung out at Pop's Stop and Shop until we saw one of Canon's finest pull up outside.

BRIAN:

After a little back and forth, we've decided that Riley should talk to the officer since I had talked to the nurse and . . . I can be a little confrontational with authority.

RILEY:

I've pressed record on my iPhone, and I'm now walking

toward the police car. The officer is an older guy, maybe in his forties or fifties, with thin hair combed over a bald spot and chips stuck in his beard.

(louder)

Officer, hello. How are you? I wondered if I could bother you for a minute.

OFFICER HAZELWOOD:

Beg pardon? You ain't bothering me none. What can I help you with, young lady?

RILEY:

(clears throat)

Do you know anything about my friend Greg Burke? We know he's in a coma, but his parents haven't really said anything about what happened to him. His friends and I miss him a whole bunch, and we just want to do anything we can to help.

OFFICER HAZELWOOD:

I'm sorry about your friend, but I can't say anything about an open investigation to nobody outside the family who ain't a lawyer.

RILEY:

(sniffling dramatically)

Can you tell us anything? Why it happened? If you have any leads? Will he be okay? What will happen?

OFFICER HAZELWOOD:

I wish I could. Truth is, there ain't much to know. I'm not telling you nothing about the case by letting you know that there's no cameras in that parking lot and nobody has come forward yet. You probably know that Jolene's does a good dinner business through the week, but the staff don't even really come in until noon most days. Chuck, the manager, just walked over to interview Greg for a job that day, and then he stayed to do paperwork. Him and his old lady live across the road there. His office is in the back, so until he heard the sirens, he didn't even know anything happened to Greg.

RILEY:

Why would someone do something like that? And then just leave him there?

OFFICER HAZELWOOD:

I wish I knew more. It's a damn shame what happened to that boy. It's been a minute since we had a hit-and-run in Canon. Town's too small, and everybody knows everybody else's business. I ain't spilling any details by telling you there ain't no details to spill.

RILEY:

Yessir. Thanks for talking to me.

OFFICER HAZELWOOD:

No thanks needed, young lady. Here's my card. Give me a holler if you hear anything.

RILEY:

And that was that. There's been no follow-up in the paper, but there's still a lot of wild and unfounded gossip at school. Some kids are saying Greg and Derek are part of a gay sex cult. And I think there are a few theories going on about aliens. We're going to do some more poking around, since I guess this has become a true crime podcast after all. Meanwhile, in the unlikely event that any listeners know or have heard anything, and you maybe don't feel comfortable going to the police, please reach out. Or if you're a Canon student and you want to talk about it, reach out. In the interest of full disclosure, we're putting contact info and a couple of articles in the show notes. The number for our local police force, and some queer-specific mental health resources are there as well.

BRIAN:

I've always been glad to have this podcast as an outlet, and incredibly grateful to the listeners who support us. Now, more than ever, that means the world. And now a word from our sponsors.

[TRANSITION MUSIC PLAYS.]

8

SKINNED KNEE
Leslie

Leslie thinks about technology.

She lives on her phone more than anywhere else. Who she is becomes evident in her wallpaper, apps, and music and the podcasts she listens to, videos she watches, and people she interacts with. Her phone is never more than a foot away, even while she's eating, sleeping, or showering. Her parents joke about this occasionally. About her generation's codependent relationship with electronics. Leslie usually just rolls her eyes or calls them boomers or dinosaurs or ignores them completely.

She pops in her earbuds and heads to the gym for release.

If only her phone could unfold into a portal she could step through to escape reality. Inside, it would look like a maze of hallways, with doors opening into different apps or communities. It would be clean, almost sterile, and slightly cold. Around each corner, new corridors would materialize with rows of doors, each one rich with potential.

Instead, she hides the world away in her pocket and walks through a landscape she knows by heart. Through doors that fill her with dread, bringing her to people she can barely tolerate. Every day is an act of survival, every moment an exercise in resilience.

She can't stop thinking about the boy from the podcast, Greg. About how he was attacked. How maybe there'll be violence no matter when she decides to come out. And what if she waits until college, comes out, and is also attacked? She doesn't want that to be the obligatory narrative. She'll never be ready to defend herself against danger she can't understand or predict. So why not now? Why is she waiting so long when hiding hurts and maybe the ending is the same no matter what?

She's angrier than she can remember ever being. It cuts a clear path through the numbness she's been cultivating. Fear and grief braid together like a whip, threatening to destroy the careful facade she's created. If a boy doing almost everything *right* could end up alone, unconscious on the cold pavement of an empty restaurant parking lot, what hope is there she won't end up the same way? Or fucking worse.

Leslie tries to let it roll off her back, tries to ride it out like she's always done, but she can feel the rage bubbling up, boiling over in a way she has never felt before. She has never thought about the podcast host in the same way she thinks about this boy. To her, Sass and Gaybor are different. Sass is out and proud. Something about Gaybor, the idea of his vulnerability, resonates with her, shakes Leslie to her core. She knows how double-edged the sword of visibility is. How it can slice you to ribbons while you're hiding for your own safety. How it feels like the skewer holding the conditional love of everyone in your life over a fire that blisters you from the inside out daily.

Canon, West Virginia, as it turns out, is about an hour's drive from her small town in Pennsylvania. She has never met either of the boys, but they live close enough that she might have seen them at a school event or at the big mall that's almost halfway between the two towns. They might have cousins in common, even.

Angry music plays loudly through her earbuds and it's almost enough to drown out the chaos inside her. What she wants is to shout or stomp or curse. Her rage is physical, but without an outlet it's like a red-hot fire trying to escape her rib cage from inside, pressing and painful. She pounds the treadmill until she's out of breath, chugs some water, wipes her sweaty face, and then lifts weights until her arms are so tired that they hang limp like spaghetti noodles at her sides.

When she comes home, her mom is unloading groceries from the car and asks for her help. Leslie slings her backpack over a shoulder and grabs one of her mom's canvas reusables from the back of the green Subaru. She's halfway up the sidewalk when the bag slips, and in trying to catch it, she trips, landing hard on both bare knees.

"Fuck," Leslie shouts. "Goddamn it."

Her mother spins around. "   , honey?" She puts her own bags down on the ground and rushes over. "Are you okay?"

And something about the worry on her mom's face and concern in her voice breaks Leslie. Her arms dangle by her sides, still limp from her workout, and blood trickles down her raw knees. Her mom's stare makes her feel like both a child and a stranger. She tries to push back the tears, but almost as soon as she takes the first deep breath, she heaves, crying so hard until she's out of air. Her mom's warm arms wrap around her like the steam from a cup of cocoa, soft as a blanket. This is not about groceries.

Leslie buries her head in her mom's shoulder, inhaling the familiar aroma of pressed powder, Chanel No. 5, and spearmint gum.

She should stop. Pull herself together and put on her game face. But every time she tries to move away, her mom's arms, shockingly strong, pull her back. Her mom's simple cotton blouse gets wet against Leslie's cheek, dampened by her tears and snot. She's grateful for this moment. Grateful for her mom's unexpected strength. Her warmth, the solidness of her, holding Leslie fast.

A few moments pass, mostly in silence. The suburbs continue to hum with passing cars and the whir of a neighbor's sprinkler. Over it all, her mom holds on. Eventually, Leslie runs out of tears. They are pressed so closely together, but Leslie could fill a football arena with the unsaid things between them.

Leslie extracts herself from the embrace and her mom smiles, wiping away a stray tear and then smoothing Leslie's hair. "Want to talk about it?"

Leslie takes a deep breath, squares her shoulders, and says the hardest sentence she's ever spoken. "I have something to tell you."

9

LIKE HEARING UNDERWATER
Greg

You woke up lost.

If you'd even call it waking up. You couldn't quite see, but you could feel your soul rattling around in your body or something. No sight, no ability to move or speak. You felt sort of . . . at peace. You could hear stuff in the dim background. It was as though someone was trying to talk to you through earplugs while you were swimming. There was a really weird smell, too. Maybe chlorine, but more sterile. A hospital, maybe? You felt trapped in the worst video game ever, the details filling in slowly, and the meta-ness of the whole situation making you question your own sanity. Best not to scratch that itch too hard, you decided.

The last thing you remembered, you were on your way back to your car from a job interview. It had gone well, and it was nice to be out of the house. It had been a while since you'd been anywhere that wasn't your house. You were still fucked-up about Derek and trying to figure out what to do with your life after all your lies were laid out in the daylight.

Okay, Greg. Just the facts. You were a relatively good-looking teenage boy. A clean-cut, all-American boy—you looked like a young Superman, your coach had occasionally said, though maybe he just meant one of the guys from those old movies. Athletic scholarship, churchgoing Christian. Good grades. Party with the bros on weekends, hold it down at home and school during the week. Or that's the story you'd been telling.

The other story, the one written in invisible ink, was different. You wondered from the shadows where you hid if it was even a story anyone wanted to hear. The story of the disembodied torso you put on your Grindr profile. On the rare occasion when there was someone new passing through East Jesus Nowhere, they mostly only cared that you had a hot body and wanted no-strings, masc-for-masc hookups. You were curious about the randos, though. You hoped they were curious about you. But, whatever. It's not as if you could get matching rainbow bracelets and post cute couple selfies on main. You called yourself Walkaway Joe after that Trisha Yearwood song, but only like one ancient queen got the reference, and you had a pretty respectful conversation about your favorite country divas. He suggested a bunch of cool people you'd never heard of and one day his profile, like that of so many previous randos, disappeared.

Until you started hooking up with Derek, the sex stuff didn't matter. And it's not like you started hooking up with Derek on purpose. Or that often. And then Coach Winsor caught the two of you.

Your breathing grew faster, and you felt trapped like that time with your dad, drunk and speeding in the car with the doors child-locked. You couldn't move, couldn't escape. There were no windows to unlock, no doors to open wherever you were, just the fact of you and your sad memories and shitty decisions. A faint beeping sounded in the background. Cool air hit your face. *Calm down, you idiot.* This was the most at peace you'd felt in how long? Forever, maybe. It was boring and confusing, but it was sort of better than reality. Or less intense, at least.

Okay, think. You had been in the parking lot. It happened so fast you thought you'd just wiped out for a minute, and then there was nothing. Did you scream? You couldn't remember. There was a lot you couldn't remember, and trying to look for specifics was terrifying and exhausting.

Hold on to the facts. You were probably okay. You were still a thinking, sentient person. Otherwise you wouldn't be able to feel your breath, your heartbeat. Maybe you were just sleeping? Probably just tired. Needed rest. But there was pain. Hurt? Yes. Needed time to heal. Were you robbed? Unconscious? No, think of the sounds, the smells. Job interview. Hospital. How? Oh God.

Funny. Wherever God was, he seemed not to be looking out for you. Not that your asshole father ever thought the Almighty had a place in your life, since you were a "godless fag" and a "shitless loser." Big change since making the JV team as a starter in ninth grade had redeemed you to him. Nothing but sports made him want to spend any time with you. And even then, it was better if he could do it as a spectator. It seemed like no matter what happened in the pre-football days, you'd been a nuisance. Too soft, too sensitive, too into things that weren't Christ or the NCAA.

So you became who he wanted. You played football with the aggressive zeal he reserved for delivering drunk armchair sermons to you. You took a more active role in his church and even worked with a couple of the other kids there to start a youth ministry at school. Started dating a girl. Broke up with her when a more popular one asked you out. Learned to stomach making out with her in the right lighting. Kept your head down. Stopped listening to movie scores and started listening to Top 40. Even dropped out of marching band and took wood shop. Actually, you kind of enjoyed wood shop. It got you out of your head. And it was a butch way to make something beautiful from something plain. You gave away the stuff you made in class like you gave away the pieces of yourself.

The realest parts of yourself were the ones you kept back from the most important people in your life. The parts that hurt. That you gave away to nebulous strangers, sent into the world on your knees. Those were the parts that got you in trouble. In the end, those were the parts that landed you here. Wherever the hell here was.

● ● ●

You didn't need to see Derek to know when he walked into the room. Even before you started hooking up, you could clock him from the other end of the football field like your body was a magnet and his was true north. His smell was so distinct you'd recognize it a hundred years from now. Not just the Axe body spray — most of your team wore some variation of that. In fact, the locker room in the field house was so thick with the scent of Axe that it sometimes made you a little nauseous. Lots of your boys were hoping to hook up with someone after the game, and half those fools didn't take time to shower before layering on a cloud of dude perfume and heading out to try and smash.

But beneath the top notes of sweat and cologne, he smelled like the woods.

Just being near him was enough to make you hard sometimes. His smell reminded you of the first time you were together. How awkward and unexpected it had been and how much it had tortured you. It was at a party at Derek's dad's hunting cabin after homecoming last year.

You'd all been drinking a lot. You always did, because you were either celebrating a Friday-night win or consoling yourself after a Friday-night loss. And anyway, you were rambunctious teenage boys. If it wasn't your God-given right to smuggle beer out into the middle of a barn, set a bunch of shit on fire, listen to loud country music, and try to hook up with cheerleaders, what was the point of even playing football? Derek's dad had said that it was basically expected that you'd all "raise a little hell" while you were young. And he'd given you a perfect place for it. Derek had said he thought it was mostly a tax write-off for his dad's business entertaining, which was some rich-people shit you barely understood.

So, you had been doing your thing, nursing your fourth or fifth beer of the night, sitting on one of the hay bales and watching your bros get drunker and wilder, wondering what kind of Snapchat stories you'd wake up to in the morning. Brendan had been doing keg stands, but Marcus and Jimmy had kept letting his legs go and howling with laughter when he toppled over, covered in cheap, warm beer. The skunky smell of weed had snaked its way through the damp musk of hay and farm animals, and you'd had to chase a couple of fucked-up dudes away from the horses several times already. The last thing this party needed was a hoof mark on some drunk asshole's forehead.

Then the loud soundtrack of party country had muted a little and there was that Kacey Musgraves song about following your arrow and making mistakes and you were just. So. Goddamn. *Lonely*. It had welled up in you like it did sometimes—all the anxiety and isolation and fear—and you had been choking back tears all of a sudden. You had stood up and vaguely excused yourself to go take a piss. No one really had noticed your retreat and you had found yourself taking long, slow, deep breaths behind the barn. A few minutes later, Derek had been there, arm thrown around you to make sure you were okay.

"Yeah, man," you had said, and cleared your throat before continuing, "I dunno. Just a little drunk. Pissed about losing to Rockwell. Pissed about my old man. You know. The usual." As soon as you had mentioned your dad, your voice had cracked and you could feel yourself losing it again. You couldn't imagine what choice words your dad would have about this sort of emotional display.

You had cried, leaning hard on the cracked wood of the old barn.

"Hey, dude. It's cool. You're gonna be okay."

When you had glanced over, his face had been so close to yours that you could smell his deodorant, something clean, alpine, and more crisp than the shared can of Axe most of the rest of the team passed around the locker room after home games. You had been so busy thinking about how his warm body would feel next to your cold one. It had surprised you both when you leaned in and kissed him.

You'd avoided this all your life. Not looking at guys in the showers if you could help it. Hooking up with Christy Benjamin that one time so she'd tell all her girls about it and her girls would tell your boys. To keep people from knowing your truth, you dated Beth Turner on and off for the last couple of years, staging dramatic breakups and reconciling publicly. You'd affected a cool-but-aloof stance on dating that you justified to your friends by claiming bros before hoes, and to your parents by saying that you didn't want to get tied down before college. Tamping down and repressing any visible desire for boys surrounding you. And then, in a single drunk, sad second, you fucked it all up. Your dad was right after all.

Derek had pulled back abruptly. In a perfect world, the ground would have swallowed you whole or you'd have made an excuse and then you'd both have laughed it off and blame Natty Ice. Derek was your bro, your best friend. You had opened your mouth to speak, but the flood of excuses had gotten stuck in your throat. The world was far from perfect. It was messy and painful most times.

"Dude, no homo." There had been a lifetime in the silence that passed before he finally spoke. "Are you gay?"

You had thought about denying it. Thought about shoving him into the wall or punching out his lights or something else suitably butch. You could even tell people he tried to kiss you and spin it to your advantage. As long as you said it first, it would be his word against yours. He'd be a social outcast, but he might survive it. You knew you wouldn't. But as soon as he asked and you started spinning your wheels about what to say or do, you were exhausted. The secret you'd been working so hard to outrun had finally overtaken you.

"I never said it out loud before," you had answered in a voice so small it didn't even sound like your own. The music had blared behind you over a crash and a collective roar of laughter. You had sighed and stared directly into his eyes. "But yeah. Yeah, I am."

"Shit." He had run a hand through tousled hair.

"Yeah, I know." You had leaned against the barn and slid down it until your ass hit the cold, hard ground with a thump. He had dropped down beside you and propped his elbows on his knees.

"I thought you were this big-deal player."

"Turns out I'm not."

Derek had gotten up in one easy motion and you had thought he might be going inside to tell everyone. You had braced yourself for the ass-kicking that might ensue. Instead, a minute later, he had come back with two beers, slid easily to the ground beside you again, cracked them both open, and handed one to you.

"Well, you gonna say anything about it?" he'd asked.

"I'm not sure what to say." You had chugged your beer, some liquid courage, hoping it would numb you, make you forget this fucking horrible night. You'd have offered a pound of flesh for the sharp burn of liquor, the blank absolution it offered for all manner of sin. "What do you want to know?"

He had taken a sip from his can and swallowed. "Oh man. Everything but the gross shit, I guess. Do you have a boyfriend? Does your family know?"

"NO." You had almost shouted. "No, nobody knows except me. And now you. Please don't tell anyone."

That said, the sex stuff was complicated. You didn't hate it, but it was mostly one-sided. It was sort of thrilling to be intimate with another human, but you hated yourself every time it happened, and you never let yourself initiate it. But the intimate moments, when you were alone in his truck or in the showers after practice or in his bedroom, played over and over in your head. You had wondered if it meant that he was gay or bi or something. And all you got was porn when you tried to search Google for an answer to your question, "How do you know if the guy you're hooking up with is gay?"

The first time it had happened, you were alone after practice, and he had said something about needing to up his protein game to have some definable abs. He dropped the towel around his waist and looked at you. "What do you think?" he'd asked. "Reverse crunches or planks?"

Your mouth had gone dry, and you had licked your lips, eyes locked with his, until he had walked slowly toward you, put your hand on his junk, and smiled. "You like this. You're into this." It wasn't a question.

Thinking about Derek, you wondered how your memories flavored the intangible soup of time in which you had been left to simmer, boil, or burn.

10

IMPOLITE TO TALK
Brian

I was quieter at school than I could remember ever being.

I felt like every word I spoke out loud moved me somehow further from my night of unexpected beauty with Greg, so I said as little as possible. Even to Riley, I was more subdued than usual. This was the first substantial event of my life I hadn't immediately told her, but it still felt too private, too intimate. And because over the years I'd suffered so much because of him. How do you explain the complexity of understanding and forgiving your bully to someone who might not approve?

In the wake of Greg's accident (that's what the news and authorities called it, even though he was found alone, barely breathing in an empty parking lot), his expulsion, the locker room incident, all that seemed to be sucked up into this vacuum of tragedy. The remaining members of the football team, dressed in their uniforms, collected donations in their helmets at nearby intersections for his medical expenses. It felt like all anyone could talk about, but my words froze in my throat.

And then people just abruptly went on with their lives. There wasn't a lot of gossip in the hallways anymore. And when it was mentioned, people treated it like a robbery or a drunk driver or something. No one mentioned the possibility of a hate crime. It was never on the table, because even if things like that happened in Canon, it's impolite to talk about them. They didn't connect the locker room incident to the accident, as though this new, fresh tragedy wiped away any trace of the previous big, gay sex scandal.

I went to the hospital after school when I could. I didn't want to make it a big thing, but I could do my homework in the silence of the cafeteria or waiting room there as easily as I could at home. The third or fourth time I went into Greg's room, his mom was sitting at the edge of a chair beside him, praying over his body.

"Brian Montgomery." She smiled warmly. "As I live and breathe. Come over here and give me a big hug. I haven't seen you since you were knee-high to a grasshopper."

"Hi, Mrs. Burke," I said, trying to get away with a quick side hug. She stood up and held me at arm's length before wrapping me in a warm, firm hug. She smelled like the same perfume she wore when I was a kid. "How's he doing today?"

"The doctors say no changes, but sometimes the Lord takes time to work His miracles. Let me get a good look at you. My land, but you got tall and handsome."

"How are you holding up?"

"One day at a time." She lowered her head briefly as if needing to gather herself. When she looked up again, that warm smile was firm on her lips. "How are you? I'm tickled pink to see you. I was wondering when Greg's school friends would come see him. But aside from you and Derek, no one has been by. Derek's daddy sent over some real pretty flowers and a card. I reckoned you and Greg had lost touch."

"Yes, ma'am. We mostly did for a while. Just grew apart, I guess. But I heard about . . . what happened, and I wanted to be around. In case y'all need anything, or he does. Or, I don't know. Maybe I shouldn't be here."

She slid back into her chair. "It's awfully sweet of you. I don't especially need anything, but if you're here for a while, I'd sure appreciate the company."

We sat for the next hour or so, chatting. She asked about my mom and Riley, and I asked about Greg's dad and church, and avoided mentioning the reason Greg was there or the incident at school with Derek. She had enough on her plate to have all that brought up again.

She excused herself, and for the first time, I really looked at Greg. He was attached to a lot of machines, and some of the bruises that were there during our night together had faded, only to be replaced by new, darker bruises. Where his eye had been black before was a yellowish green, and his other eyebrow was swollen with a freshly stitched-up cut. An oxygen tube sat just below his nose, and his mouth was stretched around another tube. More of them went into his arms from bags hanging on an IV pole, and wires bunched up the thin, blue fabric of his hospital gown. The machines around us hummed and beeped in robotic harmony.

I touched his cheek, cool and stubbly.

The door opened and closed behind me.

"He loves you, you know?" Mrs. Burke said.

"I'm sorry?" I jerked my hand back like I'd touched an oven.

"When y'all were young. He thought you hung the moon. He'd come back from playin' with you and Riley, and everything would be 'Brian this, and Brian that.' I thought it was so sweet, but it must've driven you crazy, him following you around all the time."

"No, ma'am. He was my best friend." I took a deep breath and looked from Greg to his mom. "Do the police know what happened?"

She stared out the window, the blinds only partly shut. Rain hit the glass planes, almost hypnotizing. When she answered, a deep pain was evident in her voice. "They think he was hit by a truck. Because of how high up his injuries are. They're calling it a hit-and-run."

"What do you think?" I felt bad for asking. But when did ignoring the obvious question ever answer it? "Do you think it had something to do with what happened at school?"

"The timing's funny, ain't it?" She pulled a tissue out of her pocket and gently blew her nose. "I can't really say for sure, but I hope not. I don't like to think about people around here being like that. I always thought of Canon as a good Christian town with good Christian values."

"*Christian* is pretty subjective, Mrs. B."

"Sure, you're right." She nodded. "But I grew up here, so I reckon I'm familiar with most of the people in this town. I can't imagine anybody I know nearly killing my son and then looking me in the face afterward. That is, without showing any remorse."

"You should sit." I grasped her elbow and guided her to sit on the chair beside Greg. I took a seat in the recessed hospital window. "I'm trying to figure it out, too."

Mrs. Burke opened her purse and retrieved a roll of LifeSavers. Riley and Greg used to fight over the red ones when we were kids. She removed a green candy and offered it to me. Lime was my favorite.

"Thank you." I took the candy, popped it into my mouth, and smiled down at her.

Her eyes went to Greg, then to me, and she offered me a tight smile. "You're welcome, honey."

"Mrs. Burke, this isn't all from the accident." I gestured toward Greg. "I saw him after he was expelled but before he ended up here."

"Brian," she said, returning the candy to her bag, "this is none of your concern. It's family business."

Family business? I almost swallowed my LifeSaver. Hot embers of anger ignited in my chest. When we were growing up, he was my family, too. And didn't queer people make their own chosen families all the time? Greg never got a chance to choose his and the one he was born into kind of sucked at protecting him, clearly. So I pushed back my sense of decency, my empathy for what this woman was going through, and I gave Greg a voice since someone had conveniently removed his.

"With all due respect." Anger quaked my voice, so I took a breath to calm my words. "Mrs. Burke, I think it's more than family business. Do the police know Mr. Burke has a history of child abuse?"

Her eyes widened and she gripped the handle of her purse tighter. "Alan? He disciplined Greg. He never touched him in that way. That's not why Greg is . . . the way he is."

"Gay," I said. "Greg is gay. I didn't mean to imply that Mr. Burke sexually abused Greg. But he did hit him. Mr. Burke beat Greg when we were kids, and that's what happened after the locker-room incident, isn't it?"

Mrs. Burke's gaze shifted to her purse, to Greg, to everywhere but me.

"He didn't even fight back," Mrs. Burke whispered, still not looking at me. "His daddy just kept wailing on him, and Greg didn't even fight back. I had to pull Mr. Burke off him."

I waited for her to go on. She sniffed, tugged a tissue out of her cardigan's pocket, and dabbed at her wet eyes. "The last time Greg's daddy came after him, Greg was fourteen or fifteen. I don't remember what they were fighting about, but my son stumbled up from the floor and spat blood at his dad. And then Greg hit him back. Just once, but hard enough that Mr. Burke went down. Until Greg was expelled, it never happened again."

"Do you think—"

"Mr. Burke caused a lot of harm," she said. "But he didn't do this. He dropped me off at the nursing home where I work and went straight to the chapel. Our pastor said he arrived at nine to clean the place. Besides, Florence at the store across the street said his car was parked in front of the church all morning. He doesn't have friends who'd let a drunk driver drive their truck, and he didn't use Greg's car, because Greg took it to go to the interview."

Noises from the hallway caused her to pause. A group of people whispered as they passed the door, left ajar for nurses to keep an eye on Greg. Sharp beeps from some medical device went off somewhere in a room nearby. She continued, "The police already asked me all this, Brian. I know you want to help, but I think the most I can ask for right now is your prayers."

"I don't really pray," I said. "I'm not even sure I believe in God. Not, like, a bearded-dude-in-the-clouds kind of God, anyway."

"Well, then I hope you'll keep coming back." Her eyes went to Greg. Eyes full of pain, with regret maybe, but definitely love. "I know you and him ain't as close as you used to be. But I hope you'll keep visiting. He could use a good friend right about now."

"I'll keep coming back. I promise." The words were aimed at Mrs. Burke, but we both knew that they weren't for her, but for Greg. "And listen, I'm sorry if I was rude just now. I just want to find out who hurt him."

"I know, sugar." She placed her open palm on Greg's hand. "He's lucky to have a good friend like you." Responding to that seemed like a spiderweb, so I stuck with something I felt I could commit to.

"I'll keep coming back until he does."

11

WHITE DIAMONDS
Greg

You were floating in a room with no walls.

Sometimes it got darker, like someone had pulled the blinds down on a window you couldn't see. But there were always, always faint sounds and smells. You'd sussed out that you were in some sort of hospital after wondering for a while if you were dead.

Time felt weird here. It felt both endless and instant. How long had passed between now and when you woke up here for the first time?

One cool thing was that you could fill in the details around you. You wondered if that was actual magic, if you were trapped in some sort of purgatory world, or if you just had a great memory or imagination. Ultimately, the why didn't matter nearly as much as the breaking up of time. And the way that sounds and smells could create the world around you.

The first time it happened, it was the smell of your mom's perfume. She'd been wearing White Diamonds since you started buying it for her every Christmas. You were ten when she mentioned *Cleopatra* was her favorite movie, and Liz Taylor her favorite actress. It was the first secular thing you remember her loving. After that, you checked out every Liz Taylor movie the library had in its limited stock. You watched them together in the couple of hours between when you got home from school and when your dad returned from work every day. Neither of you ever mentioned it to him, and as far as you knew, he never found out.

You were six when your dad caught you trying on your mom's shoes. They were the white patent leather kitten heels she wore to church on special occasions, and even though they were enormous on your feet, you attempted to do some sort of soft-shoe shuffle you'd seen on television. Face red, your dad lifted you out of the shoes by your shoulders. He shouted and shook you so vigorously it felt like you were on a carnival ride. Your mom yanked you from his hands and stepped in between the two of you. She sent you to the safety of your bedroom, and you could hear him shouting at her even with your head under the pillow. After that, you could feel him watching you, waiting for you to show signs of tenderness, of vulnerability.

It surprised you he didn't say anything about the perfume you bought for your mom, though. Complain you were wasting money on shit like that. But he wouldn't comment about how you spent your earnings, because he thought that working hard was a character-building, Christian value. He let you get a paper route to earn the money to buy a bike, and then you were practically unstoppable, mowing lawns and pet sitting, socking away money to buy a laptop and name-brand clothes to fit in with the popular crowd.

White Diamonds was something you'd always associated with your mom. The scent filled a room like a garden blossoming. Even when you knew it wasn't hers, it still made you think of her. So, the first time you smelled it within the dark void you found yourself in, her bedroom filled in around you like a picture coming to life under a painter's brush. You hated your shitty trailer. It was essentially a tin can death trap that rattled every time you walked down the drafty hallway and sounded like it might take flight anytime a heavy thunderstorm rolled through. Even disliked your bedroom, with its threadbare carpet and fake, wood-paneled walls. You loathed the entire trailer. Except for your mom's bedroom.

Dad's clothes and shoes were few enough that they fit in the small rack in the hallway linen closet. He didn't keep much more than his alarm clock and Bible in their room, and he'd been sleeping on the couch for a few years now.

Your mom decorated the bedroom with lacy blue wallpaper covering the bottom half of the wall. Braided throw rugs were placed close enough together that you could walk on them in the winter without your feet touching the cold linoleum floor. There were framed dollar-store paintings of Jesus on the walls—with the lambs and the little children, the obligatory crucifixion painting, *The Last Supper*, and so on.

On the wall opposite the bed, a variety of creams and beauty potions promising younger-looking skin or smaller pores covered your mom's painted-gold and glass vanity. She had so many soft, feathery makeup brushes they barely fit in the glass canister. Foundation sponges rested on a porcelain tea saucer with roses circling the rim, along with the heavy jewelry you yearned to try on but resisted for fear of your dad catching you. Even with all those amazing things, it was the smell of your mom's room that was the very best. The flowery scents of face powder and perfume masking the slightly dusty odor of your trailer.

When you were fourteen, your mom would come home from pulling a double shift at eight a.m. You knew she'd been on her feet for hours. Hearing her Chevy turn into the driveway one morning, you placed the sandwich you'd made earlier, a chilled glass of sweet tea, and a little bag of chips on the kitchen table so it would be waiting when she came inside. She smiled, hugged you, and sat down. You were on your way over to bring her some aspirin when your dad asked where his sandwich was.

"Uh," you stammered. "I can make you one. I just made this because Mom has been on her feet all day."

"Don't act like I ain't done nothing all day, boy," your dad said from the entry between the kitchen and the living room. His rage was sudden, surprising, and he turned it on your mom. "And don't you act like you're so much better than me, Miss High-and-Mighty."

Your mom kicked off her flats, leaving them by the table's leg. "I never said I was better than you, Al. I only just got home, and I'm very tired." She grasped her left shoulder and rolled her neck.

"Like I ain't tired? Shitfire, what the hell does a man gotta do to get a little respect in his own damn house?" Your dad crossed over to stand in front of your mom, looming over her.

You thrust an arm in front of your dad to stop him and wedged in between them, causing your dad to stumble back a few steps. Not that you had to push him or anything, liquor made him unstable on his feet. "Hey, old man," you cut in. "I'll make you a damn sandwich, but why don't you try picking on someone your own size."

He accused you then of trying to be the man of the house, and after that, there had been an invisible target on your back.

Before the trailer, you'd had a great house with a bigger room that faced Brian's bedroom window. The two of you would make faces at each other and write notes and draw pictures on your windows in dry-erase markers. Your room was a shrine to country music, with posters and band T-shirts tacked to your wall. It was the only thing you and your dad really agreed on. It wasn't exactly Christian music, but enough country singers and bands identified as Christian that your dad didn't really say anything when you spent your allowance on iTunes cards and played Toby Keith and Blake Shelton on your phone, even though you preferred Miranda Lambert and Carrie Underwood. You loved the Chicks and Dolly Parton, but you only listened to them when you were visiting Brian or Riley.

Their houses seemed so full of happy noises that when you returned home, your footsteps echoed in the silence. Furniture at their homes was vibrant and soft, and yours was plastic covered and hard. The radio in the kitchen hummed gospel hymns from a CD your mom's church had recorded and sold to the congregation at a fundraiser weenie roast to raise money for a ramp after the pastor's wife had a stroke. Your mom cooked some dish from the latest issue of *Southern Living*, and when your dad was home, some sport played on the flat screen.

That was the picture you had in your head of your mom. Wearing a gingham apron with her name stitched across a pocket on the chest and an oven mitt on each hand, pulling a steaming dish (usually a casserole) out of the oven with her head turned toward you, smiling all the way to her eyes.

You remembered her face the day you came home early from school after getting expelled. She was sitting on the couch in a thin, faded blue terry cloth robe with curlers still in her hair and her eyes red from crying. You thought you'd have to explain, but someone from the school had already called and said that you'd been expelled because of an incident with another student.

They had explained the nature of the incident in just enough detail to paint a picture in her mind, and your mom hadn't looked you in the eye since then.

SHAMPOO UNICORN
Episode 310: "What Now?"

RILEY:

Crime happens everywhere. We like to pretend that marriage equality solved homophobia, but that's messed up as hell. If you're right, and this is a hate crime, this is a way to talk about it.

[SHAMPOO UNICORN *THEME SONG PLAYS.*]

BRIAN:

Hi, and welcome back to another episode of *Shampoo Unicorn*. We're still talking about Greg, but a bit more broadly today. Before we dive in, I wanted to say thanks so much to all the people who reached out last week. When I started doing this podcast, it felt sort of like a message in a bottle—a missive I was sending out to the world week after week with no real response.

RILEY:

Well, that's dramatic.

BRIAN:

What?

RILEY:

That sounds so . . . unrequited. It's not like you were alone with a tape recorder on an island. This podcast was a way for you to use your voice, too. For you to get experience in storytelling and production. It began as a project for sophomore journalism, right?

BRIAN:

Oh, right. Those first couple of episodes were . . . weirdly formal. But at the end of the semester, I'd already bought a domain name and a couple of mics and learned how to use editing software. And it was fun.

RILEY:

I remember checking the stats for you the first few months and being pretty surprised that we'd gotten a couple of hundred listens and a handful of reviews. And even more after I did all that research about search engine optimization. And it kept growing from there. We were just screwing around, and all of a sudden, you got emails from, like, advocacy groups asking if you'd run a spot for their helpline, or if you'd put a link in the show notes to some fundraiser or other.

BRIAN:

It was so weird then to think about other people listening to me. Caring about the trivial drama of life in this particular small town. And eventually, I thought it was probably not about me at all. It was about other queer people who were living their own quiet hells in similar rural landscapes. Or maybe people who had already escaped and needed to remember what they survived. Whatever reasons people had for listening to the show, I kept getting trapped in my head thinking about it. So I just . . . stopped thinking about it. I mean, it was cool to be getting a few bucks to cover the cost of software and equipment and domain space from advertisers. And it meant I didn't have to get a standard after-school job flipping burgers or working retail anywhere, but whenever anyone mentioned the idea of a Patreon or subscription content, it made the people on the other end of the podcast too real. So I just blamed school or said no without giving a reason.

RILEY:

And now?

BRIAN:

And now I feel like this is a good place to talk about what happened to Greg. The police aren't doing anything. No one is *saying* anything, really. Nothing important, anyway.

RILEY:

So, in this episode, we're going to talk about what happened. We're not *CSI: Teen Scooby*, so any thoughts of investigation are a bit absurd. But like Brian said, homophobia doesn't have a central location. Hate crimes aren't exclusive to where we live.

BRIAN:

Right. Who knows who the fuck did this? Maybe that's not even the important question. Almost anyone could have done this. There's no shortage of homophobes in a community that nurtures what the fundies call "family values."

RILEY:

We'll talk to students, people we know, people who knew Greg, hopefully other queer people from around town.

BRIAN:

And we'll always, always, look into any reasonable and credible tips y'all might have for us. I feel like more than anything, this podcast has been about the culture of homophobia and intolerance that conservative religions and rural isolation create. But I've had years to think about it, mostly alone, so I'm curious to know how other people think this happened. Not just, like, how homophobia exists, but . . .

RILEY:

Who would have a valid reason to attack Greg, specifically?

BRIAN:

I don't know? I mean, we live in a small, conservative, rural town south of the Mason-Dixon Line. We could start knocking on church doors, I guess?

(deepens voice)

"Excuse me, Reverend Doldrums. Have you or has anyone in your congregation potentially committed a hate crime recently?"

RILEY:

Yeah, that's fair. Plus, who even knows what kind of worms come out of that can.

BRIAN:

Hard agree. There's too much to unpack there, let's just set the whole suitcase on fire.

RILEY:

Okay, so here's what I propose. We have four loose theories. Greg's coach—however unlikely; his ex-girlfriend; definitely the other party who was expelled, Jocko, or some random homophobe; and I still don't think his dad is in the clear, even though his whereabouts were accounted for. Lacking any other clues, let's look into them. Even if it turns out none of them are the right suspect, maybe one of those investigations will lead to something more substantial.

BRIAN:

Okay, Sarah Koenig.

RILEY:

I'm gonna say that makes you Ira Glass.

BRIAN:

Flattering, if I were, like, forty years older and both a dad and a *zaddy*.

RILEY:

Anyway. We'll be back with new episodes as we learn more, but in the meantime, if you have any ideas or know anything, our contact info is in the show notes. Please don't hesitate to reach out.

BRIAN:

And as always, thanks so much for listening.

    *[*SHAMPOO UNICORN *EXIT THEME PLAYS.]*

12

PRECIPICE
Leslie

Leslie thinks about fear.

Now that it's in the rearview mirror, Leslie can see that living with the fear of being found out and rejected was harder than declaring out loud that she's trans (not *transgendered*, which her dad said several times until she stopped laughing and corrected him. She wasn't mad. It's a new vocabulary for them and they are trying). It's a long word, but it's not even an especially scary word. The syllables bumping up against one another feel more like cuddling than conflict. She knows now that the constant paranoia and self-loathing was worse than coming out.

The moment between starting to come out and wrapping her lips around the words were the hardest. It was standing on the precipice of change between the way things were and the uncertainty about what the future might look like. Once she broke through her silence, though, she couldn't stop. All the things she had never said, never dared to say, fell into the chasm that had formed between her and her mom.

Much like their house, neat and with everything in its designated, dust-free place, she doesn't fit with her parents. They are straighter than a ruler, and she's bendy like a measuring tape. She sometimes moves the curated antiques an inch to the left or rotates one ninety degrees to the right to see how long before her mom will notice. The piece is always righted by the next morning. Her room is the messiest in the house. It's full of books and magazines and fitness equipment. When she turned twelve, her mom decided she was old enough to be responsible for her own space. Leslie has loved the benevolent mess ever since.

"But how long have you known?" her mom asked after bringing her inside, sitting her down at the kitchen table, and cleaning up her knee. She made a pot of tea and placed a cup in front of Leslie, sat in the chair beside her, and cradled her mug in her hands.

"On some level, I think I've always known," Leslie says, wrapping her fingers around the teacup, bringing it close and inhaling deeply. She lets the steam and the heady scent of bergamot comfort her.

Her mom is quiet for a while. Her hair is a mousy brown bob, but her eyes are big and green with laugh lines framing them. She wears classic clothes, mostly monochromatic polos and khakis or crisp blouses with pleated skirts. She removes her tea bag with a perfectly manicured hand and places it on a napkin. After taking a sip, she returns the cup to the table. "Is this my fault?" Her voice is small, and she doesn't make eye contact with Leslie. "Did I do something wrong to make you this way?"

"Mom." Leslie reaches across the table and covers her mom's hand with her own. Leslie hates how much bigger her hands are, but she's glad to be able to offer this small gesture of comfort. "Look at me. Do you think there's anything wrong with me?"

Their eyes meet. "No, of course not. You're my child and I love you."

"Okay, then." Leslie smiles. All she ever wanted was to be loved for who she truly is. "I love you, too. I've always had everything I needed.

You, Dad, and me. We don't talk much, but we're a team. I've always known that. You didn't do anything wrong. Sometimes that's just how things shake out."

In the end, it was mostly fine. Not perfect, but close enough. Leslie's mom is confused and concerned, but mostly, she feels that the gap between them is shrinking and there's comfort in this new proximity. Leslie finds resources for her parents and that night she and her mom sit down with Leslie's dad and explain their conversation to him.

"Dad, I told Mom earlier," she says. Each word is like swallowing a marshmallow whole, the words filling her mouth up so much that there's practically no room for air. "I'm trans. Transgender. I know it might be hard to understand or accept, but I want you to know who I am."

He surprises Leslie by wrapping her in his arms before she finishes speaking. He's still in good shape for his age, still golfing with his college buddies a few times a year and starting every day with a brisk run. His salt-and-pepper hair is thinning a little, but he's so tall that unless he's sitting, not many people notice. He's a quiet man. Not cold, but pensive. Leslie thinks she inherited this from him, this tendency to wait until all the cards are on the table to start building a house out of them.

"I don't care," he says, tears glossing his eyes. "I don't care what I need to do to support you. I will. I just want you to know that. I haven't been as around as I should have because it seemed like you didn't need me as much anymore, and I thought you might need space. I'm sorry." He swallows hard and shakes his head as if he's upset with himself. "I love you. And I'm sorry."

They order pizza, and Leslie and her mom spend a couple of hours online shopping for things Leslie might like to try wearing. Her dad opens his laptop and sits with them. He looks up gender-affirming therapists and medical providers and PFLAG meetings, and they build a timeline for coming out at school. This is what he's best at, creating order out of chaos. Making a plan. Strategy. He changes her dorm room for college to a single so she won't have to choose between gendered housing.

Her dad goes to bed early, and she and her mom stay up late, experimenting with makeup. Her mom confesses that she always wanted a daughter to do girl stuff with.

They spend the weekend watching trans movies and TV shows. On Monday, even though she has no one to tell outside the internet, she carries her parents' acceptance around in her chest like a warm ember of hope.

It is the first time she can remember not needing a reason to get out of bed.

13

INEVITABLE CHANGE
Greg

Your dad's scent hung in the air like smoke.

The fact of him was a pebble in your shoe. He was a hard man. You could smell shoe polish and Marlboros and the faint whisper of sour beer. When he spoke, which was rare, his voice was gravel. He never touched you anymore—not in anger or affection—but his hands were callused thick, the tips stained yellow. He looked like a grotesque stone golem of the man who had been the entire sky for you when you were younger. You were afraid he was the worst version of who you could become.

When you were a kid, you remember watching your dad for hours because you resembled each other so much that standing together was like looking into the weirdest fun-house mirror you'd ever seen. He was huge, loomed over you in body and voice. He could carry anything, do anything.

He would come home exhausted and covered in coal dust with a candy bar hidden in one of the billion pockets of his coveralls. You'd search him eagerly, climbing him like a tree, and his face would cleave into a grin when you found it. He'd unwrap the candy and take the first bite "for quality control" and listen to you prattle on about whatever happened in kindergarten or first grade that day.

Coal dust covered everything in the house. Despite his work clothes being washed in a special industrial machine by the mining company he worked for, even your laundry at home came out dingy, and your shower was permanently stained gray. You didn't mind, though. The coal seemed cheerful, like the friendly cloud that followed Pigpen around in the Snoopy comics your dad read to you.

Your dad had already been a little religious and a little bit of a drinker before he lost his job. After work, he'd have a beer with dinner. You went to the Church of God down by the highway on Easter and Christmas. He went from being this filthy mountain of a man to someone calmer and cleaner within an hour after he got home. He'd hug your mom from behind while she was cooking and plant a kiss on her cheek, then settle in at the kitchen table to read the paper and help you with homework until it was time to eat.

When you were in fifth grade, the mine closed and everything changed. Your dad was home all the time. He was always there. He saw you off to school in the morning and greeted you at the bus in the evening, but after a few weeks it stopped being fun or cool. He'd grill you about your day while he chain-smoked and took long, painful swigs from his whiskey glass.

Eventually, the savings dwindled, and your mom began working at the nursing home. She'd started off in custodial and gone to night school while she was doing that. She became a certified nurse's assistant, a licensed practical nurse, and then a registered nurse, racking up letters after her name like a doctor or lawyer. You were so proud of and impressed by her. Your dad said he was, too, but when he drank too much, he'd call her a certified ass wiper and tell her that her patients (always "them people" or "them sad bastards") were a tax on the good, hardworking citizens of Canon. She replied once that he was neither good nor hardworking, and he backhanded her into the dining room wall.

You tried to de-escalate their arguments with knock-knock jokes and riddles. Sometimes it even worked, and you couldn't remember seeing your dad hit your mom after that. But he seemed to resent everything you were, even though he was genetically responsible for about half of the shit he hated about you.

He thought you were a sissy or too sensitive, so you joined the football team to butch it up for him, started hanging out with other football players and dating girls you thought he'd approve of, and he warned you about fucking up your shot by knocking some stupid bitch up or blowing a knee out in the middle of a cornfield doing keg stands with your bros. He seemed jealous that you got good grades and would constantly ride your case about not going to church often enough. Nothing you did to earn his pride or respect seemed to work.

Your old man loved Derek, though. One of his favorite things to do was to compare you to Derek when you ran into him after a home game and he was drunk enough. Derek was stronger, smarter, more likely to succeed. Derek, for his part, tried his best to sing your praises, but your dad wasn't hearing it. He just took Derek's kind words as evidence of his superiority, and you fell further down in the fake-son ranking.

You started thinking about your dad and somehow wandered down a labyrinth of memories.

Back when you were eight, your friends came over almost every day after school to do homework and hang out. You were reading on your stomach with your feet kicked into the air. It was quiet when Brian scooched over to your side and Riley settled down on the other. As if it were a conspiracy, they tickled you until you all were a pile of laughing, silly chaos.

You were six and home sick from school with chicken pox, and neither of them had it yet. Brian and Riley delivered a box of dry erase markers, a bag of Pull 'n' Peel Twizzlers (still your favorite), and your homework in a plastic grocery sack with a note that said GET WEL GERG on the outside and GO 2 DA WINDO written on the inside.

When you followed their instructions, Riley and Brian were there wearing Halloween masks and capes made from bath towels, putting on plays you could barely follow but loved anyway. Then you wrote notes back and forth on the windows until you realized that your reading and spelling skills weren't quite up to the task, so you mostly just drew pictures for one another. After Riley had gone home and Brian had gone to bed, you crept out from beneath your covers to see that Brian had drawn one last picture—the three of you holding hands and walking up a rainbow to a fluffy cloud where Dolly Parton was waiting for you all.

You were seven, hanging out with Riley, and you were thinking about when you got to high school. You knew there would be dances and stuff. You were not sure where Brian was, but it seemed like a good time to get a leg up on your only other competition.

"Will you go to prom with me?" you'd asked.

Her eyes flicked up from the page she was coloring, her green crayon still in motion. "What?"

"When we're older, will you be my prom date?" Your heart beat faster and you crossed your arms as though it were visible through the thin wall of your chest and the fabric of your Pokémon T-shirt.

Riley laughed, not unkindly. "Dude, that's not for a long time."

"I know, but I wanted to ask before anyone else."

"What about Brian?" She seemed genuinely confused now.

"He'll find someone else to go with. He's funny. I'm not funny. And I love you the most." Her mom was making some sort of chicken dish a few rooms away that smelled amazing, and whatever soap opera she was watching blared on the small kitchen television. It was getting late, and you'd have to go home soon.

"That's silly. We'll all go together, of course. We do everything together. And we all love each other the most." That was enough for you. The thought of the three of you, stalking the anemic halls of your future high school arm in arm. That was the best prom you could imagine.

In third grade, you were in different classrooms for the first time and Kevin V asked Stephanie H to be his girlfriend. He wrote really bad poems for her and got her a Ring Pop, and the rest of the girls in your year thought it was so romantic. Some of the boys started talking about girls they'd kiss, like, if they had to. You didn't mind kissing girls, you just knew you didn't mean it in the same way other boys might. The idea of pairing up was intimidating, though.

By the time you were in fourth grade, pairing up with someone seemed inevitable and you knew you were no match for Brian if you had to fight for Riley's affection. Maybe the three of you would be able to work out a schedule. You could each take two days of the week with a break on Wednesdays for Riley to be single or date someone else if she wanted to.

When you talked to Riley and Brian about it, they expressed similar concerns. Brian suggested that the three of you should just practice kissing to get it over with and see what the fuss was all about. You'd all treated your classmates' obsession with kissing like a weird, annoying fad, but they truly did not seem to be getting over it. Riley's mom was at work, so you'd each kissed Riley and then each other. It had been so weird for things to be so quiet and reverent and heavy with expectations that you all started laughing. Laughing so hard you held your sides and rolled around on the floor making fun of the serious look on one another's faces and the peanut butter on Brian's breath.

Then you'd gone into Riley's mom's bathroom and given yourselves very fancy hairdos with her styling products and taken a bunch of pictures on an old iPhone. Hair frozen in place, you were terrified to go home with your hair gelled into little spikes and artful curls. So Riley and Brian stripped down to their underpants (and Riley's training bra) and you'd done the same. They ran into the backyard with shampoo and conditioner with you chasing after them. You had a great time giving yourselves shampoo versions of the styles, mimicking them with gel and mousse. Your favorite had been spikes all over your head that made you look like a scrawny Statue of Liberty, Riley's had been an impressive pompadour, and Brian's single hair spike was impressively tall.

"You look like a punk unicorn," you said, pointing and laughing.

"Whatever." Brian shrugged, a challenge in his voice. "I think I look cool. And you and I both know it. Besides, unicorns are magical, just like me."

You bumped your shoulder against his. He tackled you, and the two of you rolled over the grass, wrestling. For the rest of the evening, thinking of him made your chest warm in a way that made you sincerely believe magic might be real. After Riley left, you and Brian lay under the picnic table in his backyard taking turns kissing one another gently on the cheeks and eyelids and forehead and ears.

For science.

14

BREAK FORTH IN SONG
Brian

I became a fixture at the hospital.

Sometimes Greg's mom was there. Occasionally there were people from school. Beth, or one of the other cheerleaders. Once, I saw Greg's dad. He was standing outside Greg's room, his foot propped against the wall behind him, leaving a boot print on the institutional paint, and his head leaned back so far that I could see his Adam's apple bobbing through his tangled black beard. I'd already gotten off the elevator and his eyes locked on me before I could call it back. Instead, I nodded slightly and walked down the hall, past Greg's room. After, I rounded the corner, took the stairs back to the ground floor. He hadn't needed to say a word to make me feel unwelcome, just like when we were kids.

There was a different energy in Greg's room when someone else was present, so if I saw that his mom wasn't alone, I just kept on walking to the cafeteria. Say what you will about hospital food, but Canon General makes a mean tapioca pudding.

I wasn't really looking for anything on these visits, not researching the investigation (though my eyes and ears were always open, of course), but being present in some way meant something, even if it was just to me. Like a vigil, as if bearing witness to or holding space for something. It felt important to keep showing up, to honor the promise I'd made to Greg and his mom.

Some moments, when I was alone with Greg, trying to find him under his slowly fading bruises and the machines attached to him, I'd sing or talk to him so softly that only he would be able to hear me. It felt like a secret, and I felt silly the first couple of times. Once, I held his hand and lightly squeezed it, hoping he was aware of my touch. That he'd know he wasn't alone. Also, that maybe it could bring him back from wherever he was.

Sitting in the chair beside him with my laptop on my knees, I answered emails and social media responses about my podcast. I can't say when it happened, but people started noticing—started caring for—Greg, and the lack of police response. They'd asked about donating money or time, and asked how they could help.

Reading messages and comments of support and encouragement from strangers to Greg healed some gaping wound I hadn't even realized was scabbed over. It's not that I ever got used to being harassed—called a fag, having my books knocked out of my hands, et cetera. It's that I sort of built up a shield that granted me a few seconds to act unaffected or deliver some withering response. Being funny, being clever made me feel like that was enough. Like none of the bullying or microaggressions I encountered mattered that much because school would be over soon. I just had to brace myself to get through it so that when I got to college, my real life could begin. I wondered where Greg carried his hidden wounds.

What I didn't realize until I had the space and silence to think about it was that my detachment had cost me time and authenticity on some level. Somewhere in the heartache of worrying for Greg, I started to mourn the things I hadn't let myself feel.

Reading the emails felt like a balm. They didn't fix things entirely. But I liked to imagine I was reading them to life, leaving phantom guards there to watch over him.

I imagined Joe from Montana to be a chubby young cowpoke who would feel comfortable leaning casually against a window, squinting into the sun with a wheat stalk sticking out of the corner of his mouth. *I know everything feels real shitty right now*, he wrote. *And I don't want to tell you things get better all at once. Because that ain't always how it happens. Sometimes you got to go along to get along, even when it's hard. Then one day you look up and you're almost thirty, but you got a good man and a good dog and a pretty goddamn good life. What I'm saying is, hang in there. I'm rooting for you, man.*

I pictured Erin to be a tiny dark-haired lady who loved big books, small animals, and oversize nightgowns. I read her letter to Greg in a soft Southern accent, which is how I believed she would sound: "'The hardest thing about the world is surviving it. The best thing is the people you meet along the way. Your podcast is a gift to folks walking a hard path. Keep your head up, pal.'" I could almost see her standing beside Greg's bed, fingers combing his hair out of his face, both protective and affectionate.

Matt from Philly wrote that Greg's attacker deserved to burn in a thousand flaming hells, but also that he hoped Greg was able to find pockets of quiet grace and reflection in the hardest moments. He wished Greg unexpected laughter when he needed it most. I thought he might be the sort of guy who was most comfortable standing at the door, making sure everyone was safe.

I read their notes to him, and I hoped he heard them. I hoped that whatever song his heart and brain were singing to him would bring him back soon. Hoped the chorus of the people his attack had brought to him would lift their voices to sing him home.

15

KEEP SWIMMING, LITTLE FISH
Greg

Wake up.

You could hear Brian's papery whisper in your ear. It tickled in a sexy, playful way. More than anything you wanted to sit up and lean into that voice your ears hungered for. It sounded like home. His tone was a sound you wanted more of; it was also annoyingly nearby and unreachable like a fly you couldn't swat. Things were getting closer and more vivid now, but you could still feel yourself swimming in your memories. It felt like how you would imagine being suspended in the middle of an ice cube might. You were weightless, but the feeling was more of a prison than a pleasure. Your vision seemed clearer, so it had become a bit more like swimming in beef broth than tomato soup—less dense, less cloudy, but more annoying and frustrating for its slightly greater tangibility.

Why was he here? And where exactly was *here*? It's not like you could ask him, but for whatever reason it eased your fears to feel his presence. You needed to get back to your life and start piecing stuff together. It was as though you were swimming toward an exit—as if you had your eyes closed underwater. Swimming as far as you could in one direction would help you figure out where you were, but unless you could open your eyes you were likely to slam into the walls of your nebulous prison.

Still, there was something comforting about having Brian so near. He knew you in a way that even Derek and Beth didn't. He knew who you were. Sure, he probably hated you and had every right to do so, but you never had to pretend around him. Didn't have to pretend to like music that you felt ambivalent about or enjoy drinking warm beer or hitting on girls so your bros wouldn't catch on to your secret.

He knew the kid you'd been before you turned into such an epic fuckup. You used to feel the most at peace at his house and sometimes you pretended it was yours. That his mom was your mom, casually scruffing his (and occasionally your) hair when the two of you were doing homework at his kitchen table. The endless supply of pizza and Chinese food since she couldn't, and often didn't have time to, cook. The lived-in, loved-in mess of their house where nothing was tidy and almost everything was stained and worn. It was just the two of them, but you loved the chaos.

Brian was such an intense kid—always on, always performing, always demanding attention, affection, and an audience. You were happy to give it because he was so generous with his toys, video games, and less tangible stuff like time and companionship.

You didn't understand how one person could make so much noise and mess. But he had been constantly in motion, moving from one idea to another of how to entertain yourselves. He was obsessed with science one week and history the next. But micro-focused—not just science or history, but stuff like molecular gastronomy or the history of the library at Alexandria. And while they were not subjects you'd pick, happy to stick with times tables and learning the presidents, his fascination was contagious, and he'd always find a way to make it fun for you and Riley.

Or maybe that was Riley's influence. She was calmer, could tamp down on Brian's wild enthusiasm when he started getting so rowdy that you might get kicked off the school bus (again) or cause (more) property damage or (another) fire. She was as brilliant as he was and every bit as funny, but she was more cautious and helped serve as a conduit through which his wild enthusiasm settled into class projects or plays that the three of you put on for one another. Productive stuff. Brian would find a bunch of chemicals and wonder what he could combine to make an explosion. Riley would put the stuff with Mr. Yuk stickers back and challenge him to make rainbow slime out of borax and glue and glitter. Then you'd spend the rest of the evening betting on which would stick to the ceiling for the longest time or who could fit the most spaghetti noodles through theirs.

The three of you loved being together, riding your bikes through the neighborhood, or especially hanging out in Brian's clubhouse in the woods behind his house. It was the best place you'd ever been, a safe haven from adults and other kids. Brian's mom trusted the three of you not to get into too much trouble, the treacherous little cabal that you'd proven yourself to be, and mostly left you alone.

Regardless of where you were, the presence of your best friends was the safest and happiest place you could imagine. Comparatively, going home from Brian's felt like returning to Earth after you'd been on the moon for years. The feeling of weightlessness and ease was gone, and your feet were anchored to the ground by the heavy gravity of your parents. You were thinking in particular of Brian's soap opera phase. Where everything he said or did was matched with an arched eyebrow or a pronounced head toss. He loved to swivel toward an invisible camera and often he'd respond to whatever you'd said as though you were in a dramatic lovers' quarrel.

"Bri, come on. Help me finish my homework so we can go meet Riley at the clubhouse." You struggled with math, but all the subjects seemed effortless to both Riley and Brian.

"What are you implying, you scoundrel?" Brian narrowed his eyes as though you'd just leveled a curse at his whole family.

"Seriously, dude. This sucks. I don't understand fractions at all."

"Or do you understand them perfectly," Brian said, slamming a hand down on his kitchen table beside your worksheet. You jumped because you were so used to avoiding conflict, but if he noticed, he didn't show it. He draped one of his mom's scarves backward so that he was wearing it around his neck and the length trailed down his back like long, soft, woven pigtails.

You groaned. "Why are you like this?"

"Fish gotta swim, birds gotta fly, darling." He grabbed your math sheet and started filling in the answers. "And after we're done here, we should also take wing over to meet our favorite goldfinch."

You untied his head scarf and tried it on. "Perhaps we shall, darling." You could never capture the drama like Brian, but he loved it when you played along.

Hearing Brian—feeling him so close to you—returned the feeling of floating. Like if you could just get a better grip on where he was, you could swim up to him and out of this place. It was frustrating, but underneath that, you felt hopeful, and that was almost enough.

SHAMPOO UNICORN
Episode 311: "Small-Ass Town"

BRIAN:

Greg's mom looks like you might imagine. She seems taller than she is because of her ramrod-straight posture and her silver hair pulled back into a loose bun. She's usually wearing a long denim skirt, sometimes with big decorative buttons running down the side, sometimes not. Always in a T-shirt from some church event or radio station contest with various soft cardigans layered over top. She looks like the kind of woman who would make awesome cookies, and from childhood, I can confirm that she does.

MRS. BURKE:

Now explain to me what this is for again? Some kind of radio show? Do the police know anything about this?

BRIAN:

It's for my podcast, Mrs. Burke, which is kind of like a radio show. We are looking into what happened to Greg, since the police really don't have any leads. They don't know about it, mostly because it flies below their scope of interest. Is that okay? Do you mind that I'm recording this?

MRS. BURKE:

I guess not? I reckon I don't exactly understand what this is for or how it will help, but I don't suppose it could hurt, either.

[SHAMPOO UNICORN *THEME SONG PLAYS.*]

RILEY:

(in voiceover)

This week, Brian spoke to Greg's mom, Mrs. Burke, about Greg's attack. He asked what life inside their house was like. Then Brian and I returned to the scene of the crime. After that, we asked Coach Winsor about the incident between Greg and Derek at school and the correlation between that and Greg's attack.

BRIAN:

How did you find out about Greg?

MRS. BURKE:

Mr. Burke called me at work after the police came and told him what happened. One of the other nurses drove me to the hospital, and I met Mr. Burke there.

BRIAN:

Where had Mr. Burke been?

MRS. BURKE:

He'd been cleaning the church, like I mentioned when we talked before. Everyone in the congregation takes turns doing it, and it was our family's turn. He dropped me off at work and went to do that. We'd taken Greg's car away after he was expelled, but when we decided he needed a job, we gave it back so he could go to a job interview.

BRIAN:

What happened next?

MRS. BURKE:

When I got to the hospital, I couldn't see Greg because he was in surgery. They wouldn't let me see my own son. My baby. Some people came out to ask us for insurance information, and then the police asked us a lot of questions.

[PAUSE.]

MRS. BURKE:

Honestly, it's all kind of a blur. I remember sitting in the waiting room for what seemed like forever, and then a doctor came to get me so I could see Greg. He was asleep. There were so many tubes and wires and IVs. It's hard to look at him sometimes. Hard to know that my boy is under all that medical . . . stuff. I know he's in a coma, but I prefer to think he's just sleeping through all this. He looks so much like he did when he was just a boy, sleeping.

BRIAN:

Do the police have any leads? Have they found anything out?

MRS. BURKE:

They haven't checked in with me since the day after it happened, but I guess they would've if they had any leads or questions or anything.

BRIAN:

Did you . . . Um, can I ask if you knew he was gay?

MRS BURKE:

I don't want to talk about that. It's no one's business.

BRIAN:

With all due respect, Mrs. B, if that's why he was hit, it's relevant. And as a gay kid in the same town, if someone is committing hate crimes against gay people, it is my business.

MRS. BURKE:

You say it so casually. How is it so easy for you to accept?

BRIAN:

[PAUSE.]

It's just part of who I am. I never had to accept it because it was never unacceptable to anyone in my life. Has it been hard for y'all to deal with Greg's sexuality?

MRS. BURKE:

I wondered if he was like that. Mostly I tried not to think about it. I believed it was a sin, but now I'm not sure. It's something I struggle with. Maybe it always has been. Maybe it always will be.

[SEVERAL MOMENTS OF SILENCE.]

MRS. BURKE:

I wonder if this could have been avoided if he were different, you know? Him getting kicked out of school, needing a job. He would have been in class any other day.

[A SHORTER MOMENT OF SILENCE.]

MRS. BURKE:

I've grown up knowing homosexuality was a sin. It was just a fact. The sky is blue, the grass is green, and homosexuality is a sin. But still, we were taught to love the sinner and hate the sin. Alan—Mr. Burke—struggled with that. We mostly didn't talk about it. But I worried about it, prayed about it. Greg was different from most other little boys growing up. He was more sensitive, softer. I thought I'd done something wrong. Not been hard enough on him or henpecked him too much. And it's funny—how much time and attention I've given to that, and how little I care about it now. I just want him to wake up. I just want him to be all right.

BRIAN:
(quietly)
That's understandable. What about Mr. Burke?

MRS. BURKE:
[PAUSE.]
You should know that Mr. Burke's daddy took a firm hand with him, too. They were both raised to respect discipline.

BRIAN:
Spare the rod and spoil the child and all that?

MRS. BURKE:
Yes.

BRIAN:
And you?

MRS. BURKE:
I think it worked. We didn't often have to discipline Greg. He was a good boy. A good son. He got good grades, got into a good school. We spanked him from time to time, sure. But mostly, he was a quiet, well-behaved child.

BRIAN:

Do you think he was afraid of you?

MRS. BURKE:

Of me, no. Maybe he was a little afraid of Mr. Burke, who is, admittedly, a stern man. After the mines closed, he was different. It was easier for him when Greg was younger and Mr. Burke was working. I think he preferred me to do most of the parenting.

BRIAN:

But, let's be clear: He did beat Greg.

MRS. BURKE:

He *disciplined* him. Maybe he went a little overboard, but it was from a place of concern. You got to understand that when we were growing up, we learned morality was black and white, and being a homosexual was a sin that would lead to God only knows what. If Mr. Burke was hard on him, it's because he wanted him to have the sort of wholesome life that comes from being a good, God-fearing man. He felt like he'd done something wrong, like he'd somehow failed Greg as a father. And he could never square that away.

[PAUSE.]

MRS. BURKE:

(trying not to cry)

Social media, movies, and television shows have taught you all different things. I made mistakes. I do know that. But I did try to be the best mama I could be to my son. I did everything in my power to keep him safe.

BRIAN:

I didn't mean to offend you or hurt your feelings. Some of these questions are uncomfortable. This isn't me judging you. I'm just trying to ask the hard questions that might help us find some answers about what happened. Do you think Mr. Burke would speak with me?

MRS. BURKE:

Brian, I don't. He's barely speaking to me right now. Mr. Burke is angry and upset, and he doesn't do nothing here lately but come to the hospital and go to church and pray and worry about Greg.

BRIAN:

Will you explain what I'm doing and ask him? You can give him my phone number, too.

MRS. BURKE:

I wouldn't hold your breath, sweetheart.

BRIAN:

Can you think of anyone who would want to hurt Greg?

MRS. BURKE:

Honestly, no. He was such a good kid. Maybe Derek, the boy who was involved in the incident at school. I know this whole thing has made his life real tough in a lot of ways. Otherwise, I can't think of anyone. But maybe I don't know my son as well as I think I do.

BRIAN:

What about his girlfriend?

MRS. BURKE:

Why would she . . . do anything to Greg?

BRIAN:

Well, they were supposed to go to homecoming together, and I know they dated off and on.

MRS. BURKE:

I can't imagine that sweet girl doing anything to hurt Greg. Even when they weren't together, they were close. He told me they texted a lot about school, whatever's on Netflix, and all that.

BRIAN:

What about Coach Winsor?

MRS. BURKE:

Absolutely not. He hated that Greg got expelled. Greg loved being on the football team, and really looked up to Coach Winsor. And I know Tommy thought the world of Greg. Wrote him a real nice letter for college. Sent flowers to the hospital and everything. If anyone is as upset as Mr. Burke and me, it's Tommy Winsor. He brought me a bunch of books for parents of homosexual children. He told me he wished more than anything Greg had just been able to talk to him.

BRIAN:

Okay, thanks for taking time for me. Please let me know if there's anything I can do, okay?

RILEY:

(in voiceover)

For the record, I think Brian could have gone harder in this interview, asked more challenging questions. But he said Mrs. Burke was grieving, and she might also have been afraid of Mr. Burke. Of the two of us, he is the more compassionate, and so I try to follow that lead because it's how I'd want someone to treat my mom if I were in a coma.

The next day, we went to the parking lot where Greg was found, to see if we could pick up on anything that the police might have missed, or to see if being in the place where it happened would give us any other clues or ideas.

BRIAN:

Mic check one. Mic check two. Are you recording?

RILEY:

Yeah, levels are good.

BRIAN:

Okay, I'm going to start by describing the geography of everything.

RILEY:

Good idea.

BRIAN:

Jolene's BBQ is a fairly small restaurant. It used to be a small ranch-style house, but the owners, Chuck and Ann Hill, bought and remodeled the house next door when it went up for sale almost ten years ago. It's been an institution in Canon forever. It's named after the Dolly Parton song, of course. Chuck and Ann met at a Dolly Parton concert years ago.

Jolene's is in a mostly residential neighborhood, exempt from zoning largely because of how much people love the owners. The houses are mostly neat, ranch-style architecture surrounded by white picket fences, scattered with rosebushes. More tire and porch swings than the average American neighborhood maybe, but I guess people do like to sit around swaying in gentle motion. Their place is on the corner, with their yard bordering the parking lot to the restaurant. Employees park in the back, along a white-painted wooden fence that separates the property from the railroad. It's a small-ass town.

Jolene's shares its parking lot with the only other business in the neighborhood, Todd's Meat Market. It's been there since Todd Senior opened it up back in the forties, and it's now operated by his grandson, Todd III: Revenge of the Todds. Hunters bring their kills to him for butchering. Residents petitioned to get them to move, but nothing really came of it. There are plenty of jokes about the Meat Market being the only decent place to find a date in Canon. And lots of other meat-related jokes, as you might imagine. It's kind of a local thing.

RILEY:

Most of the block across the street is taken up by the Canon United Methodist Church and the playground beside it. There's a small parking lot between them, not enough to hold all the congregation, and often on Sundays the overflow winds up at Jolene's. It's convenient, since that's where most people are heading for brunch after church lets out anyway.

Because there is such limited visibility behind Jolene's, where Greg parked his car and his body was found, there are no eyewitnesses. Chuck walked over from his home to the restaurant, interviewed Greg for a dishwashing position, and then stayed to finish up some paperwork.

[SOUND OF FOOTSTEPS.]

BRIAN:

The employee lot is pretty small. There's not much visibility on the Hills' side of the restaurant. It's blocked off by a big green dumpster. It's one of the smaller types, so it doesn't have doors. It's just got two flaps on top that fold over. On the other side, the parking lot is empty.

It's not huge—it holds maybe six cars. Looking at the area now, on a Saturday morning before the restaurant opens, you'd never know anything happened here. There are no skid marks, no glass or chipped paint.

I truly don't know what I expected to see when I came here.

(*sighing*)

Uh, the building is maybe sixty feet wide and the distance from the back of the restaurant to the fence measures about twenty feet.

[FOOTSTEPS FALLING IN TANDEM, CARS PASSING DISTANTLY IN THE BACKGROUND OVER THE FAINT SOUND OF BIRDS CHIRPING.]

BRIAN:

From most vantage points back here, I can't see the road. There are no visibility mirrors, so that means that a random car probably wouldn't be able to see someone crossing if they were in a hurry. I hadn't entertained the idea that it could've been an accident, like maybe he was just hit by someone who was rounding a corner too fast. Wrong time, wrong place. That sort of thing. The timing seemed weird. But now that I'm here, actually walking around in the space, it looks like a definite possibility. I'm sure that occurred to the police, too. Ugh, maybe this was a stupid idea. Do you think this is stupid?

RILEY:

No. I think you have a right to be worried, because no one really understands what happened. It's normal to want to find out. And maybe we will. I don't think asking the questions on everyone's mind is a bad thing.

BRIAN:

That's a good point. Do you think it's still worth it to talk to Coach Winsor?

RILEY:

I don't know. Mrs. Burke seemed pretty sure he didn't have anything to do with it. And honestly, I agree with her. He doesn't have any sure motive, and it just doesn't seem to be part of his character.

BRIAN:

Hard agree. Coach Winsor has been a really good example of allyship goals. He doesn't mind if I walk laps instead of playing team sports where I might be pelted with nonconsensual balls and he's given every person who ever called me a fag in his presence in-school suspension.

RILEY:

I think that's a good idea. We're going to wrap up here.

BRIAN:

As always, thank you for listening and for your messages of support. They mean more than I'll ever be able to say, and there's comfort in feeling like there's a community out there in the world for me even if it seems as if there isn't always one in this single-stoplight town. As always, if you have any feedback, comments, or suggestions, our contact info is in the show notes. Please get in touch.

*[*SHAMPOO UNICORN *EXIT THEME PLAYS.]*

16

HATCHING
Leslie

Leslie thinks about action.

Brian's investigation of the hate crime in Canon is so close she can feel it breathing down her neck. She feels closer to him than she has at any point in her fandom of the podcast. He's a person she can (and does) look up on social media. He's a boy her age. She can imagine his courage—imagine squaring up to the fear of violence. Swallowing back the things that wake him in a cold sweat. Weighing justice against safety. She would like to know him. Brian. His name is Brian. She has a hard time keeping that straight, knowing him as Sass for so long. Just as her parents find it difficult to call her Leslie, after she's been   all her life. But they try and she appreciates their efforts and counts herself lucky to have such supportive parents. And lately they've been really nailing her pronouns.

Now that she has the clothes she wants, it's a struggle not to wear them all the time. She's not quite out at school yet, but she's gone all this time without really rocking the boat. What are a few months more? Is it worth the fight to graduate as Leslie, not   ? How would she even start the process of coming out to a school full of strangers she's been icing out for four years? On the other hand, every day she sits in class answering to a name that makes her want to collapse in on herself is torture. Maybe she could just email her teachers and tell them her name and pronouns have changed. If she demands their respect and compassion, maybe they'd give it to her. Leslie doesn't know how to make the choice between what's right and what's easiest.

How was it for Marsha during the Stonewall riots? Did she think while she held a brick or high heel or shot glass in her hand before she threw it? Maybe she tossed it into the air a couple of times, testing its heft? Or maybe it was heart and head working together, and she just threw it to hear the shattering of glass without a thought for how it would change everything.

People do small brave things all the time, by standing up to a bully or stepping in when they see someone who needs help. What would that look like for her? Now that she's named herself out loud, she chooses clothes that feel more comfortable at home. At school, she wears clothes that are on the femme side of ambiguous, and if anyone has noticed, no one has said anything. This is the culmination of four years spent trying to be invisible.

Now that she's almost ready to be seen, she wonders who else she's not seeing. If there are other people struggling like she is, or if she's been wearing blinders for the last four years and never noticed them. She's a ghost wandering the halls, looking closely at people she's tried hard not to see.

She's never been in therapy before, but her mom set her up with someone and having a place to process things out loud is new. Saying things out loud that she's held with white knuckles to her chest for years feels like such a relief. When she is in her therapist's eggshell office, on the overstuffed chair by the door with light filtering in through vertical blinds, it's as though her whole body can finally relax. It's the release of a held-in sneeze.

Her therapist, a thin, white-haired woman in flowing rainbow skirts and ankle boots named Carol, asks for a specificity she's never dared to name before. The office smells like lavender and patchouli, and the lamps are all covered with gauzy scarves, casting a pastel glow around each of them. Here, Leslie can relax her spine, let out her breath, and soften her face.

"What now? What do you want? What are your best- and worst-case scenarios?" Carol asks, putting her pen down and leaning forward.

"I'm a woman," Leslie says for the first time. Her voice is too deep, too loud for the quiet office, so she lowers it to almost a whisper. "Or, I guess, a girl, a normal trans teenage girl. Whatever. I just want to look like I feel. For other people to see me the way I feel."

"And you've come out to your parents. They're supportive, you said. What about school?"

"I only have a few months left of school. I can suck it up until then. I mean, I want to start hormones so that I can start college in a skirt. I like yours, by the way."

"Thank you, it was an anniversary gift from my wife." Carol smiles warmly. "What do the next steps forward look like for you?"

"I have an appointment with a doctor to discuss the medical stuff. And we're sorting name-change documents out now. I have to take out ads in newspapers and pay a fee. But I should be done with that stuff by the time I start college."

The steps forward are fairly prescribed. Leslie's known the legal, medical, and social steps of transitioning since she first started poking around on the internet. But now that her shell is cracked, she wants to burst out of it and stomp-dance on the dust of its broken pieces.

The things she's doing now are small, but after years of doing nothing, they are significant. Her lips are slathered with a tinted Chapstick and a little highlighter shimmers on her cheekbones most days. She and her mom watch YouTube beauty videos for trans girls and give each other dramatic and often hilarious makeovers. She can tell that all the beauty stuff makes her dad uncomfortable, but she knows he's trying in his way, as well. Her dad's way is practical, occasionally awkward. He is overly apologetic for misgendering Leslie, for calling her   .
He buys her pepper spray and signs them up to take a self-defense class together. He refers to her and her mom as "his gals," though he has never referred to them collectively before. She sees him looking at her when he thinks she doesn't notice.

She isn't sure if he's looking for his son or his daughter; she's mostly just glad to be seen.

17

A HOPE SO BIG
Greg

Being touched was weird.

There were so many ways and combinations to press your skin against someone else's. And so many things it could mean. Most of your touching happened in the name of football. Your body slamming into another body at high speed, competition for an oblong leather ball and an arbitrarily decided upon set of points. It felt both violent and sexual sometimes. Both of those were ways that bodies could touch. Touch could mean comfort, could mean passion, could mean longing, companionship, or friendship or familial comfort.

Or it could be punitive. Painful emotionally, sure. It could feel so much like wanting to be held that your skeleton might walk through your skin. It could feel like a punch landing squarely in the tender meat of your side, your face, your windpipe. Pain so precise it could only have been planned. Pain so common it changed you profoundly, that you built calluses against until you felt protected by your stubborn, stupid survival instincts.

Feeling hands on your body from inside this place was weird. It was weird before now, even when you were awake. Touch was strangely intimate for the amount of loneliness you constantly felt. You were so lonely that your seclusion held space like a silent companion. You occasionally hooked up with men who caressed you like a purchase they were considering. Your body was something they looked at with anticipation and greed, and they unwrapped you like a product they coveted or a gift they'd been waiting a long time to open. They treated you with ownership, with pride. Sometimes you felt empty even while you were with them. It wasn't like you both didn't want the same thing, but sometimes it felt as if they carried pieces of you away with them. You feared there'd be nothing left of you by the time you graduated.

Hookup apps took you all over the place. The actual hookups were often superfast and random. Just when you needed to blow off steam. You'd been in all sorts of cars, both front and back seat. Been in seedy motel rooms with carpeting you were sure you'd bring home bedbugs from and hotel rooms so chic and streamlined and beautiful they made you ashamed of the ratty secondhand clothing you wore into them. Thanks to Derek, you knew almost everywhere you could pull off the side of the road and park for any amount of time without garnering too much attention. You had hooked up with him at fishing spots and in duck blinds, in the locker room and all over his house. But never in yours. You drew the line there.

When you tried to imagine what having sex with someone you loved might feel like, there was only once in your history that really stuck out before the night you spent with Brian. It happened at Rugg's Peak.

If any place in Canon was haunted, it was there. It's where your dad took you hiking, fishing, hunting, and camping when he was feeling especially paternal before he got laid off from the mines. You were young then and he was still the dad you loved, long before he became the father you feared. Long before he started filling the empty places in himself with cheap whiskey and the Holy Spirit. You took Derek up there once after he struck out with some girl at a party and just wanted to get off.

"Man, this place is awesome," Derek had said, glancing around as he unzipped his jeans. "I can't wait to bring Christine Hobbs up here. I've been trying to get into her pants for months."

Images of him with Christine Hobbs tortured you the entire time you were together that night. You didn't know (and didn't want to know) who else he'd brought back to defile your sanctuary. It served you right for trying to turn whatever you and Derek were doing into something real. What you did together was about convenience for him, and about identity for you.

The problem was Canon. If you lived in a big city, or even just somewhere that didn't constantly crack your chest open with its beauty, you might care less about making a life for yourself there. Or making a life you could come back to after college. Truth was, you'd gotten scholarships to a couple of pretty good schools but leaving scared the shit out of you. To start, who would run interference when your dad got hammered and came home to use your mom as a punching bag?

And there was the problem of how to be yourself at college. All three of the schools you'd gotten offers from were in-state and you might not be the only Canon High grad there. The scholarships were all athletic, of course. You weren't failing anything, but you weren't an honor roll student, either. What would your teammates think if they knew you were into dudes? College probably wasn't that different from high school.

You couldn't count the number of times your bros called one another a fag or a queer or a cocksucker as a playful insult. It only took one person finding out to ruin your entire life.

So, yeah, you were afraid to stay and afraid to go. If that made you feel restless, Rugg's Peak settled all the scattered places inside you. It put your broken pieces in some semblance of order that made sense. It was where you ran time and time again to be humbled by the big sky and the mountains stretched above you.

You'd driven up there with some dude from out of town who was just visiting for his great-great-someone's four hundredth birthday. He was what you'd call a corn-fed country boy, beefy strong but biscuit soft. He was about your age and had made you feel more wholesome than anyone you'd ever been with. He offered you his number and to keep in touch, but you were a total dick about it because it wasn't like you were ever going to see him again. How would you explain your fucked-up family and your football facade to someone whose bland beauty seemed outweighed only by his normalcy?

It was enough to be held and to hold someone for once under the open sky. To take more time than the usual awkward fumbling. To be totally naked and vulnerable in front of someone else who was a mirror that you didn't mind looking into. The world felt limitless with that boy's thick chest pressed against your lean back, with his arms wrapped around you, warming you against the hint of a chill to come.

What you remembered most about that boy was the kissing. Other dudes weren't too interested in making out, but he had kissed you with such hunger you thought it might consume you both. Even after you were both spent, he took a long time kissing your body. Soft, gentle kisses that made you feel worshiped. It was the closest you'd ever come to the spirituality your mom found comfort in at church. It made you think that maybe God wasn't a person or entity, but a feeling. It was what you reached for when you thought about the future—a hope so big it made you almost believe in the possibility of something bigger for yourself.

A hope so big, it started to fill up the emptiness inside you.

18

HEART AND HEAD
Brian

Overnight, I was suddenly the most popular I'd ever been.

An NPR affiliate in NYC picked up Greg's story in a feature about small-town homophobia and somehow found my podcast. They interviewed Riley and me and played it on air. We listened to it alone in Riley's car and screamed when it was over and then went out for ice cream. We flailed excitedly about and wondered if our subscriber count would go up and what it might do to our sponsorship options. I hoped aloud that we'd get wildly rich or famous but thought more realistically we'd see a short spike and then level out again.

I could not have been more wrong. By the next morning, my DMs were blowing up. I had to turn off notifications and mute my phone. Our followers almost doubled. The constant dings and vibrations were distracting in school, and they made my mom and eventually even Riley annoyed with me.

It seemed more and more people had heard about *Shampoo Unicorn*, about Greg's attack and the questions we had about it. I enjoyed reading other people's stories. Loved that they were sharing them with me. I wondered if I might do something with them later.

Dreland was an older man who once was a salesman and lived in Queens with his partner. Someone had gifted him tickets once to see Alvin Ailey's *Revelations*, and he'd been so changed by the performance, and by knowing that there was art that embraced both his Blackness and his queerness, that he took classes and became a professional dancer a short time later. His partner was a librarian. They met at the home of a mutual friend. It had been love immediately for Dreland, though his partner took some convincing. Dreland said the idea of building a life together was the hardest thing he'd ever been tasked with selling.

Vinicius was a boomer from a family that held military service among their most defining characteristics. He enlisted right out of high school as well. He met his first serious boyfriend in basic training, and they had stayed mostly together through split assignments and deployments, though they had an understanding about seeing other men when they weren't able to be together. When they were both in their midtwenties, his boyfriend was killed in the Korean War.

Because Vini was deeply closeted, his ability to grieve was limited, so he served out the rest of his enlistment and moved home, where he opened the small bakery they'd talked about starting together. He felt more welcome at the VA than ever before, and though the machismo could be suffocating, he had been reunited with men from his unit through the organization.

O was a programmer from St. Louis. They loved coding languages and working outside the gender binary in their real life. They had felt like an extra piece to a complete jigsaw puzzle. There were no neat borders for them to exist within. Rather than try and fit all their identities into one box, they lived online, where they could be more than one person, more than two people, on any given day. They joined a radical anarcho-collective and all bought a home together where they shared cats and computers and were mostly polyamorous. They talked about digital privacy and radical consent at house meetings, and while they weren't always happy, they were never bored.

Alex was from a wealthy family, and there were expectations of who he should marry, where he should attend school, and what his life would look like. He had been reading by the pool when the gardener had accidentally dropped a branch in his lap. He wasn't hurt but looking into the face of a boy the same age and height as him, weathered by work and life, changed him. They were exact opposites and there had been a moment of stunned silence between them—Alex's surprise, Josue's panic. And then they laughed. Their laughter had turned to conversation, and they never stopped talking. Josue changed the way Alex looked at the world, helped him cut a new path different from the dead end he'd been traveling.

Rahul and Sreya were twins. They had shared a womb for nine months, and secrets and jokes for all their time on Earth. When they were eleven, they came out to each other. Rahul was gay, Sreya a lesbian. When they were twenty, they immigrated to the US for college. By the time they graduated, Rahul was fully out of the closet to everyone but their parents. To make things easier, Sreya came out first. And it had been fine.

Completely fine.

Their parents had protected them from more conservative family members, had cut ties with anyone who refused to celebrate them, and eventually had followed them to the US, settled into a largely Indian community in Oakland, and hosted Rahul, his husband, Sreya, and whoever she was dating during Diwali every year.

Leslie spent all her life trying to fly under the radar. To not cause a fuss, not stick out. She spent most of her days waiting to live on her own terms. College, or just after college when financial independence was an option. Her parents weren't homophobic, but they weren't politically liberal, either. Her dad voted Republican in most elections prior to 2016 for financial reasons, and while they were generally good people, they were also very quiet. She had weighed transition against suicide for so long that when she tripped in front of her mom, skinned her knee, it caused everything to unravel. She hadn't realized how badly she needed to say the words out loud. And because her family was so silent, she hadn't realized how much she craved their love and attention. Her coming out served as a wake-up call for all of them. Her parents rallied around her like soldiers in a war she hadn't realized she'd been fighting alone. With them beside her, she stopped fighting and let them know her. Their easy acceptance was a balm that healed all of them.

As I read their stories, their emails, and sincere concern about Greg, I pictured them forming an invisible wall around his bed. In my mind, they were there, protecting him when I couldn't be. Bearing witness to whatever he might be going through in his head or heart, in the invisible places I couldn't see, even as I watched his bruises start to fade.

I had gotten a fair amount of hate mail, too. Threats and letters about sin and sodomy. I could mostly take that, because they were so few in comparison to the letters of support. I kept those to myself, even secret from Riley. But I ignored the trolls and only read the good ones to Greg when he and I were alone in the room. When Riley came with me to visit, we took turns reading them. She was a better reader, more theatrical and prone to doing accents.

I printed the letters on colored paper and taped them to the walls so it would look less sterile for when Greg did finally wake up. When I wasn't there, I imagined them as a Greek chorus, keeping watch over him, his room filled with the best wishes and high hopes of a community deeply invested in his survival. More than once, I saw Mrs. Burke reading them as well, dabbing her eyes.

"All these people are writing to you about Greg?" she asked once. "Because of your radio show?" I nodded and handed her a stack of papers. "And there are more. I'm just putting the best ones up for Greg."

She took the stack, her eyes glossy with tears, and started taping them up along with me. And as I stood beside Mrs. Burke, quietly tapping varying colors of papers to the wall, the wounds began to mend.

There were so many more ways to heal than I'd realized.

19

SELF-SCRIMMAGE
Greg

You were most at home standing on the fifty-yard line.

The field was where you let yourself put all the passion, emotion, and spirituality that you couldn't find a home for anywhere else. If there was any place you were truly present in the world, it was on the field. Your teammates and Coach Winsor joked about you not holding back. You took all your bullshit and left it in the end zone. You'd come home with bruises and sprains during the season, and you loved the physicality of it. Loved the subtle reminder to your old man that guys half his age and twice his size could rarely sack you. If your body ached, you could concentrate on that rather than some fucked-up joke that one of your bros made or wondering if your dad's latest tirade was more quantitively racist, sexist, or homophobic.

Off-season, you hit the gym hard. You ran, lifted, swam, scrimmaged, and occasionally even played non-football sports. You liked basketball and hockey the best, but racquetball was good, too. You'd looked into wrestling, but thought it seemed too homoerotic for a kid who was trying desperately not to let everyone know what a raging queer he really was.

After your dad's zillionth DUI, his license was revoked, your mom added you to the insurance, and you started driving his truck full-time. Sometimes while driving him around on errands, the ache in your body would be enough to distract you from his running commentary on how people were basically thieves and whores and bastards, and there was no place left in the world for a hardworking white man. You'd tense your abs and let the throb of too many reps push his words away. Counted backward from one hundred, rolled down the window, and let the wind drown him out.

It was sort of like that now. You were miles away from the world, but you could feel your body trying hard to knit itself back together, to pull you back through the doors of your eyelids to light and vision and reality. Your head felt distant, fuzzy, and indistinct, itching and buzzing with pain.

Your ribs hurt like they did when that big linebacker from another team surprised you and you rolled head over ass. There were sharp pains that rose up into a chorus of agony and were gradually dulled as a narcotic blanket of calm covered your body. You weren't sure what you preferred, honestly. The pain was almost unbearable, but it was at least a feeling you recognized. The numbness was comforting, but wherever you were was bland and boring and you lost track of time, of yourself and the few senses you had any control over.

More than anything you wanted to stop hurting and wake up, but you weren't sure if you had a choice or not. If you were in the driver's seat, would you choose to go back to the life you had? Was another life even possible?

Your teammates were most real at parties. You could talk freely, outside of school, sports, the expectations you put forth for one another. About the stuff you said to each other. It was almost like you were alternately performer and audience. That is, until the conversations went to girls. The fact that they enjoyed talking about sex with them and you didn't made you feel like a freak and empty inside for using the couple you'd hooked up with just for show. It seemed everyone else wore a confidence they'd been given at birth that had grown with them. You stayed quiet, not participating in their brand of conversation, and you let warm, flat beers dull the places where pain flared up.

Even when shit got too real—when you had to break up a fight between your bros or you had to physically block Sullivan from going after Lisa Hubbard after she got so drunk she could barely stand up. Rather than having a long talk about consent, Sully had called you a cockblock, and you just shrugged.

"Yo, man," you'd said, deepening your voice. He had thrown an arm around you and was so unsteady that his sway made you rock back and forth. The motion was not helping sober either of you up. "You're being a dick. You can't fuck someone who can't say yes. And even if you did, Lisa's brother is, like, six feet and a million inches tall. He could squash your punk ass like a bug. And you'd do the same damn thing if someone came after your kid sister the way you're sweating Lisa."

Later, he thanked you and you shrugged, saying you were just trying to be a gentleman. He cuffed you on the shoulder and said that you were a good dude. That was the highest compliment any of you ever paid to each other:

Good dude.

If you stayed sober to make sure everyone else got home okay, you were a good dude. When you had the foresight to bring a bunch of Pedialyte for the next morning's inevitable hangover, you were a good dude. You ran a touchdown, racking up yardage to win a game against a rival, then you were a good dude.

It started to feel like you were the team's pet homo, just begging at the table for scraps of affection. You were like a kicked puppy, wagging his tail at any occasional attention. You were the best boy.

But it was more than that. You were watching them for cues on how to behave. What you should do or say. What behavior incited ridicule? It was a bit like being an alien spy trying to fit in on a planet you weren't sure was friendly or not. In the end, they claimed you as one of their own and you were happy to feel like part of something. It was the only thing you really felt part of. You knew what you were hiding and that some of them had secrets, too.

Sully's mom died a couple of years ago and he never talked about his grief. Derek wasn't stupid by any stretch of the imagination, but he got really bad grades and reading aloud tortured him. Still, his family wouldn't admit that he might have a learning disability or try to get him support. Parks constantly excused himself after meals and more than once you'd heard him puking in a bathroom stall in some casual dining restaurant. None of you called it an eating disorder because that was a problem hot cheerleaders had, not tough jocks. Your friends were a mystery that you didn't try too hard to solve for fear they'd look harder back at you and discover something they didn't like.

Yours and your friends' problems weren't the same, and no one knew your particular secret, but your silence bonded you as much as shitty beers and sports.

SHAMPOO UNICORN
Episode 312: "King Coward"

DEREK:

Sure. I got nothing to hide. Nothing to lose. I'll be on your podcast. What the fuck? If it helps Greg, why not? And it can't freakin' hurt, right?

BRIAN:

Today, we're here with a guest we've only referred to in the past as Jocko. Do you want to introduce yourself?

DEREK:

Uh, sure. I'm Derek. I go to school with Greg and Brian. I play ball with Greg. Hi. Is it . . . uh . . . normal? Should I be this nervous?

[SHAMPOO UNICORN *THEME SONG PLAYS.*]

BRIAN:

Our guest today is possibly the most relevant to this case. If you were to pass him on the street, your first thought would be that he's very good-looking. He's often dressed in the generic uniform of teen boys everywhere—dirty sneakers, jeans, T-shirt, and hoodie. He has messy dark-blond hair. Freckles cover his cheeks and nose. Beyond that, he also spent several years calling me a faggot and knocking books out of my hands, while he or his football minions bodychecked me into walls and other hard barriers. He was the other party to the locker room incident, and if we're listing people with a motive to attack Greg, he'd be our first suspect.

DEREK:

Jesus fucking Christ. How the hell am I supposed to respond to something like that?

BRIAN:

Am I wrong, though, Derek?

DEREK:

I guess not. But I've never really thought about things like that. The school shit sucked, but it wasn't like I thought it was Greg's fault, exactly. It wasn't anyone's fault. It was just something shitty that happened. Bad timing or poor life choices or whatever. But it wasn't Greg's fault. If it was anyone's fault, it was mine.

BRIAN:

Go on.

DEREK:

I mean, he was my best friend. Is my best friend. When he came out to me, I should've been more supportive. Instead, I turned it into a different thing. There were some . . . my therapist says "sexual power dynamics" at play. And I guess she's right.

BRIAN:

Therapist?

DEREK:

Yeah, man. I mean, I know I come off as a total fucking douche. And I guess I have been. But I'm trying to be better. I know I owe you an apology. That's part of why I'm here. This whole thing with Greg was a pretty big wake-up call. So I'll answer whatever questions you have if it helps him. If it helps anyone, really. The school thought I should see a therapist at first, so my old man sent me to one. Some lady I didn't expect to help. But talking about shit made things . . . not easier, really. Just maybe, like, less hard.

BRIAN:

That's a lot to unpack. Let's start with an easy one. Are you gay? Or bi?

DEREK:

No. I don't think so. I mean, Greg and I did stuff together, but it was mostly a convenience thing. Just, y'know, dudes being dudes. But when I picture myself in the future, it's with a wife and kids. I knew he thought I was hot, and I sort of got off on the attention, I guess. What's weird is that I keep having to sort of "come out" to people as straight. If you believe what you read on the internet, lots of straight dudes experiment with other guys, but now no one really believes me. They think I'm this big closet case or something, but, like, if I were gay, the cat would really be out of the bag by now, right?

BRIAN:

Okay. So what happened in the locker room?

DEREK:

Look, I'm not going to get real specific, because that's pretty private, and Greg . . . well, he isn't here to tell me it's okay to talk about it. But the official paperwork from the school board says we were engaged in inappropriate behavior and got caught by Coach Winsor and Principal Matthews. If it were just Coach, we would've gotten suspended, not expelled. Hell, he might just have made us run laps. My bet is the board made an example of us.

BRIAN:

What makes you say that?

DEREK:

Well, I mean, I'm not a great student, but Greg is constantly on the honor roll. We're both athletes, and neither of us has any major disciplinary actions on our record. So, y'know. I think it's a gay thing. Like, homophobic or whatever.

BRIAN:

But you just said you weren't gay.

DEREK:

But Greg is. And we're two dudes. How much boy-girl sex do you think goes on at school?

BRIAN:

Uh, none?

DEREK:

Okay, maybe not regular school, but it does at football games, dances, and overnight extracurricular trips. I know for a fact that a couple of sophomores got totally busted doing hand stuff on the band bus to the Canon-Appleville game last year. And no one said anything about it. Plus, there's a dude who got caught jacking off so much in the locker room showers that half the football team calls him Splooge.

BRIAN:

That . . . is completely repulsive, and I have about two

hundred questions I'm going to ask off the air for sure. But it's an interesting point.

DEREK:

You don't think it's homophobic?

BRIAN:

I guess I hadn't really thought about it. But maybe. What are you doing with yourself now that you aren't in school?

DEREK:

I've been working at the gun range since I was old enough to, so I'm picking up some extra hours there, playing video games, and working out. Working on myself, or whatever. My therapist suggested that I find a creative outlet, so I've been playing around with that. I tried painting, but I suck at it, and I hate reading and writing. I bought some modeling clay, so maybe I'll be a sculptor. Who knows? Maybe I'll take an improv or an acting class. I know you probably won't buy this, but I'm trying to focus on being a better person.

BRIAN:

Because of Greg?

DEREK:

Yeah. I mean, before all this shit went down, I fully bought into this whole football-bro-glory-days persona.

But I don't really know who I am or what I want without all of that, because I spent most of my life trying to make everyone else around me proud.

BRIAN:

That's pretty unexpected, coming from you.

DEREK:

I know, man. I've been an asshole to you. I don't even know why. You've never done anything to me. I think it was just . . . easy.

BRIAN:

Easy?

DEREK:

I mean, like, you're kind of a little guy; I knew you weren't gonna try to fight me. And there's the obvious thing of you being gay. There's a real weird group mentality that happens when you do something to impress other dudes. They don't want to risk the social fallout of pointing out when another dude says something fucked-up. So they just stay silent, or they laugh and elbow each other or whatever. Because it's better to call someone a fag than to be called a fag, you know?

BRIAN:

Why would you think I'd know?

DEREK:

You're right. What I'm saying is that I'm sorry. My friends are cowards, and I'm King Coward. All this bullshit was fed to me by my dad and sports and TV and whatever else. It was fed to me, but I didn't have to eat it. It hurt you, and Greg, and who knows how many other people. I'm trying to make things right in whatever ways I can. My therapist says I need to think about what my actions tell the people around me about what kind of person I am.

I used to think therapy was a load of horseshit. That it was for whiners and widows. I'm learning a lot, though.

BRIAN:

Not sure I'm ready to stop hating you, and I fully can't believe that I'm agreeing with you, but therapy seems like a pretty solid first move.

DEREK:

Thanks, Brian. I especially appreciate that coming from you. In a weird way, I think you and a lot of the other kids I picked on are good examples for me. You're just yourself, all day, every day. The world has not made it easy for that to be comfortable, but you know who you are. I really admire that.

BRIAN:

So, you know I brought you on this podcast because I

am looking into Greg's attack. And because you have more motivation than anyone to hurt him. Do you have a response to that?

DEREK:

I see why you'd believe that, but I think I've proven I have less motive, because I feel like shit about how everything went down. Besides, the police already asked me about it. I was at the gun range. I punched my time card, and my coworkers can confirm I was there.

BRIAN:

Do you have any other insight about why this might have happened? I mean, the attack, sure, but like, how?

DEREK:

[PAUSE.]

I mean, I know you aren't asking about, like, time and speed and suspects and things like that.

BRIAN:

Right.

DEREK:

I think it's because there's a disconnect, you know? Like, I know gay people exist. I've seen them on TV, but until Greg came out to me, being gay was just kind of a punch line. An easy way to make people laugh. Like, shit I did to make my boys laugh and not how it might make you feel.

BRIAN:

Talk to me about the disconnect.

DEREK:

I couldn't imagine someone gay being hurt or offended by some dumb shit I said. Like it wasn't real. Like, it wasn't about you, specifically. It was for them, not about you. You were just sort of . . . incidental.

BRIAN:

That is among the most fucked-up things you have ever said to me.

DEREK:

I know. I don't feel great about it, if that helps.

BRIAN:

It doesn't. Why should your guilt matter when you just said my feelings didn't matter to you?

DEREK:

Look, it wasn't just me, okay? Lots of other people felt that way. Hell, Greg's own dad felt that way, I guess. And if I could go back and undo all the ways I've hurt you in the past, I would. But all I can do is be brave in the future when presented with the choices that made me a coward in the past.

I have owed you an apology since probably the first day we met. I'm so sorry. I'll say it as many times as you need to hear it, but first, can I confess something not related to Greg?

BRIAN:

Sure.

DEREK:

When you asked me to do this podcast, I looked it up. I listened to a bunch of episodes and subscribed. I'm a big fan.

BRIAN:

It's only been a minute since I told you about it.

DEREK:

I know, but check it out.

BRIAN:

Derek is taking out his phone, searching his apps, and now showing me . . . that he's listened to, Jesus, like, twelve episodes?

DEREK:

Fourteen! But who's counting? You're funny as fuck, man. I never knew that about you. The episode where you guys went to the state fair is my favorite so far. The food-on-a-stick review, where you sampled from all the concession stands. That apple pie on a stick sounded amazing. And deep-fried butter? That'll fuck you up. It was genius. Did y'all make it to the rodeo?

BRIAN:

The one where that clown got kicked in the face by a goat and started bleeding profusely? Um, yes!

DEREK:

Oh yeah, I did hear that one. And then all those kids started crying.

BRIAN:

OMG. Yes. They're going to be in therapy for years. Uh, no offense.

DEREK:

(laughing)

No, it's cool.

[SHAMPOO UNICORN *EXIT THEME PLAYS.]*

20

PAY IT NO MIND
Leslie

Leslie thinks about pride.

The closest pride events are, at minimum, a three-hour drive away. She wants so badly to lose herself in a crowd of other queer people, in a sea of rainbow. It's never been possible before, but now that she's out to the people who matter, now that she's written and posted a coming-out letter to the people who count, now that her parents and the few teachers she's close to know, she could participate. She'd have every reason and right to attend. It's a long drive, and she'd like to go alone, but probably her parents would also really want to join her. What would it feel like to be with her mom and dad in a parade of people like her?

Her parents' pride is so unexpected and immense that it overwhelms her sometimes. Her mom found a couple of places with generous return policies and started credit accounts so Leslie can order clothes and makeup to experiment with. Mail has become unexpectedly exciting, but she does wonder about what it would be like to just walk into any store in the mall, decide to try on a dress, and make a casual purchase. She's been thinking about how it would feel to have a special occasion to shop for clothes, to make an appointment at a salon. A wedding or date, maybe, though realistically, prom or pride are more likely.

She understands that most pride events are in big cities because it's easier to be safely out where there are larger communities of queer people. She knows statistically she's not alone in feeling so isolated and invisible in her very small town. Here she feels like she's always looking so hard for other queer people that every rainbow seems like an oasis. If she had unlimited resources, Leslie would build a caravan of floats and drive them to all the places that might need them most. Small Southern towns like hers, places in the Midwest, wherever people might be queer and scared. She'd be like a transgender Batman. BatTran. Her costume would be fierce. Someone would post her signal and she'd swoop in and face off with fundamentalists, rescue kids from conversion camps, step in front of bullies and smite them with an impressive ferocity.

What would a small-town pride parade even look like? Would it be the only lesbian couple in an unincorporated town like hers, holding a giant pride flag walking down Main Street? Would it be heavily protested by conservative Republicans? Or would it embolden people to come out—not necessarily of the closet, but maybe that, too—to see who else in town is queer, who supports them or condemns them. Small-town pride parades could be a good start. People should be able to be comfortably queer at home, wherever home is.

Most kids her age watch videos, or play games, or listen to music when they're bored. But not Leslie. For her, there's almost nothing more satisfying than looking at pictures of her sheroes or reading any of the nine billion accounts of Marsha P. Johnson at the Stonewall uprising in 1969. Some people believe that Marsha started the whole thing by throwing a shot glass in protest at someone being arrested. Or it was a brick or a stiletto. In 1987 she said she didn't come in until later. Witnesses say that on the second night of rioting, she climbed a light post and dropped a purse containing a brick onto the windshield of a police car. As with legends, there are countless variations, but the theme of Marsha will always be shattering glass and changing everything.

When Leslie imagines the scene, there's always a riotous cheer after the cacophony of shatters and then it breaks into rhythmic chants. In her mind, the bar patrons and protesters have known one another from around Christopher Street for long enough that the noise is friendly from within, only threatening if you're the other team, the police.

She wants to do something Marsha would be proud of. Something that celebrates *Shampoo Unicorn* and Greg, and, to a lesser degree, herself. She wants somewhere to wear a pretty dress and a place for her parents to see that they aren't alone. There are other parents trying to make spaces safer and more welcoming for their kids. She does not want to drive to a huge city with a bunch of people who are already out and proud and take their safety for granted. Well, she does. She'd go to anything pride related, obviously. She's desperate to know her own community. To create a space that feels important to occupy. She can't see room for her in some corporate parade in a city she's barely even driven through. But she can't figure out where in Canon she'd hold it.

She turns up the music and bites her lip as she composes the email.

> *Dear Riley and Brian,*
>
> *This isn't my first email to you. I know you guys must get a lot, so these letters are probably mostly for me. This is one of gratitude. Your podcast helped me come out to my parents. I wasn't sure I'd ever be able to do that, and now, surprisingly, it feels like my life is slowly blooming. I'm so grateful to you both. Maybe you get emails like this all the time. Maybe this is silly or boring or whatever, but*

I have been looking into making a pride event in Canon (which is not too far from where I live in rural Pennsylvania). It feels like the two of you and Greg more than deserve to be showered with celebration and happiness after everything that has happened.

I just can't quite figure out where to have it. I've been in touch with a handful of municipal offices and the thing I keep getting hung up on is space. They can't (or won't) block off public parks or streets without a sponsoring organization. I don't live there, so I don't know what organizations might be queer-owned or amenable to a pride event. I have a list of flower shops and hairdressers, but that seems like a long shot at best and like a lot of bureaucratic stereotyping at worst. So I'm emailing you who have effected such positive changes in my life, hoping to cause some in yours. I am inspired by your hard work and forever grateful to you both. Is there a queer-owned business you'd suggest I ask? Or a private space I might be able to use?

Your fan,

Leslie

21

MIGHT AS WELL EARN IT
Greg

Your dad's voice was a nightmare you couldn't wake up from.

When things were going to shit, it was always him you heard in your head. You could usually tell how deep in his drinking he was by the warning tone in his voice. The louder it got, the more he was spoiling for a fight. He'd have spent all day thinking about people who'd done him dirty or slighted him in some real or perceived way.

Your mom switched to night shifts when you were in tenth grade. She'd been nervous leaving you alone with him, but you encouraged her, saying that the shift differential would help out with the bills, but really it meant you could spend evenings away from home instead of constantly protecting her from him.

"Nice going, shit stick," he'd slurred from his recliner after you were expelled, an open can of beer in his hand and four crumpled empties on the floor beside him. "You expect to get any sort of scholarship now?"

Then there was the time he barged into your room, barely stable on his feet, stinking of cigarettes and body odor. "What the hell kind of pansy music are you listening to? Christ on a cracker, some whiny ass singing about his feelings?" He pointed at your iPhone speaker. "You need to get you some gospel music on that thing. That'll get your soft ass right with Jesus."

On another occasion, he sat at the kitchen table and nodded to the seat across from him. "Jesus Christ, sit down and talk to your old man. You're never here. This ain't some hotel for you to pop in and out of when you need to eat, sleep, and beat off."

The last time he really came at you, it had been right after your mom had switched shifts. You were eating a turkey sandwich, and your dad started in on how little you contributed to the household and what a drain on resources and a general waste of space you were. He was drooling and slurring and later you found a form letter saying that Consolidated Lumber Mills sincerely appreciated his interest and had enjoyed meeting him in an interview, but they'd decided to hire someone else. They'd keep his résumé on file, and if any positions became available, they encouraged him to reapply.

Fed up and exhausted, you asked what he'd contributed to the household lately. You had been returning a two-liter bottle of root beer to the fridge when he backhanded you into the wall so hard a framed portrait of *The Last Supper* landed with a thud, the glass inside the frame shattering against the linoleum floor.

You had a moment of calm before he called you a worthless little shit, and then you matched his rage. He swung at you, and you took the hit before returning it. Pain exploded in your knuckles when you connected with his jaw and from there you were rolling around together on the floor. You grabbed him around the ribs and buried your head in his chest, pulling your neck in like a turtle. This way, he couldn't get any head shots in, and he didn't have the reach to throw any really hard punches. He connected with your ribs a couple of times, but you felt your skeleton and his make contact when you hit him in the sternum. You were both bruised for a few weeks, but neither of you said anything to your mom, and miraculously, she never asked.

After that, you had dustups, words, even shouting matches, but when it escalated quickly his eyes mirrored the fear you'd felt for so long. Without knowing anything else, your coach reamed you out for fighting. Promising careers had been ruined for less. If you were gonna blow a knee or take a hit, the least you could do was do it on the field. Your team deserved that level of dedication.

He was right. After that, you spent all your aggression in practice and during games, and even your bros mentioned that you'd become a monster on the field. You hit parties harder, too. And tried to throw yourself into chasing girls, but that felt dishonest and shitty, so mostly you just threw yourself into football and worked out so hard off-season that it hurt more often than it didn't.

When you could, you used hooking up as a way to break the building tension. You felt wound up like a coiled spring and getting head from some nameless, faceless nobody would unwind you for a while, but it also made you feel empty. It was a self-perpetuating cycle. A hurricane whose wind howled your name in a voice that sounded like home.

From forced sleep, you could hear faint strains of organ music and somber singing. It wasn't the jubilant music of your mom's radio, but it was definitely hymns. Were there people nearby? You could pick out the strands of individual voices, lifted in song. It was almost certainly "The Old Rugged Cross," your mom's favorite song, and you could almost definitely hear Mrs. Moore's emotive wail as the song circled back to the chorus.

Your mom wasn't in the choir at church even though she had a really pretty singing voice. She couldn't make it to choir practice because it was held in the evenings after her nursing shifts had started. You knew she would have loved it, but she was content to sing along from the other side of the pulpit.

You hated going to church, but you knew how much it meant to your mom. Your dad in a nice shirt and khakis, you in a tie and sport coat. It was a picture of the family that your mom wanted, but it was a fake picture. It didn't matter what happened at home. Sundays were the image she had of your family and she asked so little, you owed her at least this.

For her, you could suffer through the smell of mothballs and old-lady perfume and the numerous hugs and cheek pinches and backslaps. Creating the narrative of a concerned student helped you escape the attention of the age-appropriate girls in the congregation who made slight, shy flirting gestures.

You talked about how hard it was to be a good Christian teen over church breakfasts, bake sales, Vacation Bible Schools, tent revivals, and wherever else your mom brought you. To outside observers, you seemed like the best Christian, the best student, the best athlete, and best son possible so that later you could be a good husband to a God-fearing woman. You almost choked on the hypocrisy of it. But it made your mom so proud, and she had so few occasions to feel that way.

The hard wooden pew tortured you while the sermon droned on and on and on. You spent all of middle school convinced that you were going to burn in hell, your soul condemned to a lake of eternal fire because of what you thought about after lights out. You were worried about yourself and Brian. But when he tried to bring it up, you left the room, left his house, left wherever you were together and went home to pray by yourself. You felt guilty, annoyed, and ashamed, but you buried all that and just tried to look straight ahead or pretend to be reading your Bible.

By high school, it all rolled off your back like water and you could almost nap with your eyes open, thinking about homework or football or, when you were feeling brave, about some of the hot Christian men in the congregation. What they might look like naked. What they might sound like when you were doing ungodly things to them. And you were as sure as not that if hell existed, you had a seat reserved in your name.

Might as well earn it.

SHAMPOO UNICORN
Episode 313: "Welcome Aboard"

BRIAN:

It's a pretty wet day, but I'm warm inside a quiet corner booth at ye olde country diner with my hands wrapped around a steaming mug of what the waitress calls high octane.

The same three or four waitresses have been working here for as long as I can remember. Tonight it's Doris, who is a sweet old woman with a lunch-lady haircut and a loud, honking laugh. She's known me since I was a kid. My mom used to bring me to the diner every Sunday as a treat for both of us. I liked to build pyramids out of the coffee creamers and try to knock them all down with a folded paper football I made from the band around the napkin-wrapped silverware. It's harder than it sounds when you're six and you're still figuring out manual dexterity.

[*SHAMPOO UNICORN THEME SONG PLAYS.*]

BRIAN:

Like most of my classmates, I've known Beth since kindergarten. We've been in classes together, probably done group assignments or whatever, but I don't really know her. I don't recall ever having a conversation of substance with her. I couldn't tell you what she wants to major in, her favorite color, or what her house looks like. The last interaction I remember having with her was in middle school when the cheerleaders were selling valentines to raise money for new uniforms or something. She asked if I wanted to send a valentine to anyone, and I said no thank you. Not exactly the stuff deep friendships are built on.

[*SOUND OF A DOOR OPENING, BELL CHIMING, AND WIND BLOWING FROM OUTSIDE.*]

BRIAN:

That's her. She's wearing a purple peacoat with black jeans and knee-high black boots. Her dark, straight hair is tucked under a beanie, but her neat bangs frame an oval face with cheeks pink from the cold.

[*A MUFFLED SOUND OF BOOKS AND A BAG THUMPING DOWN*]

BETH:

Hi, Brian. Sorry I'm a little late. My car hates to start right away in the cold.

BRIAN:

No worries. I ordered you a coffee. I don't know if you drink the stuff or not? I can order you a cocoa or something instead?

BETH:

This is great, thank you. I drink coffee like it's my job. Brrr. I'm freezing. I hate this cold snap we're having.

*[SOUND OF BLOWING ON COFFEE
FOLLOWED BY A LOUD SIP.]*

BETH:

So we're here to talk about Greg?

BRIAN:

Yeah. I was wondering if—

BETH:

Can I go ahead and get something out of the way? Something that is a fairly big deal?

BRIAN:

Yes, please. By all means.

BETH:

I knew Greg was gay. Have for a while. I was using his computer and found his search history sophomore year. When he tried to deny it, I came out to him so he'd feel less alone. And then I taught him how to delete his search history.

BRIAN:

Wait, what? You're . . .

BETH:

[laughing]

A full-on cheerleader femme queermo feminist killjoy? Yes. I mostly don't talk about it because we live in not a great place to be out and proud, as you well know. Canon is much more of a Confederate-flag town than a pride-flag town.

BRIAN:

Oh. My. God. Why am I just learning about this?

BETH:

To be quite honest, there are a couple of reasons. Self-preservation being the number one. But also high on the list is that Greg was really one of only a few guys in my social circle. I just prefer the company of other women. Our "relationship" has been mostly text- and convenience-based. When he needed me to show up as arm candy, I would, and he'd do the same for me.

BRIAN:

Who else knew?

BETH:

About me? Or about Greg?

BRIAN:

Both. And about you being each other's beards!

BETH:

Well, the couple of girls I've hooked up with or made out with know about me, obviously. But I don't know who else knew about Greg. The point of being occasionally together was to cover for each other.

BRIAN:

So, why tell me? Why now?

BETH:

What good did keeping it a secret do for Greg? And maybe my saying something will make someone else feel less shitty or alone.

BRIAN:

I certainly feel less alone. I thought I was almost the only queer person in town.

BETH:

Well, statistically . . .

BRIAN:

Statistics, smatistics . . . Why are we not better friends?

BETH:

You know why, Brian. I wasn't ready to risk alienating

all my friends or being kicked out by my parents. I'm on track to get a cheerleading scholarship that will give me more academic options than community college or the privately run Bible college in Rockwell. I saw the stuff that you went through every day, and it sucked. It's an unfair double standard, but unless you're super butch, it's pretty easy to fly under the radar as a gay lady. I do wish I had talked to Greg more about how fucking lonely it can be. I wish I had been more of a friend.

BRIAN:

Right. So, what now?

BETH:

I don't know. I came out to my parents earlier today when I decided I was going to do this. I think it's important to be visible but also to recognize that there are risks involved, too.

BRIAN:

I think so, but explain anyway.

BETH:

Well, you know. You want to be recognized for your differences, lest anyone mistake your silence for shame. But also, those differences? They're probably one of the most likely reasons that Greg is . . . well, where he is.

BRIAN:

That's a really succinct way to put it.

BETH:

I've been thinking about it a lot lately.

BRIAN:

What did your parents say?

BETH:

They sort of just found out, remember? They're very much part of a love-the-sinner-hate-the-sin kind of church. So as long as I don't talk about gay stuff or try to bring a girlfriend home, we'll probably remain at a kind of impasse. I haven't figured out how much I'm comfortable pressing it. Probably not much until I graduate. My little brother was mostly concerned with what it meant to his social status to be the sibling of a homosexual. If people would ask if he was gay, too.

BRIAN:

You know, I want to say that's fucked-up of him, but Riley has fielded rumors about her sexuality forever. Sometimes for her general proximity to me, like the gay would rub off on her. But she's secretly the coolest person on Earth.

BETH:

She seems moderately cool.

BRIAN:

Girl, you don't even know. This one time, we were in the hallway and Tater Jenkins pushed me and said, "Jesus

hates fags." And Riley said, "Jesus can suck my dick."
Then she kneed him in the groin.

BETH:

I did not know that, but it makes me appreciate what
a badass your bestie is. Tater is such a douchebag. I'm
sure he's way less intelligent than the spuds he is named
after.

BRIAN:

Right? By the end of the day there were all these wild
rumors going around that she was a lesbian or a witch,
or possibly not even a girl at all.

BETH:

I have to assume that was meant in a transphobic way,
as I doubt anyone in Canon is well versed enough
about sex and gender to begin unpacking the nature of
nonbinary identities.

(laughing)

BRIAN:

Holy shitballs. You and Riley are definitely going to
be friends. That's the smartest commentary on gender
identity I've ever heard IRL in this ass-backward town.

BETH:

Before we get too off topic, I wanted to ask if there was
anything I could do to help you all. To help Greg. I keep
feeling like this is partly my fault somehow.

BRIAN:

How do you feel it's your fault?

BETH:

I mean, we discussed gay stuff, sort of. But we never really spoke about his family. We mostly just talked about queer celebrities and how much better life would be once we got out of Canon. I feel like I could have been a better friend to him. Our relationship was fake and our friendship was hella superficial.

(sniffing)

Like, I didn't even know he was fucking Derek.

BRIAN:

To be fair, though, is that something you'd really want anyone to know?

BETH:

Maybe not. But he could have told me. You and I both know how fucking lonely it can be. How you see all your peers dating, falling in love, and making out. And you're still getting crushes and stuff, but you can't tell anyone you like that you're actually into them because then you're . . . what? A godless heathen or a pervert or a predator? It's not that way everywhere, but it is still here. We know how that is, and I should have just made him talk to me.

BRIAN:

Beth, you weren't out, either. Your cloak-and-dagger

act was probably the most amount of support he's ever had.

BETH:

Still.

BRIAN:

Still nothing. You're here, doing this brave thing, and that's a big deal. It's enough. It has to be enough. I feel like there's more lots of people could have done. He just sort of slipped through a lot of cracks. That's why I'm doing this. I couldn't think of anything else productive to do.

BETH:

I think this podcast helps a fair number of people. And that's very brave and important, too.

BRIAN:

Is it, though? I feel like I've been hiding behind a pseudonym on the internet for a couple of years now.

BETH:

Names aren't as important as speaking up. Or as using your voice to say something important that helps other people feel more seen and understood.

BRIAN:

I guess so. I hope it's enough.

Anyway, we're out of time for now. Thanks as always for listening and for the attention you spend on this podcast. I do really appreciate how much closer it has brought the world to me. I hope I bring as much to you.

[SHAMPOO UNICORN *THEME MUSIC PLAYS.*]

22

PROUD
Leslie

Leslie thinks about organization.

The first riots, festivals, and parades, in particular. She could never have predicted in a billion years that her coming out would go so well. She knows that it goes badly for people all the time. The internet is full of horror stories. She's been active in online communities that rallied around people who were kicked out by parents or worse. As proud as she is of herself, she's also proud of her parents. It feels like somehow her coming out gave them a united purpose to rally around as a team.

They're all in therapy with Carol now. They eat dinner together. Check in about their feelings. She has a prescription for estradiol and spironolactone. Her mom lays out her two pills beside the coffee pot every morning, and Leslie thrills to think of the way they are working together to help her become the woman she wants to be. They're a team, Leslie, her family, and these two new, small friends, her very own anti-cistamines. She is trying hard not to stare too long at her body, willing the changes to come, but every day, she runs her hands across her chest, pushing the soft skin together, hoping for tender growth. She feels hope swell in her chest, even if breasts haven't done so yet.

She was thrilled to get a reply from Riley about pride.

> *Dear Leslie,*
>
> *Thank you so much for your sweet email. Brian is spending a lot of time with Greg and his mom, so I've been taking the lead on correspondence that merits a response. I've never been to a pride event, really, and I know he hasn't. What a cool idea that has the potential to piss off bigots and celebrate these pockets of community that keep popping up. (Both of which are a win in my book.)*
>
> *I'm not going to mention this to Brian just yet. He's been pretty worried and distracted, as I'm sure you can imagine. I'm going to spend the weekend thinking about local businesses and organizations and maybe reaching out to other pride organizations for advice. Is it ok to cc you on those emails? Maybe we could team up on this?*
>
> *Thanks so much for such an inspired and inspiring idea! This could be amazing!*
>
> *XOXO*
> *Riley*

Leslie waited thirty agonizing minutes before responding, but eventually they traded phone numbers and began to text one another.

Leslie crosses her fingers and sends up positive vibes in the hopes that the spirits of Marsha and Sylvia will help her. Her event will need audio equipment. Which means she'll need to reserve a podium, microphone, and whatever else that requires. Decorations. They'll need those. All the colors of the rainbow, of course.

Her online shadow sisters have joined her, forming a committee and taking a lot of the load off Leslie. One of her sisters found a queer actor from New York who listens to *Shampoo Unicorn* and wants to be their speaker for the event. People from every letter of the alphabet mafia chime in to join him. One is a DJ and offers to provide the music. A couple of other musicians say they'll perform and take care of speakers and audio tech. One of her dad's friends says he'll do the flyers for free. He's doing large multicolored circle ones because people won't notice the standard 8-1/2 × 11 kind. People's eyes gloss over when they see them because everyone uses that size. It's all coming together, and Leslie's having so much fun, she might just want to be an event planner one day.

The local news, which also broadcasts in Canon, wants to interview her. It's time to ask Brian to announce it on his podcast. Why not? He has over a million national followers. Maybe they'll get people who are within travel distance to come.

This could actually happen, she texts Riley. *We could do this*. Before she can second guess herself, her phone chimes back with a message from her new friend.

Girl, we already are.

23

OKAY AFTER ALL
Brian

There were lots of letters I didn't read to Greg.

Lots I deleted, too. My podcast had been popular enough for small sponsorships for a little while. I'd been socking my half of that money away for college. I'd get a few scholarships and grants, and my mom had been saving, too. But I'd still need the money to pay for housing and books and general eating and living costs.

As with any single thing I did that flew above the radar, I got the occasional homophobic response. Usually, iTunes and Spotify were great about catching and removing them, but I had public social media accounts and an email address attached to the podcast as well. But mostly, the positive responses made the negatives worth it.

When I started looking into Greg's attack, I began receiving guesses, suggestions, theories, pointers from people in law enforcement, and offers from private investigators. I wasn't sure what to do with a lot of that stuff, so I asked Riley and Beth if they'd like to come over and brainstorm. They both said yes. Derek reached out a couple of times to see if there was anything he could do, and I'd seen him hanging around the hospital once or twice, so I thought maybe I should invite him, but when I asked Riley, she said absolutely not.

"Okay, so lots of people have wild theories. Most people think Greg's dad attacked him," I said. To keep everyone focused, I ordered pizza and brought my big whiteboard downstairs. I divided the board in half with theories on one side and suggestions on the other. "And honestly, it's probably the most likely one. I know Greg's dad beat him. Greg and his dad had fought pretty recently. But his family was sharing two cars and neither of them was damaged, so that sort of shoots a hole in that argument. And he has an alibi. He was cleaning at the church, but maybe he snuck out? I don't know. I can't see a way that this is rationally Mr. Burke's fault, even though he's a fucking asshole."

"What if Greg's dad hit him in someone else's car?" Beth asked. "Just for the sake of due diligence."

"Interesting theory," I replied, and wrote it on the board. "Another theory was that it was a premeditated hate crime. But again, there's no one to link it to, and no one has come forward with information. As you can see, I've gotten some pretty good tips from people involved in various branches of law enforcement about stuff we can do to investigate."

I paced back and forth, enjoying having others to talk things through with. "I've had suggestions to search for information on hate groups in our area on the web. Someone mentioned returning to the scene to comb the area for paint chips, but of course, there was nothing there when Riley and I checked it out. Another offered the idea of pulling footage from doorbell and security cameras nearby and petitioning the Canon police for the reports."

Riley arranged her crusts into a neat triangle, then wiped her hands on a napkin. "We probably won't get anywhere with the Canon police, but I can follow up with Officer Hazelwood. See if he's willing to give up any new information."

"I'll look into the camera angle," Beth said.

The next couple of minutes were pretty quiet, each of us absorbed in thought and food. I was thankful to have them there helping me, but there was a piece of my heart missing. A gaping piece, festering and bleeding. A piece that belonged to Greg.

I couldn't help but wish Greg were there with us.

24

GREEK CHORUS
Brian

The emails I read to Greg were more and more carefully curated the longer he was unconscious. I wanted to paint joyful stories, stories in which queer people like us faced odds that seemed maybe insurmountable at one point but turned out happily.

Ferris's story started out pretty depressingly. He was gay, his family fundamentalists. When they found a letter to him from the boy he loved, they kicked him out. He hitched his way to New York City and ended up in a homeless shelter until he found a job and saved enough money for his own place.

After he'd been working and living in the city for a while, he found his way to a gay church. He cried so hard during that first service, the pastor stayed after to speak with him. Ferris had assumed he'd have to choose between God and his sexuality. He believed if he picked the latter, he'd end up swimming in an eternal lake of fire.

Being in a church full of other queer Christians wasn't something he even let himself dream was possible. He felt safer and more welcomed at that church than the home he left behind. He worshiped there, and later the congregation put him through theology school so he could come back and lead his own flock. He met his husband through the church. Although they never had children, they certainly had a family.

Inez's first love was a girl in her high school. It was unrequited and she nursed the heartache all through college, meeting and dating women from her university's lesbian book club. By the time she was thirty, she'd been in and out of relationships and bedrooms, and believed she'd be chronically single all her life.

When she bumped into Luther at a friend's birthday party, they were drawn to each other immediately but held off on committing to a relationship because they were both out and proud homosexuals. After Inez confessed to being attracted to Luther, and Luther confirmed that it was mutual, the simple fact of their love was the most stable thing in their lives, and occasionally in the lives of the people around them, despite being a couple that appeared straight but had come up queer.

Will and Hoyt met in a bathhouse. Neither was out, and neither was especially proud of seeking out anonymous encounters with other men. Will said Hoyt was so beautiful it was like looking into the sun. He didn't approach Hoyt because he figured Hoyt was way out of his league, but he kept coming back just to look at him.

Eventually, Hoyt approached Will in a steam room, and Will was so flattered and startled that he couldn't get hard. Hoyt took it personally and it wasn't until they met in a business setting with their clothes on that Will finally gathered up the nerve to ask Hoyt to dinner. Dinner led back to Hoyt's hotel room, which led to Will clarifying his intense and nearly immeasurable crush, and Hoyt confessed that he had also been coming back to the baths for the opportunity to run into Will.

Miscommunications clarified, the two men dated for a month and a half before moving in together, then lived together for a year before having a small ceremony, committing to each other in front of their friends and family, creating a long and happy life together.

Stuart was well into a life with Walter when he met and fell in love with Bob. Assuming he had to choose, he sat them both down and told them it was impossible, and that he'd rather live alone than hurt either of them. Bob and Walter, united in their love for Stuart, told him that was a ridiculous thing to say, and Bob moved in a few weeks later.

All three of them lived together as "bachelor roommates" in the 1950s, came out as a gay hippie love commune in the '60s, and formed the base of a local chapter of the Radical Faeries in the '70s that helped unite their community in the '80s surrounding the AIDS epidemic and the long-suffering deaths and grief of their community.

Stuart passed away from colon cancer in the early '90s, and Bob and Walter created a scholarship fund to celebrate the life of the man they'd loved so dearly. And every year, they lit a candle, held hands, and read the applications to each other. COVID got Walter, and Bob was dictating his letter to an aide who played the podcast for him and a group of other people in the same queer retirement community.

Adam had relationships with women until he could have relationships with men. He had long and short unions, one-night stands, and casual flirtations. None of them made him as happy as sitting alone in a quiet house with a cup of steaming tea and a novel to get lost in. He stopped having relationships with people and started connecting to books, words, and the worlds the authors created. Finding the love and comfort he had been searching for the whole time within their pages. Later, when he discovered the word *asexuality*, it felt like coming home. He learned to love himself, and that turned out to be the relationship he needed most.

Louis and Don met during the Stonewall riots. Louis had been knocked unconscious by flying debris and nearly trampled before Don grabbed him by the armpits and pulled him to the side. Don leaned Louis against a tree to prevent him from choking but knew little else about first aid.

I wanted to go back in, do something radical for my community, Don wrote. *I was standing at a turning point, and I wanted to be present. But then I thought,* What is a community but a collection of people? *If I could help this one guy, who knew what ripple effect it could have on my community. Maybe I'd be saving the gay MLK.*

So Don waited until Louis was conscious, then stagger-carried him away from the fray and hailed a cab to get him to the hospital. Don waited to make sure Louis wasn't seriously hurt. He lied that Louis was his brother so they'd let him into the room. *When Louis finally woke up the next morning, he looked up at me and said I was his favorite face he'd ever seen. I still suspect the concussion had something to do with it.*

I curated and collected stories with the happiest endings, with the most relevant beginnings, stories that captured the scope and breadth of how many ways there were to be queer. I read them to Greg, sitting on his bed, in the chair beside the bed, perched on the windowsill. I was there so often that I got to know the nurses coming in and out of his room.

I stopped reading when his mom came in and spent time with her, letting her talk and get her feelings out. Initially, I thought it might help me find some clues, some hitherto uncovered nugget of truth that would reveal everything. But instead, I just listened. It felt like maybe no one had listened to Mrs. Burke in a long time, and rather than talk about religion or sexuality, she mostly just shared stories about Greg. About how much she worried for him as a child because he had been so sensitive, about how she tried to come between Greg and his dad when Mr. Burke was on a tear, and about how many regrets she had now.

She asked about me, too. Curious how my mom had dealt with knowing that I was "different."

"Gay," I clarified. "I'm not that different from other boys my age. But I'm gay, for sure. So say the word. It's not hard. Say *gay*."

Her eyes widened at my request, and she stared at me for the briefest of seconds. "Gay," she said, and the way she said it was as if it were foreign and she'd never spoken it before.

I smiled. "See? That wasn't hard to say."

"No." She returned my smile. "It wasn't. I never admitted that Greg might be gay because I never met a gay person."

"Oh, you have. You just didn't realize it." I leaned closer to her and dramatically whispered, "We walk among you. We're everywhere."

She laughed and threw her head back so hard a bobby pin flew out of her bun, her brown eyes tearing up from the effort, dampness wetting the wrinkles around them and glistening in the light coming from the nearby window. "Stop it. I'm a mess." Her gaze went to Greg, then to me. "I promise to do better. For Greg, and for you."

"That's a start." I got up, tugged a few tissues from a box next to the sink, and brought them over to her. She took them from him and dabbed at her eyes. "Thank you."

After that, I reckoned we might all be okay after all.

25

SIMPERING SYCOPHANT
Greg

Your mom's soft crying came from somewhere nearby. The longer you were here, the less frequently you heard it. Was she crying less frequently? Less loudly? Was it because she was getting used to this as a new normal? Or was she taking her sadness elsewhere? Hard to tell.

The last time you'd seen her cry, you were twelve and Brian had kissed you on the cheek after his birthday party and you had felt yourself stir. In that way. In a way you hadn't wanted to acknowledge because it had felt too complicated, but you couldn't ignore. You had walked home from Brian's party, elated and confused at the same time.

Dinner at your house was always subdued. You weren't big talkers, largely because your dad was so explosive. Anything could set him off.

"How was Brian's party?" your mom had asked, forking a chicken breast onto your plate.

You had looked at your dad. He hated Brian, and you had seen his jaw clench in response. "It was fine, Mom." Best to keep it short.

You were still in the days of worrying about an eternity of hellfire and brimstone, but everything about your friendship with Brian felt good and wholesome and non-scary, unlike the sharp edges of home and church that could sometimes leave you bleeding when you bumped up against them too hard or from the wrong angle.

"Pass the potatoes," your dad had said, his deep voice jolting you out of your thoughts.

Your mom had noticed that you were extra quiet and that your eyes had been glued to your dinner plate, pushing peas into designs before squashing them with mashed potatoes and finally shoveling them into your mouth.

"Greg, what's wrong, sweetheart? Did something happen at the party?"

"No, ma'am," you had replied. Eyes still locked on your dinner plate.

"Are you sure? You can tell me if something's upsetting you."

You had finally looked up and seen her eyes clouded with concern. Maybe it would be okay. Maybe it didn't matter. Maybe it was even normal, and you'd grow out of it like you prayed every night.

"Y'all would still love me no matter what, right?"

Your dad had looked up at you, eyebrows furrowed at the mention of love. He had stared at you, clenching his jaw, before he looked back down and stabbed a piece of meat loaf with his fork.

"What's this about, son?" He had taken a long pull from his beer and set the bottle down hard enough to thud loudly against the table.

"I mean, nothing. Probably nothing."

"What are you talking about, boy?"

"I was just thinking about Brian. And wondering if I might be . . ." Long silence. "If I might be like him. Sort of."

Your mom had started to say something, but your dad had held up a meaty hand to silence her before turning his steely gaze on you like a pistol. Her eyes had been wet and threatening to run over, and you hadn't known if it was because she was afraid for you or afraid of your father. You had been most afraid that she was crying because she was so disappointed that your dad was right. "Listen good, son. I'm only going to say this once: I think that boy's mom is too soft on him and it's making him a fruity little queer. But he's not my son and you are, and I want you to have a good life. The kind of normal life that only good, God-fearing men get to experience."

You had been trapped in your seat, as though the weight of his attention was pinning you there like a specimen.

He had gone on. "I'd see you dead and buried before you turn to a life of sin. I'd rather you died than turned into a faggot, son."

You had felt hot, embarrassing tears spring to your eyes, and you had set your jaw against them. *Do not cry, you little shit*, you had told yourself in your dad's voice. If you cried, you proved him right. If you cried, he won.

"Look at me when I'm talking to you, boy."

You had, letting your eyes get cold and hard, thinking about anything else to keep from listening to your dad. You hadn't known if you were strong enough to fight whatever was happening to you in the presence of occasional other guys. Or to fight your dad when he figured out who and what you were. To fight your church, your feelings, and your fears.

You'd totally zoned out thinking about all this when the back of your dad's hand sent you reeling back into real life. He had hit you so hard you'd fallen off your chair and landed on your knees, and when your vision cleared, your mom had been sobbing over you. You had wanted to comfort her. You had wanted, as always, to protect her from your dad. You had needed her to hold you, though. No matter how much you towered over her. You had needed her to wrap her arms around you and tell you she loved you no matter what and everything would be okay. She didn't.

You'd blinked back your own tears and counted your dad's steps as he'd stomped out of the house and blessedly hadn't returned until after you left for school the next day. Neither you nor your mom had ever spoken of it again.

That day had changed everything for you. You spent the next several years trying to be someone your dad would be proud (or at least not ashamed) of. When that didn't work, your dad's words had been the thing that finally allowed you to realize what you wanted most—escape.

You were so goddamn tired of the nothingness of your current state. Of how you were a prisoner of your past, subject to the memories that floated in and out of your brain like some sadistic jellyfish.

You heard Brian again, and you wondered if he was haunting you like one of Scrooge's ghosts. The spirit of sins past. Not that you and he had ever sinned together. You'd just sinned against him every time you didn't defend him and let Derek or some other dick knock him into a wall or slap whatever he was carrying out of his arms. You weren't the culprit, you were just a simpering sycophant, and in a lot of ways, that was worse.

The words formed on your tongue. *I'm sorry. Please forgive me.* But when you tried to force them out of your mouth and into the world, they sat there like a communion wafer, melting until they were once again part of you.

You didn't know what you believed anymore. You used to believe in God and the magical trio of your friendship with Brian and Riley, but those things proved to be fleeting. You believed in your parents until your dad started to knock the shit out of you when your mom wasn't around. Even though you loved your mom more than anyone, you no longer believed in her ability to protect you. You had sports, sex, and beer, but those were all the means to an end, and the end was always changing. What was left? Just you, alone. Which wasn't a lot to believe in. But it was as good of a place to start as any.

You'd have loved to try something different. You'd have loved to have that option. But you were stuck in your stupid fucking brain, which seemed ironic when you thought about how many times the only thing about you that had been important was your stupid fucking body. You wanted to wake up and change everything. But there you were, in that forced rest like some sort of weird-ass Sleeping Beauty. Oh God. How cliché. Would it take Brian kissing you for you to wake up? You wanted to laugh, but of course, you couldn't do that, either.

Turned out the joke was, as always, on you.

SHAMPOO UNICORN
Episode 314: "I'm Beggin' of You, Please Don't Take My Ham"

BRIAN:

The last person to see Greg before he was hit was Chuck Hill, owner and head cook of Jolene's. As we've maybe said before, Jolene's is a well-loved establishment here in Canon. All the specials are named after Dolly Parton songs, and they're pretty punny. I can't remember a time when the parking lot wasn't packed after church services on Sunday. I've had so many pulled pork sandwiches and root beer floats that it feels like I could measure my life by them.

When you enter Jolene's, the first thing you notice is how good it smells. The scent of fried things and that savory-sweet barbecue smell hangs in the air, but there's also the aroma of fresh flowers that the restaurant has delivered every week.

[SOUND OF DOOR OPENING, BELL RINGING, DOOR CLOSING, SOFT TWANGY COUNTRY MUSIC PLAYING IN THE BACKGROUND.]

BRIAN:

I'm meeting Chuck Hill today to talk about Greg. I've met him before, of course. He and his wife are well-loved around town for the food they make and for being the sort of solid citizens who donate trays to prom fundraisers and host trunk-or-treat events during Halloween for kids who live too far away to go door-to-door. Chuck is a tall middle-aged guy with a handlebar mustache. He's quiet, always hiding under the brim of his ubiquitous baseball cap. Ann is the more talkative member of the couple. It's not that Chuck is surly or mean. It just seems very much like he'd rather not be bothered.

He agreed to see me, when I called, only because Ann was out of town caring for her mom, but when I came in just before they opened, a youngish waitress with a name tag that read BECCA smiled and unlocked the door for me.

BECCA:

Hey, hon. You're here to see Chuck, right? I'll let him know. Grab a seat at the counter. You want a soda or some sweet tea or some coffee?

BRIAN:

I'm okay. Thank you, though.

BECCA:

Okay, I'll be right back.

BRIAN:

While I wait for Chuck, I'm looking around, wondering what this space would look like to someone who didn't grow up with Jolene's as a mainstay of their lives. I'd never call it fancy, but in Canon, it's one of the few restaurants that isn't a chain. There are no tablecloths on the unvarnished wooden tables ringed with the ghosts of sodas past, but the food is undeniably good.

*[SOUND OF DOOR OPENING, FOOTSTEPS,
CHAIR BEING PULLED OUT, TWO CUPS
BEING PLACED ON TABLE.]*

CHUCK:

Hey, Brian. Coffee, right? One cream, five sugars?

BRIAN:

Mr. Hill, hi! I'm surprised you remembered that.

CHUCK:

Call me Chuck. Just because we've never met formally doesn't mean I don't remember most people who come into my place. Besides, it's a small town.

BRIAN:

That's interesting! You're so quiet, I never imagined.

CHUCK:

Just because I don't say much doesn't mean I'm not constantly watching what's going on.

BRIAN:

(sipping coffee)

Oh my god, this is perfect.

CHUCK:

Told you, I'm constantly watching people.

BRIAN:

That's really impressive.

CHUCK:

Thank you. But we're not here to talk about me, right?

BRIAN:

No, that's right. We're here to talk about Greg. You were the last person to see him before the accident.

CHUCK:

Did you know I went to school with his mom and dad? Had a little bit of a crush on his mom and was even gonna ask her to the junior prom. But she'd just started dating Greg's dad.

BRIAN:

OMG. I can't imagine Mr. Burke as a teenager.

CHUCK:

He wasn't a bad guy, actually. His dad and my dad were miners together, so we'd known each other from company picnics and things like that. There aren't a ton of options for kids in this area, so everyone just assumed most of us would go to work in the mines as well.

BRIAN:

Mr. Burke did. Were you ever a coal miner, Mr. Hill?

CHUCK:

Chuck.

(sipping coffee)

No, I enlisted in the army right after high school. My brother did, too. He was a year older. He was killed in the Gulf War under Bush Senior. I was never deployed and returned home after my enlistment was up. Took advantage of the GI Bill and met the missus at community college where we were both studying business.

BRIAN:

I never knew any of that. I'm sorry about your brother, Mr. H — Chuck.

CHUCK:

Thank you. There's no way you'd know about it. All that stuff happened way before your time. I don't talk much about ancient history, but it's sort of the backstory of how this place got started.

We keep circling back to me, but I really wanted to talk about Greg. It makes me sick to death that he got hurt here. I've always felt safe here, always hoped other folks did, too. Like I said, I knew his parents and watched his dad change after the mines closed. Thought it might be a good opportunity for Greg to put some money away if he needed to get out of his house, or for college or whatever.

BRIAN:

What happened at the interview?

CHUCK:

Not much more than an average interview, honestly. I've hired dozens of people over the years, and I can almost predict exactly how every interview will go. This was no different. Seems like a real sweet kid. Honestly, he reminds me a lot of Ann's brother. He's gay, too. He had a real bad time growing up around here. Moved to Manhattan and hasn't been back since. Can't say I blame him, honestly.

BRIAN:

And you didn't hear anything when he got hit?

CHUCK:

I wish I had. I wish I could have gotten to him faster, could have gotten plate numbers or anything. But my office is in a weird space between the walk-in fridge and the walk-in freezer, so there's a lot of ambient noise on the quietest of days.

BRIAN:

And there are no —

CHUCK:

No security system, no. We live right next door, and we've never really needed it. The worst vandalism that's ever happened was that someone stole Ann's Baby Jesus from our Christmas nativity, but she just replaced it with a baby doll from the dollar store and it didn't matter much at all.

How's Greg doing? I sent over some flowers, and I've been by a couple of times with some sandwiches for Mrs. Burke.

BRIAN:

No real change just yet.

CHUCK:

I know it's a cliché, but it feels surreal that something like this happened in Canon.

BRIAN:

Why? It's a rural small town in the Bible Belt.

CHUCK:

I know. And look, like I said, Ann's brother is gay and

he grew up not too far from here. So he wouldn't be surprised. But honestly? I still am. I serve brunch to most
of the heaviest Bible-thumpers after church every week.
They're terrible tippers, but they're always kind to my
staff and me. I guess I had fooled myself into thinking
things had gotten some measure better since her brother
left.

BRIAN:

I'm sure they are. But you're also a cisgender straight
white man. And you're a business owner and esteemed
community member. I promise that if you asked Becca
how often people got racist with her, she'd give you an
earful of wild stuff the good Christian people of Canon
have said to her.

CHUCK:

I . . . hadn't considered that. I will ask her.

BRIAN:

Look, I'm not trying to make any wild sweeping state-
ments here. But it's easy to assume other people have
good intentions because you do. I know you see and
hear a lot. I know you watch really closely. But you
might miss a lot of stuff if you're not looking for it.

CHUCK:

You're right.

*[A MINUTE OF SILENCE PASSES, WITH JUST AMBIENT
RESTAURANT SOUNDS IN THE BACKGROUND.]*

BRIAN:

Thanks for taking the time to talk to me today, Chuck. I know you're really busy. And thanks for the coffee.

CHUCK:

I'm glad to have the opportunity to do so. Please let me know if there's anything I can do to help. And let me make you some lunch. On me.

BRIAN:

Well, if you insist.

[SHAMPOO UNICORN *EXIT THEME PLAYS.*]

26

PLUMETTE WHO?
Brian

Beth texted me several times during the week to make sure I was okay, to see if I would be interested in studying together, and to ask if Riley was in any way queer. I answered yes, yes, and you'd have to ask her, but I didn't think so? However, when we crashed into a diner booth in Rockwell the next day, Beth said that Riley was flattered but uninterested.

"I get it, though," I said, cracking open the menu even though I knew I'd order a cheeseburger, fries, and a chocolate milkshake just like I always did. "Riley is smokin' hot. Like sexy in a way I don't understand and will never be."

"I don't want to objectify her or anything, but she's just so much herself. I hang around with girls who are constantly trying to be less. To weigh less, take up less space. And Riley seems so comfortable with who she is. I just assumed that some of that would be queer, too."

"That makes sense, and you're not wrong about her being comfortable with her sexuality. Unfortunately, it just happens that she is mostly heterosexual."

"Ah, well. If I needed proof she's not perfect, there it is."

I laughed just as the server came over. The boy was about our age or slightly older. Tall, thin, with a nice smile. He took our order and hurried off as if there was a fire in the kitchen. We folded our menus and slipped them into the silver ring holder at the side of the table.

Unrolling the napkin from the silver, I studied Beth. Freckles dusted her nose and cheeks, and a small gold stud rested in the crevice of her nostril. "You mentioned that you've dated and hooked up with people before. How do you meet people? You know, to date?"

Beth leveled a sardonic gaze at me. "The same way anyone meets people. The internet. Have you ever had a boyfriend before?"

"I have not."

"All right." Beth pulled a tube of sanitizer out of her bag and doused her hands. The sharp smell cut through the grease that hung in the air. "Tell me about your first kiss."

"I'm not actually sure it counts. I was in fourth grade when Riley, Greg, and I practiced by kissing each other. That was how I knew definitively that I was into dudes." I still hadn't told anyone about being with Greg in the woods. It felt too sacred to say out loud. It felt like it was not my story to share, and I was afraid saying it out loud would make it sound cheap. Maybe it would be less so once he woke up. If he woke up. When. Definitely when.

"How did that happen?"

"While watching *Beauty and the Beast*. Riley mentioned both Gaston and the Beast seemed like good reasons for Belle to stay single and just collect books. Greg said maybe she shouldn't have kissed either of them, and she only picked the Beast because he had a good library."

Beth gave me a confused look, her forehead crinkling with the effort.

"Who was she supposed to kiss if not Gaston or the Beast? It wasn't like her provincial town was crawling with eligible bachelors."

"I think Greg's take was a gay comment if I'm being honest. Anyway, one of us decided to just try kissing to see what it was like, and so that's how that happened. We giggled a lot. Both Greg and I kissed Riley, and then Greg asked if he could kiss me. I was surprised that he wanted to, but I readied myself, closing my eyes and pursing my lips. When his lips touched mine, it was so fluttery and soft that I knew I wanted it to happen again."

"With Greg, or with another boy?"

"Well, since I was in fourth grade, I wasn't sure. I knew I couldn't keep asking Greg to kiss me, though. He left right afterward, and I didn't see him for a whole week. I decided to just play it cool, though, and neither of us ever mentioned it again."

The server brought our milkshakes—mine chocolate, hers straw-berry—and set them down in front of us.

"Need anything else?" the server chirped.

I shook my head, and Beth said, "No. Thank you."

She stabbed the straw against the table and removed it from its paper sleeve. "And you haven't kissed anyone since then?" she asked. "You know there are, like, websites and dating apps, right?"

"Yes, I live in the same world you do. I downloaded Grindr once, saw that Mr. Preston was on there looking for 'greedy bottoms who could take every inch of his—'"

"Wait." My statement registered with her. "Mr. Preston from middle school? The geometry teacher?"

"Yup. He obviously didn't know it was me, and I didn't tell him." I rolled my eyes. "I deleted the app immediately and never looked back. Now I'm much less freaked out. Because, y'know, people should be allowed to get freaky with whomever they want as long as it happens between consenting adults. And I was never more aware that I wasn't an adult, but I was maybe someone that adults would want to bone, and that felt weird and creepy. Also, it's a small fucking town. Today's hook-ups are going to be next week's awkward public encounters."

"Sure. " Beth picked up my straw and tapped it thoughtfully. "But that could be anywhere. You're less likely to run into people you know at the post office or supermarket, but even in bigger cities, you're more likely to bump into someone you know within the queer community."

I sighed. "Fine, yes, probably. But wouldn't it be nice not to have to worry quite so much about it?"

"I mostly don't, but I think it's different for girls. When people find out that girls are making out or hooking up, they're more likely to assume it's just a phase or that they're doing it for attention from boys."

"If you're white and follow fairly traditional gender markers."

"Ah." Beth nodded. "That's true. I'm lucky enough to check both of those boxes, so it's never really been an issue for me. Which isn't fair, I'll acknowledge."

"Thanks for that."

"What?"

"Acknowledging it." I traced the rim of my glass. "I think most people get defensive by default."

Beth was quiet for a minute. "I wouldn't be too sure that there aren't romantic prospects around here for you."

"What do you mean?"

"Our waiter's been checking you out for the past ten or fifteen minutes."

I looked over my shoulder to catch him staring. He looked away and blushed. I turned back toward Beth. "What?"

She shrugged. "He's cute, you're cute. I don't see the problem here. You could leave your number with the tip."

I thought about it for the rest of the meal and decided against it at the last minute. I could leave my number. Maybe he'd text. Maybe we'd flirt, go on my first date. But I wanted the rest of my firsts to be with Greg. In spite of all the obstacles, in spite of the past, in spite of so much, my impractical, hopeful heart still beat harder when I thought of a future where we could see things through. Maybe we'd be better at being friends. Maybe we'd be incompatible and wind up practically strangers at our twentieth class reunion.

But we deserved the chance to find out.

27

NOT QUITE BEDFELLOWS, STILL QUITE STRANGE
Brian

Our dynamic duo had somehow become a trio.

Riley, Beth, and I had defaulted to meeting up after school on the days when Beth didn't have cheerleading and Riley didn't have academic bowl practice. (On those days, I visited Greg.) I'd make sandwiches or a big pot of popcorn on the stove and we'd spread our homework out at the table, and when we were finished, we'd play video games or watch TV.

I was sitting between them on the couch, holding an enormous bag of chips, when the doorbell rang.

"Expecting anyone?" Riley asked.

"Nope." I handed the bowl to Beth. But when I answered the door, it was Derek.

"Uh, hi," he said. "I know we aren't, like, friends, or anything but I didn't know who else—"

"Schillinger? What do you want?" Riley was at my back in a second with her hand on my shoulder. "What are you doing here?"

"I come in peace." He put his hands up. "I just found . . . Look, can I come inside?"

Riley crossed her arms over her chest, but I stepped aside and let him in.

"Oh, hey, Derek." Beth clicked the television off and followed us to the kitchen table where she set the bowl down in the middle of our homework detritus. "What are you doing here?"

"So, look. I've been thinking a lot about Greg and my part in him ending up where he is. I've been trying to look for clues about who might have done this to him. Listening to the podcast and working in the shadows. Like Batman!"

"Why?" Riley's arms were still crossed, her laser eyes leveling a gaze at him that I'd only seen once or twice in our entire friendship.

"Well, I mean, what else am I going to do? I'm not in school and I only work part-time. There are only so many hours you can work out or play video games before your brain catches up to you."

"Sure," I said evenly. "Do you want something to drink?"

"No, but I wasn't sure who to tell about this. I mean. I tried to tell the police, but they were pretty dismissive."

Beth stepped in and pulled out a chair, the voice of reason. "Tell the police what, Derek? Start at the beginning."

He took a deep breath and sat down, moving his backpack from his shoulder to the floor. He opened the bag and pulled out a laptop and opened it. "Okay, so like I said, I'm trying to be a better person. To do things that, like, start to fix all the bigot bullshit I've pulled in the past. I need to make some sort of amends for the ways I've acted. So I've been listening to a lot of gay podcasts. Not just yours. And I've been looking into who might have done this to Greg. I talked to the police, but they said they didn't have any leads and were 'allocating resources elsewhere.' Whatever the fuck that means."

"It means they don't have any obvious leads and they're not going to waste time digging for leads for some gay kid, the same way they wouldn't arrest the guy who punched Devonte Harris last year, in spite of there being two separate witnesses who heard that guy call Vonte the N-word." Riley sighed and sat down.

He pulled up a video and paused it. "Okay, watch carefully. After I play this, I'll go back and tell you what I saw. After, you can tell me if it makes sense to you or not. I had to watch it several times myself."

On the screen, the camera pointed at a porch railing, a fence, and then the road in front of Grayson's supermarket. "That's Gretchen Pagnoni's house, isn't it?" I asked.

"Yeah, Gretch owed me a favor," Derek replied. "Shhh."

We watched a few cars pass coming from both directions, nothing exciting. And then suddenly, a silver pickup truck with a badly dented hood sped by from the right side of the screen to the left side. It was speeding so fast the tires squealed.

"Hold on, I'm going to play it from the beginning again," Derek said, pushing a couple of buttons.

This time, we all inched forward in our seats. I tried to make out any of the faces of the drivers, but the cars were too far away — even the slowest moved too quickly. When a silver truck passed from the left to the right, Derek hit the spacebar, pausing it.

"Okay, this is the same truck heading for the parking lot. The time stamp says nine fifty-one a.m." He hit the spacebar again, restoring the screen to motion. This time, we were expecting it, the crinkled hood and the speed. "The time stamp here is ten twenty-two. Nearly thirty minutes later, but merely seconds after the time Greg was hit."

"Holy fucking shit," Riley said.

"Holy fucking shit," Beth repeated.

"Did Officer Hazelwood mention this at all?" I asked.

Riley shook her head.

"Can you see the truck's plates in the video?" I asked Derek.

"I already thought of that," he said. "The truck's too far away and moving too fast. I'm sorry. I didn't know what else to do, so I thought maybe you could do something with it on your podcast."

He seemed to deflate in front of us. "Is this stupid? Maybe I'm being stupid. But it seemed like it could mean something and then they—the police just—"

"Hey." I put a hand on his arm, and he startled. "It's a good piece of work. This is probably the vehicle that hit Greg. That's important. And I can see you're trying to help. And that's not nothing."

He looked from me to Beth to Riley. Beth nodded slightly. Riley didn't look at him. "You're not forgiven. But this could be something," she said finally.

28

LIVE TO FIGHT
Greg

You'd always been at least a little lost.

You'd hidden so much, so well, that when your bullshit had all finally come to light, you had been dodging debris in a hurricane until you weren't. Then you had just been alone. Your parents had been silent. You had not been permitted the escape of sports or even the mindless distraction of school. It had been you, all alone in your house, confined to the bare wood-paneled walls of your bedroom.

And because nothing lasts forever, your parents started making plans for you. You'd get a job, go to community college. To church. You'd make do. You were on your way to start making do, fresh out of the interview when the truck came from nowhere. A fast-moving silver blur. You had hopped out of its path and, right before everything went dark, you saw it swerve to make contact. It was like a geometry equation, the hood lining up like the dotted line of a test question. Like the driver was trying to position you for maximum impact. You couldn't remember getting hit, nothing after seeing the grill coming for you fast.

Your brain sparked with images.

Did you fly? You kind of remembered a feeling of floating, then dropping hard, the crunching of metal, a sensation of rolling off something. Then it all went black.

You'd been lost in memory, in smell, sound, and sensation for an indeterminate amount of time. And one day, you stopped being alone. You weren't sure when, how, or why they showed up, but you could feel that there were people near you. Whispering stories, quietly encouraging you, telling you that there was courage in your perseverance. They weren't ghosts; they felt too vibrant, too full of life for that. And they weren't real, because they weren't corporeal, either.

Hush, child. Who we are doesn't matter. What we are is more important. We are stories, possibilities, history, and hope.

You asked if you were dead and they said no, that you were resting, but it was time to wake up now.

Go home, they said. *Put things right, live to fight another day.*

It was quietly encouraging at first, and then they started pushing you. Lifting you on hands as gentle as hummingbird wings, easing you out of this blank space, and toward lights, shapes, sounds amplifying, sensations intensifying.

You tried to talk, to shout, anything, but you were choking and straining almost as soon as you could focus your eyes on the nearest solid shape, curtains on a long track. There was a violent beeping next to your head, some mechanical sounds, and then you slept again.

Time blinked, and you were awake. Foggy with pain and confusion, but awake. Your mom's blurry face loomed over you, but her voice still sounded distant. "Oh, thank God. Thank God, thank God."

She was crying, and you heard someone say something to her, and a shadowed figure pulled her back a little.

"Mrs. Burke," a woman's soft voice said. "Would it be okay with you if we took Greg's vitals? I know you're pleased to have him awake, but we need to take care of him. We'll be done as soon as possible."

"Oh my goodness, of course. Thank you for taking such good care of my baby. This is such a miracle. I'm going to step out while you do that and make some calls. I'll be just outside the door."

You wanted her to stay. Sensing her there made you feel less alone. The light was too bright, so you closed your eyes as strangers messed with you. Something cold on your chest, something squeezing your arm. All letting you know you were still alive.

"Can you hear me, Greg?" that same woman with the soft voice asked. "Open your eyes. I need to know you're still with us."

You opened your eyes.

29

WAITING SEEMS ETERNITY
Leslie

Leslie is thinking about time and space.

These intangible ideas that would be impossible to explain, but when you feel the passage of time and the broad expanse of space that can fit into your chest, it's so overwhelming it stops you in your tracks.

Every day with dysphoria feels huge—like your body is too big for you, like it's just a shell you are waiting to shed like a corn husk or a snakeskin. She knows she's not yet in her final evolution, that curves will spring forth where there are none, her hair will change. She knows what to expect. But every day that she doesn't eat or drink so she won't have to darken the doorstep of her school's boys' restroom feels infinite. She's parched all the time now, and quenching her thirst means deciding on a bathroom and that's where she feels the most vulnerable. Conspiring together with Riley is a nice way to distract herself from this balancing act.

She can feel her hips rounding out, even as her hip bones and clavicle become more visible. It is hard for Leslie to keep her hands away from her hips and chest. The new body that is ripening like summer fruit. She pulls the string of a thong over the blooming hips, just under her more androgynous panties, and hides them all behind baggy jeans. Her nipples are sore and sensitive, which gives Leslie an excuse to wear enough layers to cover her bra. Thank God the weather is finally cool.

She still sits alone, tries not to be called on, but when she goes out, she releases her hair from the bun that holds it captive in spaces where she, too, feels like a captive. She doesn't wear dresses yet, but she's experimenting with fashion that feels within reach. It's a thin line, reaching far enough to be comfortable in your own clothes, but not so far that you attract attention to yourself. She's been driving to the closest big city, to the mall, the big one with two whole floors and a carousel in the middle, to shop. She's been sitting in coffeehouses and bookstores, trying on the idea of presentation.

The first time she's gendered correctly seems like it should be historic. Trumpets and fireworks and lightning and thunder. But it's not like that at all. It's just a small peak in the landscape of her day.

She is reading about Freddie Mercury, thinking about how it must have felt for him to stand, leather-clad and shining with sweat, in front of an audience cheering his name. Celebrating him for the clear hope and power of his voice. Maybe the wind was cold against his hot sweat, maybe it was a natural high, or maybe he needed a drink to steel his nerves. The books and videos can talk about the facts of history, but Leslie would like to crawl between the pages, into the lines to feel what Freddie felt, to feel the bass riff controlling his heartbeat and the crowd filling him like a balloon, so full of courage he could float away.

"Ma'am, do you want a refill? Oops, sorry. I meant *sir*," the waitress corrects, with no real malice. It seems like a simple mistake, the sun glaring off the giant plate-glass diner window. There doesn't seem to be any intentional transpohobia behind it.

She wants to tell this teenage girl, around her age, clearly embarrassed, that it's okay, Leslie's a girl like her. Leslie would like to ask about her makeup, would like to compliment her bold clothes—a violent rainbow of clashing neon colors—her long, wavy hair and golden skin, her tall black combat boots, but instead Leslie just blushes. The girl's name tag says GEORGIA, and Leslie wonders if she's queer. "I better not."

"Okay, I'll get this out of your way, then," the girl says, taking Leslie's cup. "Again, I'm really sorry."

Leslie grins at her. It's a small embarrassment for the waitress, but it's monumental for Leslie. Like she's been hiding in a forest too thick to be seen through, and then one day, the leaves fall from the branches and reveal her to the rest of the world. She knows it won't always feel like this. That sometimes being seen will be painful, but for now, this is enough. Her joy is so sweet she can taste it, like a handful of sun-ripe raspberries.

"It's okay. You were right the first time."

30

WHERE YOU BECOME I
Greg

Your mouth was a desert.

A kind-looking nurse with laugh lines around her eyes and a brown bun streaked with gray held a straw up to your lips. "It's just water, Greg. Sometimes people find that their throats are really raw after being intubated. Take a few small sips for me, okay?"

You nodded and took the straw between your lips. Water never felt colder or more liquid before and until it hit your mouth you didn't realize how parched you were.

The nurse pulled the straw away. "I know, sweetheart, I know. Easy."

You nodded again and she held the straw back up. You took slow sips, pulling away occasionally to breathe. She asked if you wanted to try and talk, and you nodded. Your voice sounded like rust from acid rain.

You cleared your throat and tried again. "Hi."

"Hi, yourself." The nurse smiled. "I'm Kristen. I'm your nurse this evening. You must have a ton of questions for me, and I'm glad to answer the ones I can. I'm going to take your vitals and ask you a few things first. Is that okay?"

You nodded.

"Great. Can you tell me your name?"

"Greg Michael Burke."

"Do you know what day it is?"

"The day or the date?"

"The date."

"No."

"The day?"

"Also no."

"Do you know where you are?"

"The hospital, right?"

"Correct," the nurse affirmed. "I'm going to take your blood pressure and vitals now, but before your mom comes back in, I want you to tell me if you'd rather her not be here. Or your dad. In fact, if there's anyone you feel is a danger to you, please let me know now, or tell any member of the staff at any time."

"What?" Your mom was the least dangerous person you could think of. "My mom?"

"Or anyone, Greg. In light of recent events. Do you remember what happened?"

The interview. The job. The parking lot. The hood lining up to make a better impact. You could feel your breathing get fast and shallow as the blood pressure cuff cut into your arm. "Oh my God."

"Greg." The nurse stopped the pressure cuff and unhooked it. She put her face in front of yours and a hand on your cheek. "Look at me. Deep breaths. Focus. You're doing great."

You stared into her eyes, felt anchored by her cool, paper-soft hand.

"Good, good. That's better," she said. "I'm going to finish your vitals, and then your mom will come back in. Are you hungry? We can start you out with some liquids, and if you can hold those down, after the doc comes by in the morning for rounds, I bet he'll clear you for almost anything else that sounds good."

You nodded.

Your mom poked her head through the door. "Can I come in?"

"Of course," Kristen said. "I'm finishing up here, then I'll grab some food for you. Maybe sorbet? The cold will soothe your throat. And some tea, too, okay?"

After she left, your mom watched you silently, her eyes glassy. She took a deep breath, crossed the distance between you to sit on the chair beside your bed, took your hands in hers, and kissed them.

"I don't think I've told you often enough how much I love you," she whispered, her voice holding back an ocean of hurt. "You're going to be okay, and that's the most important thing."

"Mom, I—"

"Shh. I've been planning what I would say when you woke up for a long time. And I want to make sure you never doubt that I love you. I have a second chance to make things right for you. You're not a baby anymore, you're almost a grown man, but I should have done more to keep you safe. I will from now on."

"Did Dad do this?" you whispered, just as much afraid of the answer as you were of the question.

"No, baby. He couldn't have. But I understand why you'd ask." She shook her head and her grip on your hands tightened slightly. "He was at the church. A witness saw his car out front when you— Anyway, the police investigated her statement and it was checked out. He won't hurt you again. I saved up a little money. I left him and got a place just for us. I promise you'll be safe there."

There were so many things you wanted to say, but you were too tired to speak. You were relieved she left him. At least, after you graduated and went out on your own, you'd know she was safe. Until then, you'd be around to help her adjust to life without Dad. Without his anger. Without fear.

Maybe there was even room for a little bit of hope.

SHAMPOO UNICORN
Episode 315: "Why We're Doing This"

*[*SHAMPOO UNICORN *THEME SONG MUSIC PLAYS.]*

BRIAN:
(whispering)

We're in Riley's car, parked across from the liquor store. We've been following Greg's dad for the better part of two days. So far, he's only left the house to come here, to church, once to the supermarket, and once to the post office.

RILEY:

Shh, here he comes.

BRIAN:

What we see is Greg's dad, wearing a pair of slides with

socks, sweatpants, and a MAGA T-shirt with a couple of holes and a stain on it. He's an older guy, with unkempt graying hair and a two- or three-day beard. He looks awful.

RILEY:

He looks dangerous, or unstable. Maybe both.

BRIAN:

He always looked dangerous or unstable. But this is the first time I've seen him since I was a kid. He looks like he hasn't combed his hair in a while. He was never especially well-groomed, but it looks like even the bare minimum has been ignored here. Mr. Burke looks unhinged.

RILEY:

What do you remember about him from when we were kids?

BRIAN:

He didn't like me. Thought I was "too sensitive." Greg preferred to hang out at my house instead of his because his dad watched us so closely. His mom was nice enough, but she was a totally different person when Greg's dad was home. More reserved and careful, I guess. Even the air changed whenever Mr. Burke walked through the door. I could feel him watching us, looking for signs of weaknesses to correct.

RILEY:

I only met his dad a couple of times, but he was always effusively nice to me.

BRIAN:

Sure, you were his one big hope for Greg not turning out to be a flaming homosexual, being the only girl he really hung around. Remember when we built that birdhouse?

RILEY:

And you nailed the tip of your shoe to the ground and Greg hammered his thumb so hard he cried? Yes. How could I possibly forget that?

BRIAN:

After you left, Mr. Burke took Greg and me out for burgers. Told us you were the kind of person we should be like—tough and no-nonsense. And that you were the type of girl we should try to marry.

RILEY:

It feels like I'm meant to be flattered by that. But I'm not.

BRIAN:

He's weird about girls. About gender roles. Well, he has these totally ass-backward views of men and women. I think losing his job messed up his sense of the world.

When Greg's mom became the breadwinner, he didn't know what to do with himself. The only righteous thing he could commit to was religion.

RILEY:

Here he comes.

BRIAN:

To clarify for you listeners, we are not in the actual parking lot of the hooch store. We're in the parking lot of the post office across the street.

RILEY:

He's coming out with a fairly big brown bag. He's getting into his car, and he's just . . . sitting there.

BRIAN:

He has both hands on the wheel and his head leaned back against the headrest. It looks pretty . . . existential. I wonder what he's thinking about.

RILEY:

Oh, what's he doing? Huh. He's lighting a cigarette and just sort of smoking and staring off vacantly.

BRIAN:

Jesus. He looks like that dude from the *American Gothic* painting. He's just missing a pitchfork and a pair of overalls. Same vacant stare, though.

RILEY:

What is our best-case scenario for this stakeout?

BRIAN:

I guess . . . we tail him back to wherever the truck he hit Greg with is being stored. And then we call the cops.

RILEY:

I would def not hold your breath for that. But who knows? Oh, he's getting ready to go.

BRIAN:

Come on! Remember to stay at least two car lengths behind him.

RILEY:

Do you want to drive?

BRIAN:

I can't drive and record at the same time.

RILEY:

Exactly. Just narrate.

BRIAN:

Okay, okay. We're turning onto the main road and . . . it looks like we are headed back to Greg's house. Goddamn it. This has got to be the worst stakeout possible.

Riley is doing a magnificent job of staying far enough back so we won't raise suspicion and close enough we won't lose him. But it seems like the last couple of days have been for naught.

[AMBIENT DRIVING NOISES FOR A FEW MINUTES.]

BRIAN:

And, as I suspected, here we are, right back where we started. Crap, crap, *crap*.

RILEY:

Hey, it's okay, Bri—

[CAR DOOR SLAMS.]

MR. BURKE:

(shouting)

What the fuck are you doing?

*[SOUND OF RILEY PICKING UP THE RECORDER,
A DOOR SLAMMING, HEAVY BREATHING,
FEET POUNDING ON THE GRAVEL.]*

RILEY:

(slightly out of breath)

Shit. Okay, loyal listeners, your intrepid host has lost his damn mind. We parked at the entrance to the trailer park, and he just hopped out of the car. I can only assume to confront Greg's dad on his own. Brian is trailing Mr. Burke, and I'm trailing Brian. The dude has a good six inches on Brian, so I hope it doesn't escalate.

BRIAN:

(from some distance away, getting louder as Riley approaches)
Mr. Burke. Do you remember me?

MR. BURKE:

(slurring a bit)
Brian Montgomery? Yeah? What are you doing here?
What do you want?

BRIAN:

I have some questions for you. I asked Mrs. Burke to ask
if you'd speak with me, but she said you were too upset.
Looks like you're more drunk than upset. Got a minute?

MR. BURKE:

What do you want? This got something to do with my
kid?

BRIAN:

Yeah. It does. Where have you been? Not at the hospital. I've been there.

MR. BURKE:

Not that it's any of your business, but I've been at
church. Praying. For my son's immortal, immoral soul.

BRIAN:

Maybe. If *church* is what you're calling the liquor store.
Where were you really when he got hit? Where are you
hiding the truck?

MR. BURKE:

What the hell are you talking about, kid? I was at church when he got hit. Reverend Greenleaf can attest to that. I was cleaning the sanctuary. I already told the police that.

BRIAN:

Who did it, then? If you didn't? Who else had a reason? I saw Greg a couple of days before the accident, and you had beaten the shit out of him.

MR. BURKE:

Look, you arrogant little fruit. I don't know what your interest in my son is, but I didn't hit him with a fucking truck. I did try to beat some of the fag out of him. I've been trying to straighten him out for years. Shame your mama couldn't keep a man around to try and do the same for your fairy tail.

*[PANTING, SOUND OF BOTTLE SLOSHING,
LOUD, DEEP GULPING.]*

MR. BURKE:

Didn't work though, did it? Still managed to get himself nearly killed because he was fucking around with some other boy in the locker rooms. I tried my best to put fear and reverence for the Heavenly Father in him, but it didn't do me no good at all.

RILEY:

Mr. Burke, can you—just—

MR. BURKE:

I can't do nothin' for him now. His mama left. She cleared out all her stuff and his, too. Said I was too dangerous and needed to learn to love my son for who he is.

BRIAN:

She's right. You should love your son no matter what.

MR. BURKE:

Why? Would she expect me to love a murderer? Or a junkie? He made his choices. He made it clear that he'd rather sit in sin now than by the side of the Lord in heaven later.

BRIAN:

Murderers? Junkies? How can you compare your son to them? They're not at all the same. And that assumes being gay is a sin. Do you really think that?

MR. BURKE:

I know that. I've known it all my life. The church teaches that "man shall not lie with another man," but also "love the sinner, hate the sin." I've tried to hold both in my heart, but I wish . . . I wish he would have picked almost any other sin. I'd rather have him in jail, or worse, than just committed to a life of wrong. Out dancing with other sinners, flaunting themselves in freak parades.

BRIAN:

You know what, we're never going to agree about this.

You're on the wrong side of history, and if you ran him over, the police will find out and you'll go to prison where you belong.

MR. BURKE:

You know, I almost wish I had done it, Brian. At least then my final lesson to him would have been the wages of sin is death. But I didn't, and it don't matter whether you believe me or not. Only person I got to answer to is my God. You should be worried about answering to Him, too.

BRIAN:

My god is a Black woman named Beyoncé, and she supports gay rights. She's also a hell of a lot more accessible than that tired old work of fiction you've been thumping people over the head with all your life. "For the wages of sin is death." Really? Straight out of the Bible, right? You can't even come up with your own words. You think you're righteous? I only see one sinner here, and it's you.

You're a sad old fool who is going to die alone, and Greg and his mom are better off without you.

RILEY:

(whispering)

Whoa. Come on, let's get out of here.

[SOUND OF FOOTSTEPS AND HEAVY
BREATHING. CAR DOORS SLAMMING.
KEYS JINGLE, ENGINE CUTS ON.]

RILEY:

Well, that was really fucking intense.

BRIAN:

(*panting*)

Oh, holy shit. Holy fucking shit. That was so reckless and so very, very dangerous and scary.

RILEY:

Sure, but also . . . brave? What made you do it?

BRIAN:

I've never done anything in my whole life to stand up for myself. Not really. I spent the last four years trying to fly low enough beneath the radar so I wouldn't get pantsed in the hall or have my locker defaced or be called faggot in gym. And you know what?

RILEY:

No, what?

BRIAN:

It didn't work. All those things happened to me. Damage control was about me doing what was best for me, not about doing what was right. If I'd fought back, escalated things, or documented things, maybe other kids would've gotten picked on less. Maybe Greg would've had some more affirmative message that wasn't coming from his homophobic dad.

RILEY:

Sure, maybe. But there's nothing you can do about it now. You can't change the past.

BRIAN:

I can let the past change who I am in the future.
(*sighs*)
Do you believe Greg's dad? That he didn't do it?

RILEY:

I kind of do. You?

BRIAN:

Yeah. I do. Like he said. I think he'd have some sort of weird pride about being able to claim it. Plus his alibi. I wanted that to be false. Wanted it to be Mr. Burke who did it, so he'd be thrown in jail and punished. Punished for all those years he actually did hurt Greg. He's guilty of so many things. I just wanted it to be him so badly so there would be some justice for all the pain he has caused. So where does that leave us now?

RILEY:

I don't know, exactly. I guess we're looking for a busted silver truck. Maybe we talk to mechanics and see if anyone has come in for body work? We can see if there's any way to find out anything from the police, too.

BRIAN:

That's a good suggestion. We'll do that before the next

episode. In the meantime, I wanted to say thank you so much to the people who are sending in advice, tips, and their stories.

Keep writing. I can't respond to everything, but know that I read everything, and all your kind words remind me of why I'm . . . why *we're* doing this.

*[*SHAMPOO UNICORN *EXIT THEME PLAYS.]*

31

CURRENT HISTORY
Leslie

Leslie thinks about time, how it is shaped by events.

Not just structures but ideas, concepts, history. There's a direct line between her and Marsha and Storme, the Stonewall uprising of 1969. Leslie's building a celebration in the memory of Marsha's act of rebellion. She's refusing shame, commemorating how far they've come in the time and distance between her life and Marsha's.

The Canon Pride parade is a go. For every single thing she's needed an adult for, her mom or dad has stepped in. Chuck Hill, the owner of a BBQ place in Canon, felt so bad about his parking lot being the scene of a potential hate crime when Riley talked to him about it, he offered her the whole parking lot for what they are calling Canon Pride Fest. He thought they should wait until June, when the world erupts into rainbow, but when Leslie pointed out that they'd be competing with bigger events, with people traveling out of town, he agreed that sooner was better. He's been rallying his patrons and has gotten a couple of friendly local businesses to help sponsor the event. When she spoke with him on the phone, he said he was thrilled to death his brother-in-law was coming down to celebrate, too. They have enough vendor space to bring in businesses from out of town. Leslie is working with a few drag queens to make a pageant and talent show.

Along with her guests from New York, Leslie has invited people from the internet to come and perform or sell their queer wares. So far, she's gotten a troupe of queer circus performers, a singer, a comedian, and a folk band. It's a random assortment, but who cares, she thinks. It will be fun.

She was initially hopeful for a gathering of fifty. After getting all the paperwork filled out (in triplicate) and setting a date, it seems like the number of attendees could be in the hundreds at least. She even over-heard someone at school talking about it, not unfavorably, and felt a little thrill run through her body. This is the most she can ever remember being excited about anything.

Leslie glances over her laptop. The café she's working from is busy, and her coffee mug is almost empty. Her shadow sisters are with her. They are standing in the daylight now, and they no longer need the coded language they've relied on to keep them safe.

She will stand tall beside her sisters, and together they will bathe in the sunlight.

32

AWAKE
Brian

The natural order of things had shifted.

Derek started joining us for our evening podcast investigation, homework, and Netflix hangouts. At first it was a little awkward—I invited him because he seemed like he didn't have any friends and was generally trying to be a kinder person by way of investigating what happened to Greg. And since it was relevant to our podcast, he just sort of attached himself to us. Riley, always the last to let go of a grudge, still distrusted him, and Beth, who had known him from the general upper echelon of CHS's social hierarchy, just accepted him being around.

After we played the recording of me confronting Mr. Burke, Derek whistled, long and low.

"Badass," he said. "That dude's been scary long as I've known him. I don't think I've ever said more than *yessir* or *nosir* to him."

"He's scary as hell, that's for sure," Riley agreed.

"We should still maybe report him to the police, though, right? Even if he didn't attack Greg, he should still be on record for all the abuse. Is there a statute of limitations for that?" Beth stood up from the kitchen table where we'd all been picking at a lasagna she'd baked and brought over. She pulled out cups from my cabinet and put on coffee. "Anyway, that leaves us with the possibility of some rando who attacked Greg. We could also ask Coach Winsor if he has any leads."

"Riley had a good idea." I grabbed the creamer, set it beside the coffee pot, and boosted myself to sit on the counter. "She said we could call repair shops and see if anyone had brought a truck matching the one in the video."

"I made a list of repair shops in a twenty-mile radius," Riley said. "There are ten body shops and a bunch of general full-service mechanics. I figure we can split them up among us and have an answer in a couple of hours."

"Hey." Derek stood up and stretched, walked toward Riley, and opened the box of doughnuts he'd brought in earlier. "My old man has a hunting cabin he never really uses this late in the season. I used to have parties there on Fridays after home games sometimes. I was wondering if y'all wanted to pull an all-nighter there next week. I feel like we could get some good detective work in."

Riley arched an eyebrow.

Derek's face reddened. "It was just an idea. I mean, it's just sitting there."

"I can't see why not," I said, and opened the refrigerator. "It feels like we're overdue for something fun. And anyway—"

"Speaking of fun, I wanted to show you something," Riley said, grinning and handing me an envelope. I opened it and pulled out a colorful flyer.

"Canon Pride Fest?" I looked at her, confused. "What's this?"

"It's an event I've been helping a podcast fan put together. She's not from here, but she's from not too far away, and she is kiiiiind of amazing."

I knit my eyebrows together.

"But obviously not as amazing as you." Riley winked. "Your bestie-hood is in no danger. Anyway, she had this idea about how dope it would be to be, like, open and unafraid in a small town, instead of driving to a big metropolitan area that has a bunch of bars we can't go to with people, like, twice as old and half as cool as us."

"Dude, we haven't taken a fruity shit the other person didn't know about in the last ten years," I said, trying to keep the petulant tone out of my voice.

"That you know of," Riley snapped. "I contain multitudes. Anyway, this is happening, largely due to your influence, so we should hype it up on the pod socials."

Derek scratched his chin thoughtfully with his thumbnail and looked at Riley. "Are we allowed to go to this thing? Since we're straight, I mean."

"It says free and open to the public in big letters." Riley pointed. "Right up top."

Derek nodded. "Cool. I bought a shirt. I was just gonna casually wear it one day and not say anything, but a pride event seems like the perfect occasion."

"What does your shirt say?" Riley asked, ever suspicious.

"Straight, but not narrow." He blushed a little, looking the least confident I'd ever seen him. One by one he met our eyes, and his shoulders relaxed a little. Riley smirked. "I mean. I'm trying."

And then my phone rang. I didn't recognize the number on the screen, but I picked up anyway.

"Hello?"

"Brian?" I didn't recognize the voice right away. "It's Mrs. Burke. Is this an okay time to talk to you, darlin'?"

"Oh, hi, sure!"

"I just wanted to let you know that Greg's awake. His doctors are doing tests and things now to see what kind of therapy he might need and how the coma might have affected him. But he's awake."

"Oh my god," I replied. "Is he . . . okay? Does he seem okay?"

"He looks so good. I can't say for sure until I know what the docs have to say, but it seems like my prayers have been answered. God is so great. Give us a couple of days and then come visit when you can. I know he'd love to see you."

"Yes, ma'am. Thank you for calling. I'll do that." I was so stunned after I hung up the phone that I couldn't move for a minute. It wasn't until Derek called over to me that I startled back to life.

"Bro, you okay? You look like you've seen a ghost."

I looked into the faces of my friends and thought about the boy who brought us all together. Smiling placidly, Beth played idly on her phone. Riley was throwing little pieces of cheese at Derek, who had been trying and mostly failing to catch them in his mouth. The couch and floor below him were littered in cheese. Beth stealthily took a video of the two of them, then winked at me.

"Y'all, that was Greg's mom." I felt warmth in my chest spread to my arms and legs, fingers and toes.

"He's awake."

33

NOT ALL HEROES WEAR CAPES
Greg

Your world was getting clearer.

The edges were coming into focus, and things were starting to make more sense. Your mom and doctors said it was because you were coming out of the coma fog. You were still hurting pretty badly but tried to use the painkiller pump button sparingly. The pain kept you rooted to earth and made things seem realer and clearer. Your doctors explained the extent of your injuries. You had pretty serious brain trauma with enough bleeding to require surgery, but they'd gotten you in quickly enough to minimize any potential brain damage.

Those had been hard fucking words to swallow. Brain damage. You fractured a couple of ribs and your wrist. Moving hurt, but you needed it. Needed to know what you were capable of doing. You begged your doctor to let you get up. Physical therapy, occupational therapy. Anything. You couldn't just rot in this hospital bed. The waiting was unbearable. Your mom was so present that you sometimes sent her on errands just to have some space.

You needed to get out of bed. To move around. Anything. Sitting here, all you had was boredom and anger. If the accident hadn't caused you permanent brain damage, the mundane laugh track of shitty sitcom reruns might. Fuck those perfect actors and their incomprehensibly normal antics.

Everything was so exhausting and there was so much to think about. Not just school or your busted brain and body, but also your dad and mom and what would happen. She said regardless of what happened, she was divorcing him. Regardless of what her church said was or was not a sin. That she'd been trying so hard to be a good Christian she hadn't realized what a terrible mother she'd been. You thought maybe she was being too hard on herself, but when you objected, she just held up a hand to dismiss your protests.

The police were trying to visit you to get a statement. Your mom and doctors wouldn't let them, saying you weren't cognitively ready to deal with it yet. They agreed on assigning an advocate to work with you on getting your statement down. But that was pretty far down your endless list of worries.

You wanted to know what was happening outside the hospital. Your mom said that Brian and Riley and Derek had come to see you, but no one from the current team roster. You were anxious about seeing Brian. And about seeing Derek. Did they hate you? Did everyone? Now that the world knew who you were, what would living in Canon be like? When you got out of the hospital and ran into your former teammates at the gas station or the supermarket, would they ignore you?

The uncertainty was part of the problem. If there were any answers at all, maybe you wouldn't swing wildly back and forth between rage and despair. You tried to be patient and kind to your mom. She was juggling a lot. Spending time at the hospital with you, working at night, and sleeping when she could. Not to mention moving entirely on her own.

You felt responsible for her sadness. She spent so much time with you unconscious that she needed you to need her while you were awake. When you didn't, or when you asked questions she didn't have the answers to, it made her sad. Since there was nothing for either of you to do, it felt like an endless cycle of shittiness.

What you finally did ask for were movies. Epic science fiction and superhero movies to get lost in—to take you both as far from this hospital as possible. Mom brought in your laptop, loaded up Netflix, and you watched first the complete Lord of the Rings series, agreeing that while elves were beautiful, you'd rather be dwarves—stoic and strong. You binged superhero movies until your eyes hurt. It was so cool to see her get lost in the magic of story and cinema, to see special effects and actors take her away from this sterile place and put her somewhere else entirely. You had forgotten about how carefree she'd looked during your Liz Taylor marathons.

Your days were so full and exhausting that in the evenings when she didn't have to go into work, you just let Mom decide what to watch. You could tell she was choosing things she thought a teenage boy would enjoy.

"Oh, Captain America," she said. "The girls I work with just love that actor. And I've heard good things about the special effects, too. Do you mind if we watch this one?"

"Sounds good, Mom. I'm ready when you are."

She'd turn off the light in the room so that the loud buzzing didn't drown out the crappy speakers on your cheap laptop, and then she'd scoot her chair close enough to your bed that the screen would bathe you in flickering blue light. When you looked over at her, she was almost always napping through the movie, but a couple of times, she covered your big hand with her smaller one and squeezed gently.

When Mom noticed your eyes getting tired, she brushed your hair away from your forehead, planted a soft kiss there, and said that you didn't need a cape or one single Infinity Stone to be her hero, and that even heroes need their rest.

34

MIRACULOUS
Brian

I had a lunch date.

Before I went to visit Greg for the first time since he was conscious, I asked his mom if I could take her to lunch for the finest provisions Canon General Hospital had to offer. She accepted my date during his morning physical therapy and after we'd both filled our trays with the most palatable of the cafeteria food—lots of tapioca pudding—I pulled the books I'd gotten her from my backpack.

"Lunch and gifts?" Mrs. Burke smiled. "What did I do to deserve this?"

"You've probably been pretty stressed out, working and moving. Being here and, uh, making big life choices and stuff. I wanted to get you some books I thought might help you with all this newness."

She read the titles of the books I slid across the table to her. *"God and the Gay Christian: The Gospel of Inclusion."* She set her coffee cup down, the paper leaving a slowly spreading ring on the Formica table. "Brian Montgomery, you are as sweet of a boy as you ever were."

I shrugged. "I was thinking about something you said when I was growing up that stuck with me. You said when you had questions or didn't know what to do, you took it to the Bible to figure out what Jesus would do."

She smiled, flipping through the pages. "This was when you were deciding whether or not to bleach your tips. I was trying to talk you out of it without making you feel silly."

"It worked, thank goodness." I picked at my french fries. "I was thinking about the Bible, though. About how it's a book. The Good Book, some people say. But just like the ones we read in school, people interpret it in different ways. And people get wrapped up in the 'right' or 'wrong' way to read it. I just think, maybe, you can't have a conversation if you're not willing to listen to what someone else has to say."

"That's very diplomatic."

"There's a Metropolitan Community Church off exit seven. I know it's not as close as your home church, but—"

"I won't be returning to Mr. Burke's family church."

"Oh? Where will you go now?"

"I went to a PFLAG meeting at the MCC. I think it seems like a really warm, welcoming place of worship. I'd like to take Greg. He hasn't liked going to church with me in years, but maybe this would be different for him."

"Maybe." I nodded. "How're you doing overall?"

She stabbed a few pieces of lettuce with her fork and examined the wilting leaves. "You know, if you had asked me a year ago how I'd feel about leaving my husband to be more supportive to my homosexual son, I might have had a different response. But I have known for a long time that Mr. Burke is not a good man. I just hate that it took this for me to make the changes that are best for my family." She placed her fork down and picked up the roll on the side of her plate. "I judged the virtue of my decisions on someone else's interpretation of the Bible because I believed more in their authority than I did my ability to know right and wrong in my heart."

"It's a hard situation," I said. "I can't imagine how it feels to make such big choices."

"Leaving was the right thing to do. Right for me, right for Greg. I let Mr. Burke convince me that he knew more about how to be a good Christian than I did. And honestly, it was easier. I was wrong."

"Are you afraid of him at all?" I couldn't stop thinking about him shouting at me, slurring his words, ranting about Greg.

"Lord, that man is crazier than a June bug. But he takes all his power from making other people scared. I think my leaving shook him to the core. How can you be a good Christian husband and father if your family leaves you? He's either got to change or die sad and sorry in his own misery."

The fluorescent lights buzzed overhead. The cafeteria was busy, with mainly people in scrubs rushing to get their lunches in during their breaks.

"I thought it was him, you know?"

"You thought what was him, sugar?"

"I thought . . . Mr. Burke did this to Greg." My voice was shakier than I wanted it to be. "I thought he hit him. But when I went to ask him about it, he just seemed like an angry bulldog, barking at the wind. I don't think it would occur to him to have done it, and I think he would have felt . . . I don't know, righteous or something."

"Oh, sweetheart." Mrs. Burke put her soft hand over mine. "Mr.

Burke talks a big game, but he'd never have it in him to do something like this. Not because he doesn't have enough anger. Lord knows he has that in spades. He just ain't that ambitious."

"I don't know what to do now. I thought I could help the police, and Greg—find out who did it. I thought that was a thing I could do for Greg. And now, I've got practically nothing." I couldn't look at her, instead focusing on the scene behind us, the other diners, mostly solo, eating while staring at their phones. The two cashiers spoke over their registers, their scrubs and hairnets mirroring each other.

"You've been here visiting Greg this entire time, Brian. You really think that's nothing? His teammates haven't come to see him. His dad didn't come back after that first week."

"I know, but I just really want there to be some sort of justice. It's unfair that he's here and whoever did this to him is just walking around free." I was absently scraping the label off my soda bottle. The intercom squelched to life, paging Dr. Bird to the ER. We both ignored it.

"You're right, it's not fair," she said. "But the most important thing is that he's going to be okay."

"This is going to seem like it's out of nowhere, and it kind of is, but do you know anyone who drives a silver pickup truck?"

"I don't think so, Brian. Why do you ask?"

"It's probably nothing. I'll let you know when I find out more about it." I didn't want to trouble her in case this lead got us nowhere. Sitting with her, with dust dancing in the air of the sun-dappled hospital cafeteria, I wondered if it even mattered. Justice would be lovely, but the most important thing was the broken boy we had in common, the one slowly working his way back to normal. Whatever normal meant.

"All right. If you know something, you should tell the police. Let them handle it." Mrs. Burke wiped her mouth and dropped her napkin on her tray. "He'll be finishing up PT right now. Let's head back."

• • •

On our way into Greg's room, we met the physical therapist—a Latino man with huge biceps, a cute undercut, and a nice smile—at the door on his way out. "He did real good today," he said. "Him being an athlete and in good shape definitely helps."

"I'm so glad," Mrs. Burke replied, smiling tenderly at him. "Thank you for working with him, Larry. It means the world to me. You've all been such angels."

Larry returned her smile. "He might be tired, but we'll pick up again tomorrow."

Mrs. Burke paused before going inside and turned to me. "I'm going to run home and get Greg some clean pajamas. You go on in and visit. I won't be long." It was a lie, but that lie was a small act of mercy. She could read a room like there were six-foot letters written on the wall. I smiled gratefully and hugged her.

After taking a breath to brace myself before entering, I yanked down the handle and swung the wooden door open as silently as I could. Detached from the feeding tubes and monitors, Greg still looked fragile and beautiful. His bruises had almost entirely healed, and his cheeks were flushed. His eyes were closed, hair swept to the side, slightly damp. The rise and fall of his chest beneath the thin blue cotton of the hospital gown was so miraculous, I felt a lump rise in my throat.

"I'm just going to rest awhile, okay, Mom?" he said without opening his eyes.

"Take all the time you need," I replied softly. "How was physical therapy?"

Greg's eyes snapped open, and he winced as he tried to scoot up into a sitting position before collapsing back onto the pillows. "Hi."

"Hi, yourself." I walked over to him, put a hand on his arm, and gestured for him to relax. Greg's grin was crooked and unsure and so beautiful that it almost stopped my breath.

He ran a hand over his hair in an attempt to smooth it down. "It was fine. I mean, it's like gym class for hospital patients who are figuring out how to be humans again, so it was hard. But fine."

"I'm glad you're a human again," I said, suddenly feeling like a tangled marionette. Not sure what to do with my arms or legs, I shoved my hands into my pockets. "I visited before. You were still a human then. Just a human at rest."

"I think we're playing it fast and loose with the word *rest*, Bri. I'm pretty fucking exhausted."

"Oh shit. I'm sorry, I could go if you need—"

"No." He stopped me. "Don't go. I'm tired, but maybe you could just sit with me for a while?" He reached for a cup with a straw sticking out of it on his bed table but fell short.

I picked it up and handed it to him. "Yes, of course. I'll stay."

His fingers were cold as they brushed mine to take the cup from me. He took a long sip on the straw and gave it back to me to return to the tray.

"Thanks," he said. "Mom told me you're trying to figure out who did this to me. That you've been talking about it on your podcast. I don't know if I ever told you that I listened to it. But I did. I liked it a lot. It made me miss you less."

The air was full of questions. We'd get to them. We had time. "I have. Riley and Beth helped. And even Derek. We didn't come up with much, though. We tried to give whatever we had to the police. We thought since we knew you, we had a good chance of helping them solve this. Do you remember anything?"

Greg shook his head. "Mostly not. I can't tell what I remember or what other people have said. Will you tell me what you found in your investigation? I wanted to listen to the series on your channel, but my mom hasn't brought me my phone yet, so I can't."

"Calling it an investigation is pretty generous, Greg." I sat down in the chair by his bed, leaving my hand on his forearm and gently stroking it with my thumb. "Mostly I questioned people who already had alibis. But Derek did figure out that it was a silver pickup truck that struck you. Does that ring any bells?"

Greg didn't say anything right away, but I could feel his mind wander away. He was staring absently at my hand and his arm, but he was clearly thinking about something else.

"Greg?"

He snapped back to attention. "I'm sorry," he said. "I feel like it's almost there, but I can't quite connect with the memory. I'm sorry. I really want to help."

"Hey," I said, and he looked at my face, his brow still furrowed. "What matters is that you're okay."

"I'm glad you're here, Brian."

"Can I hug you?" I asked. "Gently, I mean?"

He looked at me and nodded, and I stood and wrapped my arms around him. He rested his head on my chest, and when I tried to move away, he held me tighter. I lost track of how long we stayed like that, but I didn't want to let go, neither did he.

"Bumper sticker," Greg mumbled against my chest.

I pulled back and studied his face. "What?"

He swallowed hard. "The truck had a bumper sticker on its front. It was black and said 'stand and fight' in white with the NRA initials in red at top."

Now I was swallowing hard. "That's great. I've seen those before."

"So that could help?"

"Yes, it definitely can." At the same time I said that, I wondered how popular the bumper stickers were and if they were sold at many stores in Canon.

His hand grasping mine brought my attention back to him. "I'm afraid," he said. "What if they come after me here? Or after I'm released."

I sat back down, keeping a hold on his hand. "They won't."

"You can't know that."

"I'm going to mention on the show that you don't remember anything." I gave him a tight smile, hoping it would mask my worry. "If they think you can't point fingers, they'll leave you alone. Meanwhile, you should also mention that your recollection is pretty foggy to the police. And see if they can offer you protection."

"My mom asked already. She wanted to make sure I was safe." His Adam's apple bobbed as he swallowed his fear. "They said that hospital security would be enough."

I thought about it. "That's probably okay. I've had to sign in to get a pass whenever I've visited. And there's a guard in the lobby and security cameras in the parking garage."

"Hope you're right."

I hoped I was right, too.

35

NEW BFF
Greg

A couple of days passed in a matter of seconds.

Your life was a tight schedule of meals, therapies, and visitations. You filled the spaces in between with sleep. It felt like you'd never get enough rest. Even when Brian was there, your body reached for the dull comfort of sleep. You crashed a couple of times while he was around, only to wake panicked that he'd be gone. Instead, he was mostly screwing around on his phone, though once you found him fully reclined in the chair by your bed, snoring so sweetly it sounded like a song.

It was after dinner but before visiting hours were over, and you were alone in your room. The door and your eyes opened at the same time, and there was Derek, sheepishly inching into the room. You hadn't seen him since that day in the locker room, but you thought of him often and wondered how this moment would go.

"Wow, you look like shit," he said.

"I got hit by a truck, what's your excuse for that ugly mug?"

He grinned and you grinned back. You breathed a little easier.

"I was born rich, with a massive dick. It would be unfair to be good-looking, too."

"Asshole."

"Shithead."

"Douchebag."

"Butthole." And then he was across the room, hugging you and crying. And whoa, it was a lot. "I was so fucking worried about you, dude. I'm so sorry. This is all my fault."

"Hey, hey. Unless you were driving the truck that hit me, it's not your fault. You gotta loosen your grip, though, because my ribs are still broken."

"Oh holy shit, bro. I'm sorry. Are you okay?"

"I'm . . . surprisingly okay. I'm really fucking glad to see you. When you didn't visit, I thought maybe we weren't friends anymore. That you blamed me for all the locker room stuff."

"I worried you blamed me. That I had, like, sort of blackmailed you or something. Even if I didn't get that what I'd done was wrong, it was."

"How so?"

"I know everything that happened was pretty one-sided. I'm not gay or anything, but I still like getting . . . well, y'know. But I talked myself into thinking you were into it, too. But now I've had time to think about it, it seems like you were afraid I'd out you."

"Look, I don't super want to talk about that," you said awkwardly. "We're cool. I'm not mad; you're not mad. Let's be clear, we're bros, but it will never happen again."

He nodded, stuck out a hand, and you shook on it. A moment passed while your friendship adjusted to its new rhythm.

"Nice digs," he finally said, sitting in the chair by your bed, the one you thought of as Brian's seat, even though your mom sometimes occupied it. "They treating you okay in here?"

"Not bad. Kind of boring. Had a pretty serious head injury when I came in—it's why I was in a coma for so long. But I'm in physical therapy for my wrist and to prevent muscle atrophy from lying around all the time. And in occupational therapy to make sure there's not, like, lasting brain damage."

"Shit."

"Sounds scarier than it actually is, I promise. I'm doing great."

"Yeah?"

"Yeah. Plus, I've got a couple of sexy-ass scars. I'm going to tell people I got them dueling."

"Why would you be dueling? That's a hard sell, man."

"I'm not even going to explain. I think it'll make me sound mysterious." You waggled your eyebrows. "How are things with you?"

"Fine. I've been hanging out with Brian, Riley, and Beth. They're cool."

"They are cool. What are you doing about school shit? I haven't even really started thinking about it."

"Ah. I signed up for a GED tutor. My old man hired some lawyers to say that our getting expelled was homophobic. But when I told him I wouldn't blame you, or pretend to be actually gay, he flipped shit. Threatened to disinherit me after all the hard work he'd done to create a family legacy. And I was just going to throw it away for some casual faggotry."

"Jesus." You winced. "Where are you staying?"

"I'm still staying at home. I've got enough saved to get a place if I need it, but he hasn't asked me to leave and he hasn't been home much."

He shrugged. "Anything to stay away and not have to look at me, I guess. He's been out of town 'on business.' I suspect he's waiting to kick me out when I turn eighteen so that if there's even the slightest risk of a downtick in public perception, he can sell it as some sort of decision to help me 'be my own man' or 'pull myself up by my own bootstraps' or whatever.

"Why do they keep these rooms so cold?" He was trying to change the subject.

"I don't know. Preserves bodies?"

Silence filled the space between us as you both searched for something else to say.

Derek cleared his throat. "How are things with your parents?"

"Honestly," you said, "not bad. I mean, my dad's a piece of shit. But he's been a piece of shit most of my life. My mom left him. She's getting a place for the two of us. Without my old man's deadweight and anger, we'll be okay."

"That's awesome, dude." He beamed at you, and you could see him clearly now. Not the guy you lusted after or feared, but the dude you trusted with your deepest secret. He looked older. He looked tired.

"I'm so fucking proud of her. She's finally taking control. She's at a new church, too, and it seems like she's okay . . . more than okay with the gay thing."

"Yeah, well, she almost lost you, dude. That's got to be a real come-to-Jesus sort of reckoning." Derek stretched his arms over his head. "I gotta get going, bro. Can I come back and see you sometime?"

"You better come back and see me." You reached out a hand to dap. "Otherwise I'm going to have to get a new best friend."

"Yeah, good luck filling my size twelves, bro."

"Hey, Derek?"

He stopped with his hand on the door handle. "Yeah, man?"

"You're going to be okay, too." You smiled at him, and he smiled back. "I promise. The good guys always win in the end, right?"

"Am I one of the good guys?"

"You're an okay guy right now," you said. "But I can see you're working on it."

He nodded. "That's fair."

"I think maybe the working is what's important, though. Like, you're not a good guy if you're not working on it."

"You're not winning if you're not working, isn't that what Winsor says?"

"Wise man, that coach of ours."

"You're wise, too, you know?" Derek's face was as open as you'd ever seen it. "I've always thought that. Not just smart. Wise."

And with that, he left, and you were surer than ever that you were both, in fact, good guys.

36

DEREK LOVES CHANDLER
Brian

I wasn't a truck guy, but suddenly I couldn't stop staring at them.

You know how, when you get a crush on a tall red-haired boy, you're suddenly attuned to the fact that there are randomly tall red-haired boys everywhere and none of them are the boy you're looking for? That happened to me in ninth grade, and while Billy "Billiam" Willis never knew how I felt, looking for a silver pickup in Canon sort of felt the same way.

White and gray trucks were just similar enough to make me notice. We called every repair shop in town, and then when we didn't get any results, we called the next town over. There had been a couple of silver trucks (because even a broken clock is right twice a day, as my mom would say), but they were either smaller than the one that hit Greg or were in for actual mechanical repair instead of body work.

We were visiting Greg in groups and helping his mom get their new place ready. Riley, Beth, and I were taking exams and preparing for

Christmas break. Derek, home alone, and alienated from his football friends, started picking me up on his way to the gym on the weekends. Once, he asked me if I thought Riley would date him. If he had not been spotting me, I would have dropped a barbell on my neck.

"Uh, look, as diplomatically as I can say this." I strained to get the weight back to its home base. "I don't. I know you've come a long way from the jock douchebag you used to be, no offense, but she has a long memory."

"That makes sense. Still, I think I'm going to shoot my shot anyway."

"Fine, but if she's not interested, you can't let it change the group dynamic."

"I won't press it. I know." He changed the subject. "You wanna carpool to Canon Pride? Maybe we can see if Riley and Greg want to all go together?"

"Yeah, for sure."

"Can you imagine how many people's heads will explode?"

The muscles in my arms burned, but I had one more set to go. "I just worry there'll be some sort of protest or religious demonstration. Although it's possible I'm imagining scenarios that will never play out. We've never had a pride event in Canon before. Not sure how our local churches will handle it."

When we finished our workout, we made our usual stop at Pop's Stop and Shop for coffee and protein bars. We'd just pulled off the road when Derek slammed on the brakes. "Bro, look," he said, staring in the rearview mirror.

I turned around to see a silver pickup with a crinkled bumper, parked at the front of the parking lot between the median and the road. "Is that . . . Wait. That's the truck."

"Yep." Derek jumped out of the car, and I followed him.

"It's clearly been in an accident," I said, rushing to keep up with him. "Maybe the hood was repaired but the bumper wasn't."

Derek slowly circled the car, putting his hands on the dented rear fender. "This could be it," he whispered.

I felt hope spark in my chest.

We were silently circling the truck when a voice snapped me out of my hypnosis. "Hey! What the hell are you guys doing?" An older woman in a Dale Earnhardt Jr. T-shirt with a cigarette dangling from her lips stalked toward us.

"This your ride?" Derek asked.

"Yeah, what the hell are you doing touching it?"

"What happened to the bumper?"

"None of your goddamn business, kid. Now get the hell away."

I stepped in front of Derek. "I'm sorry for my friend. I'm Brian, this is Derek. We're in the market for a used truck. However, he's socially inept due to his poor upbringing. Are you interested in selling this one?"

"Selling Chandler?" She squinted at me.

"Chandler?"

"Yeah, don't you have a name for your car?"

"Oh, I don't. No. But I understand that lots of people do. I don't have a car of my own yet. Like I said, I'm in the market. But I know it's a thing."

"Hell yeah, it's a thing. You know, like . . . Chandler Bing, from *Friends*. The Chan-Chan man? Bing-a-ling?"

I smiled awkwardly. "Is Chandler available for purchase?"

"I can't imagine what you'd want with this hunk of junk. He's got some transmission problems, so it wasn't worth it to get the body repaired."

"What happened to the body?"

"My old man got shitfaced and ran into the trailer hitch. We got into a fight about who was a better band, Guns N' Roses or Metallica."

"Oh sure." I nodded. "That's a tough one. Tell you what. Why don't I take your number and I can call you after you've had time to think about it. That way if you do decide to put Chandler on the market, you'll know he's in good hands."

She seemed to think about this for a minute, doing mental calculations, and then nodded. "All right, Brian. I'll give you my number. Since you can talk to other people like a gentleman, unlike your friend, give me a call. I'll talk selling Chandler with my common-law mister."

I elbowed Derek sharply in the ribs and heard him grunt. "Yes, ma'am. Thank you."

"That's more like it," she said, and handed me a Dollar Tree receipt with a hastily scrawled number on the back.

She dropped her cigarette and stomped on it before shuffling back inside. I handed the paper to Derek, and he shoved it into his jeans pocket. "I feel like I'm going off the deep end here, bro."

I patted his back. "I know what you mean. I see that fucking truck everywhere. I think I've even dreamed about it a couple of times. But Chandler isn't it. There isn't an NRA bumper sticker on the front. Unless she removed it. Even then, I think there'd be residue or discoloration."

"I'm starting to think it doesn't exist."

"Well, sure," I said. "If I hit someone, I'd want it to not exist, either. But how do you get rid of something like that?"

"Who knows? Set it on fire? Junk it? Drive it into the ocean? Sell it for parts? Scrap it? Maybe whoever did it already got rid of the truck, and we're just out here chasing ghosts."

"Do you think we should give up?" I walked back toward the gas station as he fell into step beside me.

"I don't want to be a quitter, but I feel like the important thing here is that Greg is okay. So maybe we ask him what he wants and then decide as a group how much further we can feasibly go with all this."

"That's a good idea." I stretched, remembered my post-workout sweat rings, and put my arms down. "I feel like we've followed this lead about as far as we can. And, not to be sappy, but time we spend looking into this phantom truck is less time we spend helping our man sort his life out."

"Sure, you're right." Derek nodded, slapping me on the back. "Come on, I'll buy you a cup of coffee."

37

PO-TAY-TOES
Greg

You'd only ever lived two places, and they were polar opposites.

During your early, idyllic childhood, Riley, Brian, and you had climbed trees, started a lemonade stand, ridden bikes, and, once or twice, played Truth or Dare in the woods. You didn't live in the wealthiest part of Canon, but it was a relatively nice, objectively safe subdivision.

After your dad lost his job, when the bank foreclosed on the house, you moved to Pine Hollow Trailer Park. Through the thin metal walls, across your postage-stamp yard, you could hear the neighbors fighting, fucking, and watching movies your mom certainly wouldn't have approved of.

Your mom picked you up when the hospital cleared you to go home. The only issue from your brain injury was some selective memory loss. That was to be expected from a traumatic incident and they suggested therapy. The doctors prescribed short-term physical therapy, but overall they said you'd been very, very lucky and told you over and over how pleased they were by your recovery.

When your mom pulled into the parking lot of the apartment building, it was so clean and modern-looking that you couldn't help but feel as lucky as the doctors had announced. Your unit was on the third floor, down a wide, well-lit hallway.

Mom unlocked the door, and you helped her bring your stuff inside.

"Careful," she said. "Don't leave the door open."

You were about to ask why when a ball of black fluff attacked your pants leg with a fury that might have been more appropriate from a bigger animal. You laughed and picked up the hissing ball.

Mom came over and ran her hand down the cat's back. "Oh, hello, little man." She laughed. "Isn't he cute? It was too empty and lonely here without you, so I got him to keep me company. Besides, I know you always wanted a cat. I did, too, but I was worried about your dad's temper."

"You told me you were allergic."

"And I hope you can someday forgive me for that lie." Mom grinned. "His name is Vespers."

The small cat stopped writhing when you held him to your chest. "Welcome home, Vespers," you whispered, and his loud purr against your chest was comforting.

Your friends visited the next day. It was the first time you'd seen all of them together. Beth got there first with doughnuts. Brian came next with pizza. Riley and Derek got there suspiciously close together, with Riley's coffee and Derek's bagels from places in the same strip mall.

"Are we expecting more people?" you asked. "Or is this feast just for us?"

"Oh," Brian said. "I thought that it would be helpful if you had leftover stuff you could just eat without cooking. I know your mom is working a bunch this week." He pulled plates and napkins out of a bag he'd brought. "I helped her put some furniture together yesterday."

"And to what do I owe the pleasure of all this food and fine company?" you asked.

"Honestly," Brian said, draping an arm over your shoulder, "it's a bribe."

"Oh?"

"For your mom," Derek said.

Your stomach rumbled. "So I don't get to eat any of this?"

"Of course you do." Beth threw a couch cushion at you. "But we've been buttering her up all week to see if she'd let us whisk you away next weekend."

"Do go on," you said, amused.

"Look," Brian said matter-of-factly. "You and Derek aren't going to get to do a big graduation or any of the quote unquote"—he made air quotes with his fingers—"'normal high school rites of passage.' We thought maybe we'd kick it at his dad's hunting cabin."

"The last couple of weeks have been fucking stressful," Derek added. "And there's a heated pool and no adult supervision. It might be nice to just go chill, away from all this." He shrugged. "The old man's been mostly away since the locker-room thing. And if he's going to disinherit me or some bullshit like that, I should take advantage of my wealth while I still can."

"You make a good point," you agreed. "I'll present your case."

You watched a movie and ate some of the food they'd brought. Brian sat so close to you on the loveseat you could feel the heat coming from his body. The thought excited you and caused a ridiculous smile to plaster onto your lips, and you were glad for the low lighting. Riley stretched out between Derek and Beth on the couch, her head in Beth's lap with her feet on Derek's knees. The last time you laughed this hard with a group of friends, it was a bunch of drunk jocks. That might be the company that your dad preferred you keep, but you felt safe and comfortable here in a way neither the team nor your dad ever made you feel.

You smiled and scooted closer to Brian.

38

COMMUNITY OF FRIENDS
Brian

Riley, in the driver's seat of her RAV4, checked her rearview and shrugged. We were on our way to Derek's cabin. Greg's attack had been traumatic and exhausting. The following weekend there would be a parade, a Pride Fest I didn't have to plan, which seemed like a nice balm to help ease us back into a normal life.

"Yeah, but how many people do you think will actually come to a pride festival in Canon, West Virginia, of all places?" Beth asked.

"There's queer people all over the place," Riley said. "Canon is one small town in the middle of a lot of small towns. And the podcast has a national audience. Anything could happen."

"Yeah," Derek chimed in. Apparently, part of his wooing technique was brownnosing. "Anything."

Riley arched an eyebrow at me, and I stifled a grin. "I'm for it," I said. "I think it'll be cool."

"This girl, Leslie, has been working her ass off. I can't wait to meet her in person. And we've gotten a metric shit ton of emails since you started talking about it on the podcast."

"I'll go," Greg said.

"We're going as a group, I assume," Beth added. "We can get ready at Brian's house."

Riley pulled into the gravel driveway leading to the cabin. It nestled up against a lake surrounded by a thick forest. Calling it a cabin didn't do it justice. It was bigger than most of our homes, and only a little smaller than Derek's house in Canon. The walls were made of stone, with a wide chimney sitting on its tin pitched roof.

"Holy crap," Beth said. "You call this a cabin? Maybe for the Kardashians."

There were seven bedrooms. Derek and I put our stuff in the room with twin beds. Greg got the biggest bedroom since there was a bathroom for easier access in the middle of the night. Riley and Beth each got their own.

After we unpacked and put the groceries away, we soaked in the hot tub. We'd decided officially not to drink because of Greg's injuries and the meds he had to take. Later, we played video and board games. And a lot of Never Have I Ever and Truth or Dare. It was much tamer sober.

Calling it a hunting cabin was a bit of a misnomer. The place was enormous. It was easier to text one another from different rooms than to try and find someone. We were all hanging out in the kitchen, making s'mores over the gas stovetop, when it came to light that Derek had never used hair gel.

"But why would I?" he said, somewhat defensively. "My hair is short, and it's almost always under a ball cap."

"What other rites of passage have you missed out on, you goober?" Riley asked, shoving him.

"I think this calls for a makeover!" Beth clapped and hopped a little in place. "I have a full arsenal of products in my overnight bag. Hold that thought."

"Boy, you are getting the full beauty treatment tonight," I said. "Guyliner, pedicure . . . the works."

Derek shrugged. "It won't be my first homosexual experience."

My eyes got wide and Riley sucked in a breath, but a laugh burst out of Greg like a bird freeing itself from a net and all the awkwardness vanished.

Riley shouted to Beth, "What makeup did you bring with you? We're going to get pretty as fuck up in here."

Beth didn't respond.

"Beth?" Greg got up to find her and didn't come back right away.

"Y'all?" Riley yelled. "Everything okay?"

"I'm gonna go find them," I said after waiting a minute or two. Riley and Derek followed me. They weren't in the bathroom, and when we found them in the garage, it became apparent why they hadn't returned. They stared at the crumpled hood of a huge silver pickup truck. An NRA sticker was attached to the right side of the front bumper.

Our entrance jolted them out of their trance, and Greg looked at me first, and then at Derek.

"It was you?" The pain on Greg's face was so palpable. He wasn't crying, but he wasn't far from it, either. He inched closer to the truck, to the point of impact, where the grill was mangled and twisted. He placed a hand on the jagged metal. "You?"

Derek stared blankly from the truck to Greg. "Bro, I've never seen this truck before. Except in that surveillance video."

"No. No, no *no*." Greg's eyes focused on the truck before they narrowed on Derek. "I don't understand."

Derek circled the truck before opening the passenger's side door and pulling the contents of the glove compartment onto the front seat.

He swept empty Skoal cans and beef jerky bags onto the floor until he got to a small black folio. Derek flipped it open, and his eyes traced the page.

"My d-dad?" His brow furrowed in confusion. He dropped the folio onto the seat and continued looking through the loose papers. "Todd's Meat Market. A ten-point buck."

I watched him connect the pieces in his head. Greg was still standing with his hand on the front bumper, looking back and forth from the point of impact to Derek.

"My dad. It was my dad." He slammed the door, crying. "Greg, I didn't know. I'm sorry. You have to believe me."

Beth and Riley were standing near the door, holding on to each other. "Fuck," I heard Riley whisper. "Should we call someone? The police?"

"Greg?" Beth whispered. "Should we call someone? Your mom? What do you want to do?"

Derek approached Greg with his palms up. "Greg, I'm sorry, I didn't know." He reached out a hand for Greg's shoulder, and Greg flinched violently.

"Don't touch me," he hissed, his hands still resting on the hood of the broken car.

Derek walked away from Greg, his Adam's apple bobbing as he swallowed. "I understand. I get it. I'm sorry. I'm so fucking sorry. I'll go. I'll do whatever you want, man."

Less than a second later, Derek was standing at the side of the truck, slamming his fist into the door over and over again. The rest of us were silent, staring at him unraveling, pummeling the side of the truck with his hand and screaming with rage. There was so much blood.

I put myself between where Derek's anger was unraveling and

where Greg was staring and flinching violently every time Derek landed another wet, metallic punch. Beth looked stricken but moved over to guide Derek away from the truck. I looked at the fading bruises where Greg was just starting to heal. "Hey, let's step out of the garage, okay?"

His gaze went to my face, and he nodded. I led him away and into his bedroom, where I pushed the door shut and wrapped my arms around him. He buried his face in my shoulder and cried. His hot breath wet against my neck. There were no words for all the things I wanted to say to him, no way to keep him safe from all the dangers in the world that were bigger than both of us. Instead, I just held him tighter.

I could feel his heart hammering through the walls of both of our chests, knocking against mine until they were singing the same song. I could not protect him, but I could wrap him up in my arms. I could lend the strength of my new muscles, the heat of my body to him. I would gladly have given him anything at that moment. I cradled the back of his head in my hand and held his head against my chest until his body stopped heaving. I buried my face in his hair. I could feel my legs and back cramping, but I didn't move.

I wasn't sure how long I'd held him, but the sun had gone down. A soft knock came from the door. Neither of us responded.

"It's me," Riley said softly through the door. "Can I come in?"

I extracted myself gently from Greg and looked at him for approval. He nodded, and we went to the door together. I twisted the doorknob to let her in. It was the first time the three of us had been alone together since childhood. She reached up and slipped her arms around Greg. I snaked my arms across them both, and we stood there united for a minute.

Greg pulled back to look at her, but neither of us let go.

"We got you," she said. "Whatever happens, we got you."

39

THE IMPORTANCE OF THICCNESS
Greg

You were too frozen to speak for the entire drive back to Canon.

You didn't want to explain everything to your mom, so you, Riley, and Brian went back to Brian's house, where his mom would be fast asleep, dreaming melatonin dreams. Riley drove and Brian sat in the now-spacious back, right beside you, his fluttery hands never leaving your body for long. He ran his hands through your hair, nuzzled your face with his, touched your hands and arms soothingly. He was trying so hard to keep you from pulling away, to keep you feeling safe. And it was working intermittently. But it was also working for you in ways it wasn't decent to have an audience for. When he finally did look down at your tented pants, he grinned crookedly and buried his face shyly in your neck.

You leaned your head on his and stayed like that, eventually closing your eyes. Neither of you moved much for the rest of the trip, except to adjust for comfort. Eventually, he wound his fingers through yours and you let his hot, soft breath against your skin relax and excite you and take you far from Derek's dad's garage.

• • •

Riley ordered pizza from the place you'd eaten hundreds of pizzas from together as children. It was the flavor of nostalgia and comfort. She and Brian settled into the couch and turned on *Drag Race*, which you knew about but had never seen. Riley explained that it was a relevant and referential epicenter of queer and Black art, as curated by RuPaul Charles, as devastating in a dress as he was in a Kline Epstein Parker fitted suit. Brian said it was like the national gay sport, and while fitness was important, so was thiccness. It took exactly one full episode to become completely obsessed. By the lip sync, you had a favorite contestant and were deep in the Wikipedia page. It was the perfect comfortable distraction, somehow orchestrated by the two people you owed the most apologies to. When Brian excused himself to take a shower, sort out pajamas and linens for you, and call his mom, you were alone with Riley for the first time in years.

"Riley, I—"

"Don't start," she interrupted. "I know you feel like you have to do a big apology thing, but let me remind you that I live with a politician. I know you're sorry. Words are stupid."

"Words *are* stupid," you agreed. "How's life with the mayor?"

"Oh, you know, he's the most respectable Black man in Canon, West by God Virginia." She rolled her eyes. "So naturally he would prefer that I dress more femininely, stop hanging out with homosexuals, and speak my mind less loudly."

"Oh dang. I forgot Vernon was so . . ."

"Hypocritical?" Riley snorted. "Annoying? Mired in internal racism? Almost openly misogynist?"

"Insecure," you offered. "I can't imagine what his life must have been like, growing up around here, like, fifty years ago. But it can't have been easy."

"I know your life hasn't been easy, Greg." Riley turned to face you. "And his wasn't, either. But having a hard life is not an excuse for taking the easy way out. Do better from here on out. Or I'll give you almost as much grief as I give the mayor."

You remembered her first protest. You were ten and made environmental protest signs out of art supplies and rolled them up into an Uber Riley called to get you all to her dad's office. She sprayed a light coating of adhesive on the posters and then sprinkled them so liberally with plant-based, biodegradable glitter the trail that followed you could only have been intentional. Riley's dad never really changed his opinions about fossil fuels, but the glitter ground itself into the carpet and was still there at his end-of-the-year campaign fundraiser.

"Yes, ma'am." You grinned. "I won't let you down."

"And, Greg?" She made sure she had your entire attention. "I see whatever is happening with Brian. But if you hurt him again, if you cause him one single moment of discomfort or sadness, you will wish you had died in the hospital."

She didn't look away, and you laughed nervously.

She did not.

40

FRUIT OF MY LOINS
Brian

After so many years of his absence, I was still not used to having Greg in my home again.

It made me anxious to see him pause in front of the wall of school pictures starting with kindergarten that lined the stairs. His mom had called to ask if I'd make up an excuse to get him out of the house because she was worried about him not leaving except for medical appointments, and I agreed. I suggested a meal, the mall, a movie, and a half dozen other options. Greg shot them all down. Until finally, he didn't.

"Greg," I had eventually said over FaceTime one evening after he had shot me down again. "Is it me? Do you not want to, like, hang out with me? I can stop asking. If you're just too polite to tell me to get lost—"

"No, no. Absolutely not, it's not that." The phone had shaken as he had picked it up from where it had been resting nearby. "I want to see you *so* much. Like, all the time. But the thought of being in public makes me so fucking nervous. I think about running into someone from CHS at the movies and them knowing about all the worst things in the world happening to me, and it makes me want to puke until I turn myself inside out. And I hate how flinchy I feel in crowds. I take the stairs at the hospital because the elevators are too crowded. I'm sorry. It's not you at all. I hate that you thought that."

"Ugh." I had taken a deep breath. "That sounds awful. And we'll get back to that, but I'd like to just say I'm relieved it's not me. Do you want to maybe come over here and visit? My mom asks about you all the time. We could watch a movie and order pizza? Or I could try to cook something."

"Could we watch more *Drag Race*?"

"We can watch as much *Drag Race* as you want." I had grinned. "We could, with Riley's blessing, even start *All Stars*, season seven, the queen of all queens season."

"Maybe I can get my mom to drop me off after she gets home from work? Or I can ask Riley to pick me up."

I had cleared my throat. "I was hoping for some one-on-one time, if that's okay? If it is, I can come pick you up whenever."

He hadn't said anything right away, which had made me desperate to fill the silence. "We don't have to do anything! I don't have an agenda. I was just thinking we should talk. Check in. State of the Brian and Greg Union. That sort of thing."

"Hmm." He had laughed, low and a little nervous. "We have a union?"

I had never been religious, but I had prayed to every deity known to humankind that the earth would open up and swallow me whole.

Finally, he had stopped giggling. "I can be ready in half an hour, whenever you're free."

"I'll be there in twenty-five minutes."

• • •

And now here we were.

"It's so weird," he said, touching one of the picture frames. In it, I am still frozen at age nine, a mess of frizzy hair and acne and braces. "So much is the same, but a few things have changed. New coffee table, same photos. New couch, same gaming setup."

"New you, new me," I said, crossing the distance between us to stand closer. Six inches away, he reached for me, and we wrapped our arms around one another. Two long-legged spider boys beginning to build a web of limbs.

"Thanks for inviting me over," he said. I could smell his cologne. Something clean and woodsy. "Is Mrs. Montgomery here? I have a thank-you card and some muffins I tried to make for her with my mom's supervision in my backpack."

"She's working, but she'll be home in about forty-five minutes. Same house rules as before." I grinned into his chest. "No closed doors, ask for consent, put the seat back down after you pee."

"Do I have your consent to kiss you?" he asked, so close that his lips tickled my temple.

"Yes, please," I whispered against his lips just before they met mine. It was easy to get wrapped up in the kiss. In his heat, his smell, his heartbeat, the way his hands found their way to my waist. I felt all the blood in my body migrate to my southern hemisphere as his fingertips brushed against my back, under my shirt. I put my hands gently over his and extracted myself. "Please believe I want more of this. But I do think we have to talk before we can get back to the fun part of whatever is happening, just to clear the air."

"You're right," he said. "I know you're right. But can I just say for the record that this feels like the easiest, best thing that has happened as long as I can remember."

"I'm glad, Greg. I'm really enjoying whatever this is, too. But I do want to be clear. I know you're more experienced than I am, but I need to move pretty slow with physical stuff. Like, I want us to make sure we're checking in with each other. Not just for me. You just nearly died. Like, you were in a coma."

He looked at me and nodded, putting his hand on mine. "You're right," he said again. "And I wanted to apologize for—"

"For the stuff from before?" I asked. "With the team? I know you're sorry for that. And I do forgive you. I've been walking around thinking about what forgiveness looks like. What it means. And I couldn't be here, with you, if I didn't forgive you. I haven't forgotten, and I think I'm unlikely to. And that has to be mine to deal with. But I can't absolve you of that guilt, and we can't move past it as friends if it's a thing we keep bringing up."

"Fair. What else?"

"Well, like, what's happening here?"

"You just said we were friends." He looked at my lap, still somewhat tented. "But I'm trying to break away from sexual friendships. And I'm working through a bunch of shame and guilt, like you said. But I love this. Spending time with you. Touching you. I guess it didn't occur to me that you might be seeing anyone else, so I don't know if you were looking for a label, or—"

"I'm two thousand percent not seeing anyone else. And I don't want to. I just want to keep doing this."

"Me too." He leaned toward me and as soon as our lips touched, I heard the front door open.

"Fruit of my loins, cause of my stretch marks, I have returned home with pizza."

My mom's timing was equal parts cruel and hilarious.

41

TIGHT BROS
Greg

You were just getting used to the shape of your new life.

The new dad-free apartment felt calm; Vespers stretched out in his favorite afternoon sunbeam. You found that if you took a lot of deep breaths and concentrated on the thing in front of you, you could push through the really intense moments of panic or sadness or anger. Your mom made an appointment for you to see a therapist, and she started seeing one herself. Meditation and deep breathing were a couple of things you learned from the neatly groomed older man whose office was cozier than you'd expect from a place in a strip mall on the edge of town.

You were enrolled in an online GED prep class and were working on the math part when there was a knock at the door. Your mom was out running errands, and you were always so nervous at home alone that it would be your dad, Derek's dad, or any number of violent homophobes. You and your mom had both changed your phone numbers when you moved into the new place, but a couple of trolls got ahold of your email address and sent some pretty disturbing shit before you finally changed that, too. Brian, Riley, and Beth all texted before they came over. You checked your phone and whoever was at the door knocked again, louder. You flinched involuntarily.

"Who's there?" you asked, crossing the small living room in a couple of steps. You tried to make your voice sound brave—louder and deeper than normal.

"It's me. Derek," he said, slightly muffled through the thick wood of the door. "Look, you don't have to let me in. I get it. But I wanted to let you know that I'm here, that I'll always be here if you want to pick our friendship back up. But if you need to leave me behind to move past this, I don't blame you."

You didn't say anything, but you put your hand on the knob. You could feel your heart beating its fists against the walls of your chest.

"They arrested my dad earlier today. It was the first time he'd been home in, like, a month. I waited until I knew he was home. I thought he was avoiding me because of the locker-room thing. I didn't know he was avoiding arrest. I'm so sorry, man. I didn't want him to have the opportunity to run." You could hear the strain in his voice. "So, you know. I just thought I should tell you that. In case it helps you feel a little bit safer. I knew you'd see it on the news tonight or Brian would tell you or something, but it felt like something you should hear face-to-face."

Your mouth was dry. You reminded yourself to breathe.

"Or face-to-door, I guess," Derek went on. "Okay. So . . . I guess that's it. I'll go now. But y'know, man. I love you. You're probably the realest friend I've ever had. I just wanted to say that, too."

You twisted the handle and pulled the door open. He had already started walking down the hall toward the elevator, and when he turned back to look at you, the hope in his eyes was so bright you blinked. "Hey," you said.

"Hey." He grinned. "Long time no see. You look good."

"Better than you."

"Pfft." Derek laughed. "You should be so lucky."

"Asshole."

"Douchebag."

"You wanna come in? I was gonna order a pizza or something." You threw an arm around his shoulder.

"I could eat," he said.

Derek caught you up over dinner and then you played *Madden* until your mom got home. She smiled when she saw him.

"Hey, Mrs. B." He stood up and kissed her cheek. "Gosh, I'm sorry. I didn't mean to wear out my welcome. I didn't realize how late it was."

"Oh, sweetheart, I'm glad to see you. How are you doing?"

"Doing okay. I just came by to let Greg, and now you, know that they arrested my dad for attempted murder. I don't know what will happen. But . . . I'm sorry."

Your mom took Derek by both of his shoulders. She had to reach a little. "Listen to me, Derek. You didn't do this. I know that. And I know you might be having all kinds of feelings right now. We all are. But the most important thing is that you know this. Are you listening?"

He swallowed hard. "Yes, ma'am." His voice was a raspy whisper.

"This is not your fault."

"I know, but—"

"No buts. And if your daddy makes bail and you need someplace to come, that couch folds right out into a bed." My mom pulled Derek close, hugged him around the waist, and put her head against his chest. "This ain't your fault. You're a good kid, some real bad stuff happened, but things are gonna work out okay for you. You are not defined by your dad's wrong choices."

Derek laid his cheek on Mom's head. You could see that he was trying to blink back tears, but one escaped, ran down the side of his face, and landed in her bun. "Thanks, Mrs. B. I didn't know I needed to hear that. But I guess I did."

"You got somewhere to go, right?" you asked Derek.

"Yeah, I've been packing my stuff. I'm gonna move out. I've got some savings and whatever. But thank you so much. I'm sure I'll wind up being pretty tight bros with that couch over time."

You smiled and clapped him on the back. "Come on, I'll walk you out. Tomorrow, I'll come over and help you pack."

When you got to his truck, you put a hand on his arm. "Hey, I know it couldn't have been easy to come over here. Thank you."

He looked at your hand, removed it, and pulled you in for a hug. "You're the only person I've wanted to talk to through this whole fucking nightmare. I just missed my best friend."

"I missed you, too, man," you said, hearing him sniffle into your ear. "Look. It took some time to move past. But I was never mad at you. I just needed space with things."

"I get it. Even if you were, I get it. I feel so goddamn bad. How could I not have known? It was my dad. You're my best friend. I—"

"Stop." You pulled away so you could see his face. "You're not your dad. Whatever happened between the two of you. Whatever he did to me. Those are separate. You are a good person, and he isn't. But you aren't him. You get to decide what kind of man you become. You're not your dad."

You had never seen Derek cry before, and when he did, it was like a short, intense rainstorm. All heaving and snot and sound. You wrapped him back up in the tightest hug your still-healing ribs could manage and just kept telling him that he was not his father until his tears subsided.

It wasn't until you were walking back upstairs you realized you needed to hear it, too.

You were both better men than the men who raised you.

SHAMPOO UNICORN
EPISODE 316: "Denouement & Farewells"

NEWS ANNOUNCER:

Jarod Schillinger, a prominent local businessman, was arrested today, following the discovery of evidence he attacked Canon High student Greg Burke. It is suspected that the attack was a hate crime, but no statement has been released by either the victim or the suspect. We'll be back with more as we hear from the Canon police department.

BRIAN:

Hey, listeners. The rest of my guests are going to join me in just a little while, but before any of that happens, I want to personally say thank you to everyone who has ever listened to this podcast. Regardless of whether you were with me from the beginning or you picked us up somewhere along the way, I appreciate any amount of time or attention you've shared with me.

For a variety of reasons, big and small, this will be the last episode of *Shampoo Unicorn*. When I say that doing this podcast saved my life, I am in no way exaggerating. Being queer in a small town, in the South, in someplace rural—all of that can be really fucking lonely.

I've mentioned in the past that this started as an assignment, but it validated me in a way I didn't expect. It made me feel like my voice mattered. You did that, actually. I hope I've made you feel like your voice does, too. You can't imagine how surprised I was when you all started writing back, when this podcast escalated into a part-time job, and when it brought the community I needed to a place where knowing and interacting with queer people from literally all walks of life seemed inaccessible.

I've been walking around trying to think about how to say goodbye. How to end something that has meant so much to me, taken up so much space in my life. But . . . it's not goodbye, is it? Because the internet will still be there. Because you'll still be around and so will I. Because I will sometimes imagine that you're walking with me, and I hope you'll imagine that I'm walking through the hard stuff with you.

I want to end this with a conversation between Jarod and Derek Schillinger. I have the consent of both parties and I think it's important for closure. And then, one by one, my friends and I, the people responsible for this podcast, will see ourselves out.

There are rules regarding who is allowed to record inmates even for members of the media. We're only allowed forty minutes. Jarod, Derek's dad, would only agree to this if Derek was asking the questions. The plan is to have him record the interview, which his dad consented to. Derek hasn't seen or spoken to his father since he was taken into custody. Is that pretty much it?

DEREK:

I think so. I haven't had anything to say to him personally, but I do think it's worth it to speak with him to provide some sort of closure to this whole shit show.

[AMBIENT BUZZING AND CLANKING OF METAL DOORS.]

BRIAN:

A really big guy with a blond crew cut led us to a bank of windows with phones connected to them. It's giving very *Orange Is the New Black*. Derek looks a lot like his dad. They have the same square jaw and sloping forehead. And to be clear, Jarod Schillinger is a little bit of a local celebrity. He owns the biggest auto dealership in a three-county area. He sponsors a bunch of local stuff, Little League teams, the Thanksgiving Day parade, a bunch of football-related stuff. His billboards were everywhere growing up.

DEREK:

I hated all that shit. I didn't realize we were rich until

I met Greg. I didn't think much about that until I had a friend I could share my stuff with. My dad was such a cornball growing up. It felt like he was just always schmoozing. Or blowing off something important to me for "an important meeting."

BRIAN:

You don't really talk about your mom much. You don't have to, but . . .

DEREK:

Oh, I don't really mind. My mom died in labor with me. I don't know much about her, honestly. My dad shuts down when I ask about her. And her parents died when I was still pretty young. She didn't have much other family. I did one of those cheek swab tests a few years ago, just in case, but it seems like my dad is pretty much it. And Gramps, I guess, but he's not really up to dealing with any of this.

BRIAN:

That's pretty fucking bleak, dude.

DEREK:

I know, right? Luckily I'm *super* well-adjusted with no recent trauma history.

*[AN UNCOMFORTABLE MOMENT OF
SILENCE FOLLOWED BY BOTH LAUGHING
FOR A WHILE. THE LOUD SLAM OF A DOOR
INTERRUPTS THEIR LAUGHTER.]*

BRIAN:

When they take you back, just hit record on your phone and clip this mic to your shirt. It should pick up the conversation and filter out most of the background noise. If you want, you can narrate what you're seeing or feeling, and we can cut whatever you don't like in edits. I'll be here waiting. And, Derek? Thanks for doing this. I think it's important for the pod, but also probably for you, too.

DEREK:

(nervously)

No sweat. I'm just going to start recording here and talking through it.

[A GUARD CALLS DEREK BACK, THEN BUZZES HIM IN.]

DEREK:

It's comforting to see my dad looking less than polished, weirdly. If there's anything he's ever been consistent about, it's his moisturizing routine and barber appointments. His hair and beard are both longer than I've ever seen them. They look unmanicured. His tan jumpsuit is nearly colorless and super wrinkly. He doesn't look bad. He just looks plain. Like what he'd call every other sad luck case here. I'm watching him through the glass of the visitation room, and his whole posture is different. Stiffer or less proud, maybe?

GUARD:

Schillinger, you got forty minutes. You can exchange a hug now and one when you leave.

JAROD:

You gonna hug your old man, son?

DEREK:

I only agreed to come for Brian. And for Greg. This isn't for you.

JAROD:

Everything I ever did was for you, Derek. Even this. I know you don't understand it now. All I wanted to do was prevent you from struggling like my family and I did when I was growing up.

DEREK:

Jesus, old man. I don't want your blood money. I didn't ask for any of this. And I certainly never wanted you to fucking mow down my best friend with your truck.

JAROD:

Look, I'm not confessing to anything. This whole interview is against the advice of several very expensive attorneys, but I need you to know that the day I looked into your new baby eyes, I knew I'd do anything in the world to build a legacy you could be proud of. Our name is on the Little League field, the library, and road signs. I wanted you to be able to look around this town and know that you matter, that the world is yours for the taking.

DEREK:

Maybe it shouldn't be, Dad. Maybe the world is meant to be shared, not taken. I know you wanted to make me proud, but I'm ashamed to be your son. You'll get out of this. You'll pay some hefty fine, grease the palm of whoever matters in this situation. But I don't want anything to do with you from here on out.

JAROD:

(sarcastically)

Oh sure, son. You'll get into a great school on your bad grades with no athletic scholarship. I can't wait to see you pay for that one.

DEREK:

I'm not your son. Not anymore. I'd rather be dirt-poor working for minimum wage in an apartment with six other dudes than have anything to do with you. I don't know what I'll do. But I'll figure it out on my own.

JAROD:

We'll see how long that lasts, kiddo.

DEREK:

What I can't figure out is how Greg plays into this? Why did you try to kill him?

JAROD:

I didn't. I got into an accident. He wasn't looking

where he was going, and he crossed in front of my truck.

DEREK:

You're pretending this wasn't a premeditated hate crime?

JAROD:

I didn't premeditate anything. And I don't hate that kid because he's a fag. I hate him because he ruined my son's life.

DEREK:

Jesus Christ. Do you hear yourself? You've had my life planned since I was four years old. Do you know I don't give a shit about football? I like it because I'm good at it, but I was way more interested in art before you forced me into econ and foreign language classes. Do you know what I learned in all those business and finance courses?

JAROD:

How to—

DEREK:

That I don't need a lot of money to live a life of happiness. That what makes me happy is helping. That it makes me feel proud that I'm somehow karmically making up for all the shady business dealings and the ridiculous shit you filled the house up with to make up for the fact that you were never fucking there.

(clearing throat)

DEREK:

I think we've said all we can. There's nothing productive left in this conversation. I think you've proven
what kind of man you are. I hope you find some iota
of humanity while you're locked up. I can't imagine a
world in which you are ever relevant again without it.
You aren't welcome in my life until then.

[TRANSITION MUSIC PLAYS.]

DEREK:

(in voiceover)

I haven't seen or spoken to my dad since then. His attorney sends me paperwork regarding his estate, and I've
hired representation to add an extra layer of distance
between us. I moved my clothes and shoes and toiletries
out. I have a little studio in the same complex where
Greg and his mom live. Greg and I are in the same GED
class, and I'm looking at programs at the community
college. I'm more excited about learning a trade than
I've ever been about going to college and joining a frat
and making all these bullshit social connections. I am
looking at nursing programs. Doing something helpful,
for a change.

GREG:

Hello, I'm Greg. I feel like there's a whole lot of people
to be grateful to. I'm in therapy and just starting to

reckon with the fact of my mortality. I'm definitely more comfortable with my sexuality. I almost died and was in a coma for a while. And before that, I wasn't really living.

All my worst fears happened, and you know what? I lived through it. I lived because I was stronger than my fear, more stubborn than anyone who had any reason to hurt me. And both my dad and Derek's dad are worse off for their hate. It soured their hearts and everything around them. I thought I'd hate them—and I'd never be able to wish anyone that violent or evil anything good. But I just pity them.

Now that I'm alive, I can't wait to live—to be a good friend, to get a job, to make my way in the world, and to make the world around me better. Maybe it's because I came so close to dying, but every day feels like a gift. I don't intend to squander it.

RILEY:

We were in tenth grade when Brian told me about his idea for this podcast. It seemed like such a stretch to imagine that a couple of nerds with very cheap audio equipment would make much of a splash in the pool of polished, professional productions. But what I forgot about was how funny and talented and sincere my best friend is. I'm so glad y'all recognized it at a point when he was trying hard not to be noticed.

Brian and I have always been friends. We were always going to be, and I can't imagine a world in which he and I aren't. But this podcast let me know him in ways that he was too scared to say out loud. It let him know that other people outside of his mom and me loved him, too. Thank you, for loving my best friend almost as much as I do. Thank you for listening to us—for spending time with us and making us know that our voices, our feelings, the things we have to say are important.

I hope, in some small way, we've been able to do that for you, too.

BETH:

Hi! And goodbye, I suppose. I am so flattered to be asked to speak again on Brian's podcast. I know I wasn't a big part of anything, but this experience changed me in really important ways. Seeing Greg hurt, coming out so publicly, it was all a lot of big scary change. But it was worth it. Things are better now. I . . . I'm going to prom. With a girl I really like. I couldn't have imagined that before. I'm so excited about dancing with her in a room full of my friends, getting photos taken, and eating shitty Waffle House fries post-afterparty when we're all bleary-eyed and silly. I am so grateful to have been part of something bigger than any of us. And I hope whoever you are, listening, I hope you get to feel that, too. Because it rules. And you deserve to be happy, too.

NATALIE:

I told Brian I didn't know what I'd say on the last episode of this podcast that has meant so much to him and his friends, that has brought them all closer, brought Greg justice, and brought closure to a lot of people. But

I guess more than anything, I'm grateful to have a kid who teaches me stuff all the time. And I hope if there are parents listening to this, they stay open to learning from their kids, too. You forget, sometimes, when you get old that language changes and identities shift and the most important thing is love. To just love kids for who they are without drawing boundaries. I'm not gay, but I got pregnant with Brian before my parents would have liked me to, and that put a lot of strain on our relationship. And what I needed was their love and kindness. I'm not saying it's the same thing, but I hope that if you're listening to this and your parents aren't supportive, you find support elsewhere. You are perfect the way you are, and all you have to do is keep growing into the best person you can. You're doing great.

BRIAN:

Shampoo Unicorn, how do I love thee, let me count the ways. Ahem. It's really a lot harder to think of the right note to end on than I would have expected. I know I seem effortlessly cool, but I'm not.

(laughing nervously)

I mean, I *am* cool, but it takes a lot of effort. I live in my head a lot and think about what the right things to say and do are. I kind of always have. And this podcast has been such an unexpectedly receptive place to sort of shape my own narrative. When you're the gay kid . . . that is, when everyone *knows* you're the gay kid, they assume all sorts of wild shit about you. And I think without this podcast as an outlet, maybe those assumptions would have made me bitter. Thank you for listening to me. Thank you for every kind word you've said in social media posts and DMs and emails. Thank you for all the time and attention you've spent listening to this podcast. I'm more grateful than I have words for. I hope we'll see some of y'all at Canon Pride Fest. As always, links are in the show notes.

Again, thank you so much.

[SHAMPOO UNICORN *EXIT THEME PLAYS.*]

42

FIRST-PERSON SINGULAR
Greg

Until I saw it, I wasn't sure if there would be a pride festival.

But sure enough, Brian and I pulled into Todd's parking lot. He was closed for business today but kept the building open for bathroom access and as a backstage area where performers could get ready. The whole affair was a sea of bright colors. Vendor booths and information stands lined the parking lot of Jolene's. The restaurant was hopping, and through the plate-glass window, I could see Chuck leaning over to set a couple of dishes down on a table full of laughing, smiling drag queens.

Across the street, a bunch of people in Jesus T-shirts and camouflage were carrying protest signs that said things ranging from tired slogans like ADAM & EVE, NOT ADAM & STEVE and LOVE THE SINNER, HATE THE SIN to ones more wildly offensive and graphic. I could feel my shoulders squaring for a fight, even before I saw my dad there, unshaven and seemingly unshowered. He was carrying a sign that said NO PLACE IN

HEAVEN FOR GROOMERS, and I could feel my fists reflexively curling into balls. Brian traced my stare to the old man and back, before he put a hand on my forearm.

"Hey," he said, gently, scooting closer to me. "Hey, we don't have to interact with them at all if you don't want to. He's across the street and you have a restraining order."

I looked at his earnest face, tilted to the side, eyes swimming with concern. Just then, a motion across the street pulled our focus. My mom. My MOM. Leading a group of people in gold robes with enormous wings, hiding the protestors entirely. One of them carrying a boombox pressed play and "YMCA" started blasting.

Brian's eyes got wide. He opened the car door and hollered at my mom, "Mrs. Burke! Go *off*, queen!"

Mom caught his eye and winked without missing a step of synchronized choreo. A cheer went up from a bunch of drag queens near the stage, and the rest of the crowd joined in, cheering and hooting.

"Shall we?" Brian grinned crookedly, which made all the butterflies nesting in my stomach take flight at once. Couples of all ages and races held hands, all types of families pushed strollers containing cranky toddlers, and people served looks and occasionally cruised one another thirstily. My eyes were wide, taking it all in, and I found it hard to pay attention to where I was going.

"Excuse me," I said, bumping into a lesbian couple holding hands. "I'm so sorry."

They smiled at me and continued down the makeshift row flanked by booths and food trucks. Brian grabbed my hand and pulled me back out of the path where people were filing into the festival, milling around. A passerby handed him a brochure. "You okay?" he asked. I was scanning the crowd, which was moving with the beat to a remix of some pop song I only vaguely recognized. Working at playing it cool, but in the midst of all these strangers, I felt known, seen. "Greg, are you okay? Is this too overwhelming?" When I looked over at him, his beautiful, elfin face had cracked into a look of raw concern.

I grinned at him. "Can you believe this is really happening? Here? Now? For us?"

He smiled back. "No, I truly can't. But I'm glad it is. And that you're here for it."

"Well, I'm glad you're here with me." I could feel my heartbeat line up to the bass from the dance remix of another pop song. Sweat dampened my hairline, and I wasn't sure if it was the sun causing it or being worked up with the newness, the raw sensation of joy and fear exposing me like fresh skin.

We strolled under a rainbow flag canopy. Down the row, I spotted Riley pushing Derek playfully away from her. He laughed, grabbed her hand, and twirled her. She stopped fighting but insisted on spinning him back before they settled into a swaying motion. Next to them, Beth awkwardly twisted a strand of her hair around her finger as she spoke to a girl with cropped black hair and tight jeans.

"Hey." Brian stopped and faced me. "I don't know if this is weird timing or . . . you can feel free to say no, but . . ." He swallowed, his Adam's apple bobbing. He bit his lip, glancing around as if searching for the words to say before his eyes locked with mine. "Uh, do you want to be my date for prom? I . . . um . . . know it's a few months away and all . . . but there's no one I'd rather take."

"I thought you'd never ask," I said. "I'd love to go with you. How does that work, exactly? Do I buy you a corsage? Or since you're the one who asked, do you get me one?"

A laugh lifted his chest. "It works however we want it to."

I bumped his shoulder with mine and he bumped me back. Everything about the day felt perfect. Brian looked radiant and I could see his mind racing with prom plans. "Do we get matching tuxes or is that too gauche?" I winked.

"We get whatever we want." The corners of his mouth rose adorably.

"What if we already have what we want?" I kissed his forehead, his nose, and finally his soft, warm mouth.

"You fucking cornball." He sighed against my kiss. "We have so much catching up to do."

43

RIGHT HERE, RIGHT NOW
Leslie

Leslie is thinking about possibilities.

There isn't enough room in her head or her heart for the over-whelming waves of pride that swell and burst inside her. Anything could happen today. Everything could happen. The day is perfect; it's sunny with a slight wind that occasionally perfumes the air with the smell of BBQ from Jolene's. Leslie's parents dropped her off early so that she could be with Chuck to help vendors get set up. There are a couple of people from the city clerk's office, a few police officers, and a lot of press. That's a thing Riley and Leslie agreed on, wholeheartedly. They were doing something big—they wanted people to know they were here, gay as geese, even way out here in the country.

She knows their faces almost as well as their voices even though they are strangers to one another. Without *Shampoo Unicorn*, there might not be a Canon Pride. She wonders briefly if she can trace the cause and effect of the podcast back to Marsha P. Johnson before a lesbian couple selling cakes of rainbow flag soap asks her where they should set up their booth.

"Hi. Let me help you with that. I'm Leslie, by the way," she says, extending her hand. Her name is the sweetest-tasting thing her mouth has ever held.

She wears a skirt in public for the first time. It's knee length, black, pleated, and she is wearing it over pastel tights. She has on black Converse and a trans pride crop top. Her hair is down and free, blowing softly around her as she watches people arriving, unloading boxes, pushing children in strollers, eating snacks, and doing all manner of living.

Her parents are around, helping people sign in, find their space, handing out bottles of water, condoms, rainbow pins. Her dad is wearing rainbow suspenders and it's all so unbearably sweet that she needed to break away for a while to breathe on her own the air of hope that fills her past the point of inflation. She's watching people pass, watching herself be seen. Occasionally saying hello or offering directions. Finally, she spots a familiar face. She and Riley traded emails at first, and then tentative text messages until Riley finally wrote: *Omg, can we just decide we're friends? Call me biiiitch and send me all your best memes.*

And that was that. They are texting friends who occasionally FaceTime but today, Riley's hair is pulled high on her head in two Afro puffs wrapped in rainbow ribbons. Leslie recognizes the boy standing next to her as Derek, and the boys holding hands a few steps behind them as Greg and Brian.

The sight of all of them takes her breath away. They had all meant so much to her, informed so much of her recent life, that it is incomprehensible that they are strangers. She takes a deep breath and tries her best not to fangirl. She is trying to come up with the perfect first line when

Riley breaks away from the group and wraps her in a hug so tight and sudden that she laughs involuntarily before returning the embrace. Of course. It can be easy like this.

"Look at those boots. Look at that cat eye! Bitch, we have got so much to talk about."

There is something there, tickling her brain. *Bitch* she knows. She knows all the ways *bitch* can hurt. This is the first time *bitch* feels like home. Like a girlhood she can occupy. She could be a bitch. She could be *that* bitch.

Leslie hip-bumps Riley. "Yeah, we do," she says.

"This is Leslie. She's responsible for all this." Riley gestures at the celebration around them. "This is Brian and Greg and Derek and Beth. My friends. And now, I guess, your friends, too."

Brian's hand is warm with possibilities. The beat gets faster. The sun shines brighter. "It's nice to finally meet you."

ACKNOWLEDGMENTS

This book started out as a love letter to queer people, influenced by the ones I grew up with. There's a bittersweet ache to surviving people who still haunt you, and I have conversations with their ghosts on the daily. I hope I do them proud.

Like a lot of trans people, I have a complicated relationship with my family. I love them, and I'm grateful for all the ways they influenced my life. My grandmother taught me kindness. My grandfather had an unshakable confidence in me. My mom let me read whatever I wanted, had faith in my general competence, and taught me that the worst thing you could be was a bigot. I've spoken with enough therapists that I think my gratitude finally outweighs our shared generational trauma. I am also very grateful to cousins, classmates, and church members for their kindness, then and now, as I was sorting myself out.

Zines and zinesters gave me a place to use my voice before I was even sure I had one. When I was a queer hillbilly kid who felt like there was no possible future joy in my life, stories and letters and mixtapes and slam books and all the other ephemera you can cram into an envelope landed in my lap like messages of hope in a bottle. Riot grrrl is still such a big part of my identity, and I try to walk through my days paying homage to the DIY ethos of punk rock.

If gratitude were a pie, the biggest slice would have to go to Ryan Lovett, who is my favorite person on Earth.

Erin Entrada Kelly is one of my favorite writers, my platonic soulmate, and the most incredibly kind and fierce advocate for my work I've ever known. It's incredibly daunting at times to have a BFF who is very famous and important, but Entrada believed in me, and in these characters, even when my faith wavered.

Grace Gordon was one of my first coconspirators and cocollaborators and is the costar of some of my best bookish memories. I'm proud of her every day.

Matt Godfrey will tell you that I'm not always easy to befriend. I am prickly and sometimes absent, but his persistence and vulnerability make him one of the best dudes (and hands down the BEST, most feminist dad) I know.

Rahul Mehta and Sreya Alladi kept me grounded and focused every Tuesday for years. Just kidding, we mostly giggled, and once Sreya and I said the word *bidet* so much that Rahul asked us to never say the word *bidet* again. There aren't enough words to describe how much I love you both.

Nia King, Joe Hatton, Alex Smith, JC, my zine event-planning people and tourmates: I am humbled by your friendship, and knowing you all makes me a better person because every day I wake up and think about what I can do to deserve you. I hope I make you proud.

Big Blue Marble Books in Mount Airy is one of my favorite places in the whole world, and I count the time I spent working there among my happiest memories (in particular, bookseller Thanksgiving, when we feasted on Indian food during inventory). On some of my worst days, I could count on Nif to offer a warm hug that I swear left me healed and fortified. Elliott batTzedek is one of the most talented poets I've ever met, and I'm lucky to have her as a mentor and friend. Mariga Temple-West is a talented writer, but her real superpower is being unabashedly weird and funny and totally herself. And Sheila Allen-Avelin is one of the smartest people in Philadelphia, and I hope we never run out of things to talk about.

I had the best classmates and teachers at Rosemont. Christine Salvatore's poetry class taught me how to dance with language, and Carla Spataro's grueling novel workshop forced me to stay in my chair and adhere to an outline and how to endure the grueling work of a first draft. Tawni Waters is so kind and helped me figure out where Sass's story really started. Michal Dyson, Stacy Wong, Nicole Hill, Kourtney Gush, Cory Thorton, and SO many classmates that it would be impossible to name them all without a transcript. Thank you so much for sharing your work, and for being so careful with mine.

Pitch Wars changed my life and my relationship with writing. Brenda Drake was a mentor for five minutes and then became a friend I'll be grateful to for the rest of my life. I'm not always great at keeping in touch, but I'm such a big fan of the writers in my cohort and I remain grateful to have shared creative space with such legends.

I am so deeply grateful to the following people for the profound influence they had in shaping *Shampoo Unicorn*'s final form: Farrin Jacobs, Sylvan Creekmore, Leslie Stevens (who loaned her name to my favorite character), Dirk Keaton, Alex DiFrancesco, Lia Belardo, and so many friends who read embarrassingly rough drafts. I'm so grateful to my agent, Andrea Morrison, who has been the best advocate for *Shampoo Unicorn* and might be the kindest person in publishing. Kelsey Sullivan and the editorial team at Hyperion heard and believed in these voices when I most needed them to, and for that, my gratitude is profound.

Every single barista I worked with taught me something, and some of them lent names to SU's Greek chorus. I continue to be impressed with and proud of each one of you. Thank you, thank you, thank you. I am so proud of all of you.

And YOU. However you found yourself here, thanks for spending time with these characters. I hope you had a nice time. I am so grateful.

Respectfully,

Sawyer